The ph...
of a fire-ravaged vessel at sea.

"What happened?" Bolan asked.

"Langley says they were lured off course by a false distress signal," Brognola replied, "then smacked with some kind of fuel-air bomb most likely delivered by an aircraft. The ship was dead in the water within seconds."

"Any suspects?"

"The China Sea's crawling with pirates. They'll rip off anything that moves on water, then ransom the ships and cargo to the highest bidder."

"Beijing's got the case to buy its missiles back."

"Not an option, I'm afraid." Brognola shook his head slowly. "Seems this deal was commissioned by another party, with an eye toward private use of the cruiser-killers." He hesitated. "And if Langley has it straight this time, our Navy is the sole target."

Don Pendleton's Mack
Bolan ®

BALLISTIC

A GOLD EAGLE BOOK FROM
W⦿RLDWIDE ®

TORONTO • NEW YORK • LONDON
AMSTERDAM • PARIS • SYDNEY • HAMBURG
STOCKHOLM • ATHENS • TOKYO • MILAN
MADRID • WARSAW • BUDAPEST • AUCKLAND

Recycling programs
for this product may
not exist in your area.

First edition January 2013

ISBN-13: 978-0-373-61558-2

Special thanks and acknowledgment to
Mike Newton for his contribution to this work.

BALLISTIC

Printed in U.S.A.

Against naked force the only possible defense is naked force. The aggressor makes the rules for such a war; the defenders have no alternative but matching destruction with more destruction, slaughter with greater slaughter.

—Franklin Delano Roosevelt
Aug. 21, 1941

Our enemies made the rules for this fight. Now they have to live—and die—by them.

—Mack Bolan,
"The Executioner"

For Sergeant Christopher Abeyta, 1st Battalion,
178th Infantry Regiment, 33rd Infantry Brigade
R.I.P. March 15, 2009

PROLOGUE

East China Sea: 3:14 a.m.

Still hours short of sunrise, the *Shenyang*—a Type 051B Luhai-class guided-missile destroyer of the Chinese People's Liberation Army Navy—cruised at a comfortable nineteen knots across smooth water toward its destination in the vast Pacific Ocean. At the helm, Commander Han Shushin wondered, as always, why he couldn't sleep his first night out from port.

It couldn't be a by-product of inexperience, since Han had spent twenty-two of his forty years in naval service, rising to his present rank of *Hai Jun Zhong Xiao* aboard one of his homeland's twenty-six active destroyers. The PLAN was his life, and he felt more at home on the sea than he did on dry land with his wife and children. He knew every bolt and rivet of the *Shenyang,* and he could recite its vital statistics from memory upon command.

As practice, silently, he did so. The ship was 153 meters long, 16.5 meters across the beam and displaced 6,100 tonnes. Its two steam engines could drive the vessel at a maximum speed of thirty-one knots. The *Shenyang*'s crew of 250, including 40 officers, serviced its ZKJ-6 combat data system, its Type 381 Radar 3D search radar—dubbed Rice Shield—Type 360 air-surface search radar and Type 344 multifunctional fire-control radar. If those systems detected hostile targets, the *Shenyang* was ready to strike with sixteen antiship missiles, sixteen surface-to-air missiles, two antisubmarine rocket systems, six torpedo tubes, one dual 100 mm gun and four dual 37 mm guns.

Also, on this trip, something new.

Lieutenant Commander Gido Tingjian joined Han on the destroyer's bridge. He was accustomed to Han's first-night insomnia and didn't question it, making his silent rounds to check the various radar displays. He was approaching the Type 360 station when a blip appeared on its screen and the operator called out, "Contact with a vessel, sir! Eight degrees to port, at ten kilometers."

Han joined Gido to stand over the radar operator, peering at his screen. The ship was definitely there, still unidentified, but on their present course they stood to miss it by ten kilometers or more.

"Its speed?" Gido inquired.

The operator tapped his keyboard and replied, "At present, it is stationary, sir."

"Lying at anchor?"

"I can't tell, sir. But it isn't moving."

Suddenly, as if on cue, the *Shenyang*'s radioman chimed in. "I have a distress call, sir. From the *Sleeping Dragon*."

"The *Sleeping Dragon?*" Gido said. "I'm not sure I like the sound of that."

"What's the emergency?" Han asked his radioman.

"Taking on water, sir. Their operator says they're in danger of sinking."

Han muttered a curse. Maritime law required him to assist a vessel in distress, regardless of its nationality or any inconvenience that the *Shenyang* might experience as a result. That meant off-loading crew and any passengers the *Sleeping Dragon* had on board and delivering them to the nearest port before Han could proceed with his assignment. No small problem, when his mission had been classified Top Secret by his masters in Beijing.

"Shall we respond, sir?" Gido asked, giving Han the option to refuse.

"We have no choice," Han said regretfully. "Acknowledge the distress call. Alter course to intercept the vessel. Full speed ahead. Stand by to take on passengers."

At top speed, the *Shenyang* should be within visual range of the *Sleeping Dragon* in approximately fifteen minutes. Whatever happened next would depend upon the damaged ship's condition at the time—or whether it was even still afloat.

At least it was a calm night for a rescue. If the *Sleeping Dragon* was afloat and wasn't on fire, the transfer should be relatively simple. Officers would be assigned to keep the rescued crew in line, see to whatever injuries they had sustained, and make sure none of them went wandering around the *Shenyang* unaccompanied, peering at things they weren't meant to see. As far as putting them ashore, since ships from the People's Republic of China were unwelcome at Taiwan, the nearest port of call would be Kuchinoshima, in the Japanese-controlled Ryukyu Islands. Call it nine hours off-course, plus whatever time was wasted in port, obtaining permission to dock and explaining the problem to Japanese customs officials.

First things first, Han thought. They had to find the *Sleeping Dragon* before anything transpired. If she went down before they reached her, all Han's problems would be solved. It felt perverse, secretly hoping the disaster might unfold that way, but Han didn't believe in wishes coming true, and thus experienced no guilt.

At 3:33 a.m., he heard the lookout's call reporting the lights of a vessel on the horizon, a kilometer ahead. Seconds later, Han's own message to the night watch brought men to the forward railing, ready with the lines and other gear they would require to transfer passengers to their ship. No sign of fire was visible so far, though it could be ablaze belowdecks without Han observing any flames from where he stood.

"Sir," one of his observers on the bridge called out, "there seems to be a helicopter on the rear deck, and... yes sir, it's lifting off!"

"A helicopter?" Han frowned at the news, uncertain what it meant. If men aboard the *Sleeping Dragon* needed to be rescued, why would any of them waste time launching aircraft that would never be permitted to touch down on the *Shenyang?*

A trap?

"All hands to battle stations!" Han commanded, wincing at the instant blare of the alarm his order had initiated. Now he saw the helicopter, rising from the dark hulk of what seemed to be a freighter, lights extinguished except for dim ones on the bridge, where human figures scuttled, barely visible. The small aircraft rose swiftly, soaring toward the *Shenyang,* and was over them in seconds flat.

"Sir!" came the warning shout. "They're dropping something toward our deck!"

Han observed the object falling, judged it to be roughly the size of an oil drum. His eyes were tracking it when it exploded, thirty feet above the forward deck. Its thunderclap blew out the bridge's windows, forcing Han to squint against a storm of flying glass, but he still saw the roiling cloud of flame advancing toward him, gaining ground so swiftly that he didn't have a chance to scream.

CHAPTER ONE

Tioman Island, Malaysia: Midnight

Tioman Island was located twenty-one miles off the eastern coast of Peninsular Malaysia, in the South China Sea. It was twenty-six miles long and eight miles wide at its broadest point, densely forested and sparsely populated by humans. In 1958 its pristine beaches served as stand-ins for Bali Hai in the film *South Pacific.* Two decades later, *Time* magazine called it one of the world's most beautiful islands.

Tioman was all that—and more.

Mack Bolan, aka the Executioner, killed the outboard motor on his Zodiac inflatable boat as he cleared a gap in one of Tioman's coral reefs, beloved by scuba divers on vacation but deadly to small craft after dark. From that point on he would be paddling, hoping that the cloud cover remained in place until he reached the island's shoreline.

If the full moon caught him on the water, and a lookout happened to be watching, he was dead.

Bolan would happily have waited for another night with no moon overhead, but he was on the clock and heard the numbers running down relentlessly toward doomsday. Stalling for a better night wasn't an option.

It was now or never, and the cost of failure was unthinkable.

Beyond the reef, two hundred yards of glass-calm water separated Bolan from the spot he'd chosen as a landing site. It wasn't Tioman's most scenic beach, which half explained his choice. A mangrove marsh met the sea to his left, home of soft-shelled turtles and walking catfish, with ample places to conceal the raft while Bolan worked his way inland on foot.

The other half of his choice was based on proximity to his target: a village of sorts, occupied by thirty to forty armed men he was coming to kill. Among them, possibly, one who could shed some new light on his mission, point him toward bigger, better targets.

And if not, at least the forces of his enemy would be reduced in number.

Call it a win-win scenario—if he survived.

Bolan reached the mangroves without incident and rolled out of the raft. As he dragged the jet-black rubber boat under cover, warm water lapped at his thighs. He hoped the island's king cobras weren't swimming around the mangroves at this moment. As quickly as possible he tied off the boat and carried his gear to dry land.

Bolan was dressed in midnight black from head to foot, his face and hands darkened with combat cosmetics. He carried a Heckler & Koch HK416 assault rifle, issued as standard equipment to Malaysia's PASKAL—navy—and PASKAU—air force—Special Operation Forces, chambered for 5.56 mm NATO ammunition. His sidearm was another standard-issue item, the Heckler & Koch USP autoloader with 9 mm Parabellum ammo, carried by members of the Royal Malaysian Police PGF counterterrorism group. Fragmentation grenades were clipped to his web gear, and a classic Mark I trench knife completed the deadly ensemble.

Moving inland, the Executioner was dressed to kill. Now, all he needed were targets.

SYARIF HAIRUMAN WAS running out of patience. It wasn't a quality that he possessed in great abundance at the best of times, and his frustration with the prisoner's persistent stubbornness now verged on homicidal rage. Unfortunately, he couldn't afford to kill her yet, or his head might be next to roll.

He needed information, but had nothing to report so far. When Khoo Kay Sundaram demanded answers, in a few short hours from now, failure to offer him substantive information might prove fatal. So, he drank another double shot of black spiced rum, set down the glass and turned back toward the hut that served his captive as a prison cell.

Clearly, he'd gone too easy on the woman until now. No matter how she squealed at anything Hairuman did to her, she still defied him. Her affrontery insulted him, both as a man and as a field commander of the pirates feared by every merchant sailor working the South China Sea.

This day he vowed to get results.

Before it was too late.

The guard outside the prison hut saw Hairuman approaching and rose from his slouching stance into a rough approximation of military bearing. It was the best Hairuman could expect from the riffraff available to him. Piracy wasn't a gentleman's trade, and there were more important points to discipline than standing at attention.

Guarding a prisoner, for instance.

If the rifleman allowed her to escape, or if he interfered with her in any way while standing guard over her cage, Hairuman would be pleased to beat him senseless, then set him afire as an example to his other men. Nothing impressed them quite so much as shrieks of agony, accompanied by the pervasive stench of burning flesh.

Outside the hut, Hairuman told the guard, "I need a generator. One that cranks by hand."

Reading his mind, the pirate muttered, "Yes, sir" and hurried off to fetch the torture instrument. Hairuman let himself into the hut and found the woman as he'd left her, bound with rough hemp to a simple chair with legs set wide apart, preventing her from tipping it by any rocking motion of her body, side to side.

"I'm glad you waited for me," Hairuman remarked, taunting his prisoner. "All rested now, and ready for another game?"

"Prick!" she spit at him. "Son of a bitch!"

"Such language from a lady," Hairuman replied, smirking. "You shock me. In return, I think *I* must shock *you*."

His man returned then, entering the hut with both hands full, the generator in his right, a coil of cable in his left, dangling a pair of copper alligator clips.

"You see?" Hairuman said. "It's come to this."

Her eyes flicked back and forth between the equipment and Hairuman's face. He smiled at her and said, "You leave me little choice, unless…you care to speak now? No? So be it. Let us see if this can loosen your tongue."

BOLAN COULDN'T TELL whether the first target he met was standing watch, or simply answering a call of nature. Either way, he didn't pull it off. The soldier came up behind him, clamped a hand over his mouth and drove the Mark I's seven-inch double-edged blade through the gunman's foramen magnum into his brain. The guy died on his feet, and Bolan eased him silently to the earth.

One down. A drop in the bucket.

The Executioner wiped his blade, resheathed it and eased his rifle off its shoulder sling. The sounds of men in camp were loud enough for him to steer by as he crept in through the trees. A moment later, firelight made it easier, accompanied by smells of whatever the crew had had for supper. Stew, he guessed, but didn't speculate on what would be available as meat.

Crouched in a glade with trees obscuring the tropic night's display of stars, Bolan surveyed his target. He counted huts and tents to start, then started counting heads for those still up and moving after midnight. Twelve—make that thirteen—but if the huts and tents were occupied to full capacity, the island camp could easily accommodate three times that number.

On the verge of moving in to raise some hell, he saw one of the campers moving toward a hut located on the north side of the camp. There was nothing unusual in that, except the long-haired man was carrying a hand-crank generator and a coil of wire that looked like heavy-duty jumper cables. Bolan tracked him, noting that the camp had no electric lights, and no antennae topped the hut to mark it as the site's communications shack.

That only left one option, and while Bolan couldn't have cared less what punishment the camp's inhabitants inflicted on one another, instinct told him he was onto something else. Something he needed to investigate before he launched a blitz attack.

He circled to his left, remaining out of sight, watching his step. There could be cobras, but the greater danger was a careless noise that would rouse the enemy.

Not that they seemed to give security much thought.

So far, Bolan hadn't identified a single lookout, and he had begun to wonder if his targets—nothing more than common pirates—had evaded capture for so long that they believed themselves invincible.

Or, possibly, protected by some unknown persons in authority.

It wouldn't be the first or last time bandits had struck a bargain with the law, but if this bunch thought they were skating on their crimes, they were about to get a rude surprise as soon as Bolan found out who was in the target hut, about to have a shocking night.

The man lugging the generator and its cables stepped into the hut, then reappeared a moment later, empty-handed. He sauntered off in the direction of the fire, where half a dozen others sat, passing a bottle. Seconds after he had joined them, everyone was laughing, obviously tickled by the thought of torture going on a few yards distant.

Bolan marked the attitude and their positions, filed away for future reference. If he had time and opportunity, the joke would be on them, but none would be in a position to enjoy it.

Seconds later, he had reached the rear of the hut and crouched there, listening. Two muffled voices, male and female, argued in the Malay language, all incomprehensible to Bolan. Even so, he didn't need a translation to recognize the sound of ripping fabric and the woman's sobbing.

Time to move. He watched the idlers by the fire as he emerged from cover, ducked around the hut and burst through its door.

MAIA LEE GAPED at the stranger who had barged into the hut. Despite the war paint on his face, she recognized him as a white man. When he spoke, saying to Syarif Hairuman, "I hope you don't mind if I crash the party," Maia knew he was American.

After her initial shock, her first thought was of her appearance, bound up in the chair, her blouse ripped open seconds earlier. Before she had a chance to cringe, with no hope of covering her partial nudity, Hairuman spun to face the stranger, challenging him with a burst of rapid-fire Malay. The man in black responded with a long stride forward and a hard jab with his rifle's butt into the pirate's face.

Maia heard bones crack as Hairuman fell, his head striking her knees before he rolled aside. The pain of impact barely registered, her mind was in such turmoil as the stranger raised one booted foot and brought it down against Hairuman's neck. She thought the second crack had to be her captor's spine, and felt him shivering against her ankle as he died.

The new arrival drew a wicked-looking knife, brass-knuckled on its handle, and she cringed instinctively as he circled behind her. Then the blade was sawing through her bonds, releasing Maia's arms to let her clutch the tattered remnants of her blouse in front. Legs next, as he began to speak.

"I don't know whether you can understand me—"

"I speak English," she informed him.

"That's a bonus. Are you up for getting out of here?"

"If we can manage it," she said, rising on shaky legs.

"I like our odds," he answered, and he flashed a smile so brief that Maia wondered if she had imagined it.

The tall man stooped and drew a pistol from Syarif Hairuman's belt holster. She watched him check it, drawing back the slide to put a live round in the chamber. "Any chance that you're a shooter?" he inquired.

"Try me."

He handed her the pistol, which she recognized as a Beretta 92. The gun was heavy, reassuring, in her hand.

"Once we go through that door," he said, "you can shoot anyone but me."

"Who sent you?" Maia asked him.

"We can talk about that later," he replied.

"All right. Thank you," she added, heartfelt.

"Better wait until we're clear for that," he said.

She got the message. They might not survive the next few minutes, but at least she had a fighting chance. She wouldn't die trussed up for slaughter like a hog at market.

"I'm ready when you are," she said.

"Okay. Let's get it done."

TIONG KRISHNAN WAS SIPPING rum and waiting for a chance to speak with Hairuman. Krishnan, the fighting unit's second-in-command, supposed that Hairuman would be preoccupied for some time, while he had the woman to himself, but drinking was as good a way as any to kill time. If Hairuman hadn't emerged within an hour—

The first gunshots startled Krishnan, causing him to slop rum on his knuckles as he spun to face the sound. He was in time to see a stranger, all in black, emerging from the hut where Hairuman had caged their prisoner, an automatic weapon in his hands and spitting death across the compound. And behind him, firing a pistol, came the woman.

"Stop them!" he shouted at the others. "The woman is escaping!"

Despite his orders, Krishnan saw most of those who were awake in camp diving for cover from the bullets rattling past them. As he fumbled for his own pistol, he saw one man fall, a head wound spouting crimson, while another tripped and fell headlong into the fire.

Cursing at his useless men, Krishnan squeezed off two shots at the escaping figures, mortified when neither of them found their targets. Livid, he ran raging through the camp, shouting into the flaps of tents, kicking the doors of huts, routing the other pirates from their beds. They stumbled out to join him, many of them barely dressed, clutching their weapons awkwardly and wearing dazed expressions on their faces.

Krishnan pointed to the dark woods where the woman and her male companion had already disappeared, shouting for everyone to follow them and bring them back, dead or alive. Where could they go, within the next few minutes, on an island, when they were outnumbered and outgunned?

Krishnan himself ran to the prison hut and peered inside. Lamplight revealed Syarif Hairuman sprawled on the dirt floor, bloody-faced, his head cocked at an angle that revealed his neck was broken. Where the woman had been bound, slashed ropes lay on the ground like lifeless snakes around her chair.

How in the name of Ma Zu had this happened?

More importantly, how could he possibly explain it to Khoo Kay Sundaram? Krishnan's own life could be on the line through no fault of his own, but he wouldn't blithely submit to execution for some other person's error.

Why had no lookouts been posted on the camp's outskirts? Complacency.

Why had no guard joined Hairuman in questioning the woman? Because Hairuman wanted her to himself.

That was his ticket to survival: blaming Hairuman for everything. Krishnan, after all, was only *second* in command, and Sundaram himself demanded strict adherence to his quasi-military form of discipline. Krishnan had no authority to countermand instructions from his chief.

That rationale might save his life, but Krishnan knew he'd be on firmer ground if he retrieved the prisoner and killed or captured her rescuer. To that end, he bellowed orders at his men, slapping and shoving those who dawdled, until all who still survived were up and running in the general direction of the woman's hasty flight.

Krishnan stopped by his own hut, retrieved his stubby VB Berapi LP02 submachine gun and ran to catch up with his men. From the direction they were headed, Krishnan knew their path would take them to the mangrove swamp and the lagoon beyond, a dead end for the pair he was pursuing.

And if more of Krishnan's pirates died to bring them down, what of it?

Life was cheap, and they were all expendable.

"How did you find me?" the woman asked, as they ducked and dodged through forest undergrowth.

"Save your breath for running," Bolan cautioned. "Any luck, we'll have the time to talk about it later."

"And if not?"

"Then it won't matter," Bolan said. He listened, added, "Hurry up. They're coming."

"Please, at least tell me your name!" the woman said.

"Matt Cooper," he said. It matched his passport, New York driver's license and the credit cards he carried. If a search was run—the least of Bolan's problems, at the moment—all the documents would check out fine, including credit history.

Which wouldn't help him one damned bit if he was dead.

They had a lead, thanks to the chaos they had left behind them, and the men he'd shot, but it would quickly be reduced by any kind of competent pursuit. Smart money said the pirates knew Tioman Island better than he did from having studied it on various documents, and they were motivated by a fear of lethal punishment to bag him and the woman, one way or another.

Under other circumstances, Bolan could have told her that he'd found her accidentally, had no idea of who she was or why she'd been detained for questioning by men who had become his targets thirty hours earlier. No time for that while they were running, though, no breath to waste on explanations, when each one might be their last.

They were still making decent time, but there would be a lag after they hit the mangrove swamp. The Zodiac raft lay waiting for them, but he still had to untie it, drag it to the beach and launch it, making sure the woman was on board. Each moment gave his adversaries time to close the gap, and even when they'd launched, the rubber boat would be a relatively easy target on its long run to the reef.

Another danger: if the pirates reached their powerboats and followed him to sea, Bolan had every reason to expect that they would overtake and sink him on the dark and lonely run back to the mainland. He was thinking *blood* and *sharks,* but stopped that train of thought before it took him down a dead-end track to panic and despair.

He stopped, turned toward the woman and said, "Go on without me. Make for the lagoon. With any luck, I won't be far behind you."

"The lagoon?"

"I've got a boat hidden. We have a decent chance to make it if I slow them down."

"I'll help you," the woman said.

"No. Listen—"

"You want me to get lost out here? What happens then?"

Scowling, he said, "All right. Find cover, then, and do exactly what I tell you, *when* I tell you. Otherwise, we're both as good as dead."

CHAPTER TWO

Blue Ridge Mountains, Virginia,
thirty-three hours earlier

Mack Bolan held the rented Prius hybrid at a steady thirty-five miles per hour, cruising south on Skyline Drive toward Stony Man Farm. The farm had been established shortly after Bolan's orchestrated "death" in New York City at the climax of his one-man war against the Mafia. It was the headquarters and nerve center of operations known to few Americans outside the D.C. Beltway—and, in fact, to very few inside it. As for those who knew that Bolan lived, albeit with an altered face and name, they could be counted on the fingers of his hands.

After the President of the United States, the high man on the ladder at Stony Man was Hal Brognola, Bolan's second-oldest living friend. The big Fed had been frontline FBI when Bolan went to war against *La Cosa Nostra,* and had met him for the first time in Miami, when the Executioner had dropped in uninvited on a summit meeting of the syndicate. From that point on, their paths had crossed repeatedly, and Brognola became an ally in the struggle that began when Bolan lost his family to Massachusetts loan sharks.

The rest was history.

Bolan finally was admitted through the gate into the

Farm property and drove toward the farmhouse. The first sign of life that he saw beyond the gate consisted of three figures waiting for him on the long front porch. Brognola in the middle slot, a gray man from his hair on through his Brooks Brothers attire, standing with his hands in pockets, no smile as he spied the Prius, tracked its progress; on his right stood Barbara Price, the Farm's mission controller. Sparks of sunlight glistened on her hair. The denim jumpsuit she was wearing fit as if it had been tailored for her slim athletic form. To the big Fed's left, Aaron Kurtzman—aka the Bear—sat in his wheelchair, dead legs a cruel memento of a hostile raid on Stony Man. He was the Farm's resident cyber-genius, supervising staffers who could do almost anything conceivable with a computer—and some things that *weren't* conceivable to lesser minds.

The trio on the porch waited for Bolan as he stepped out of his car, leaving the key for someone else to tuck the vehicle out of sight. Nobody moved until he'd climbed the porch steps, then the hands came out all around to shake his.

How long since he'd last visited the Farm? Two months, maybe three? He often met with Brognola off-site, in the vicinity of Washington.

"No problems on the drive down?" Brognola inquired, his tone perfunctory.

"Smooth sailing," Bolan said.

"Good deal. We may as well head for the War Room, then."

Bolan was last into the house, catching a sidelong glance from Barbara Price that bolstered his impression of a crisis on the boil. He trailed the others to an elevator, joined them in the relatively spacious car and stayed away from small talk on their short drop to the basement. In the War Room, Brognola moved automatically to his chair at the head of a conference table with seating for twelve. Bolan sat to his left, Price on his right, while Kurtzman powered his chair to the far end of the table, large hands hovering over a keyboard console there. His first touch brought a giant flat-screen television on the nearby wall to life, its silent screen sky-blue.

"What do you know about a Chinese missile called the Hsiung Feng III?" Brognola asked.

"Rings a bell," Bolan replied. "Something their navy's using now?"

"Correct. *Hsiung Feng* translates as Brave Wind. It's manufactured by the Chungshan Institute of Science and Technology, in Taiwan."

"Taiwan?" Bolan frowned. "They're selling weapons to Beijing now?"

"It's an oddity, I grant you," Brognola replied. "Chungshan develops systems for Taiwan's civilian space program, such as it is, but it also works closely with the PRC's Ministry of National Defense. So far, the company has produced China's whole range of antiship missiles— Hsiung Feng I, II, IIE and now III. They also produce the Kung Feng and Thunderbolt-2000 Multiple Launch Rocket Systems for China's army, plus the Sky Sword infrared guided air-to-air missiles for Beijing's air force. On the side, they build Taiwan's Sky Bow surface-to-air missiles. Talk about your glaring conflicts of interest."

"I guess it works for them," Bolan observed.

"Whatever. We don't know much about the HF3, except that it's a Mach 2 class supersonic missile designed to target surface vessels. It uses a rocket-ramjet propulsion system, with two side-by-side solid-propellant jettisonable strap-on rocket boosters for initial acceleration and a liquid-fueled ramjet for sustained supersonic cruising. It's a wingless design with four strake intakes and four clipped delta control surfaces aft. Uses an X-band monopulse planar array active radar seeker with digital signal processing. Carries an SFF/EFP warhead—that's Self-Forging Fragment Explosively-Formed Projectile, if you're curious—weighing around five hundred pounds. Top range, right now, is something like eighty to one hundred miles. We think."

Bolan had to smile. "I thought you didn't know much about it."

"Bare bones," Brognola replied. "First time it was displayed in public, it came complete with a sign that read Aircraft Carrier Killer."

Not good. During the Vietnam War, America's Navy had scrapped its classic battleships, retiring the big-gun boomers in favor of long-range aircraft carriers, supported by missile-bearing cruisers and destroyers. A guided missile that could neutralize that power might change everything in the Pacific—and around the world.

"Sounds grim," Bolan acknowledged. "But I'm betting we're not about to tackle the Chinese navy."

"You'd win that bet," Brognola said. "There's nothing we can do about deployment of the HF3 to Chinese ships. Unfortunately, someone else has intervened to grab a couple for themselves."

"Someone?" Bolan echoed.

Brognola looked past him toward Kurtzman. "Aaron?"

Kurtzman's fingers danced over the keyboard, bringing the flat screen to life. Its first image was newsreel quality, shot from the air, depicting the blackened hulk of a fire-ravaged vessel at sea.

"That is—was—the *Shenyang,*" Brognola said. "A

Chinese Guangzhou-class destroyer, designated Lu-yang I class by NATO for reasons best known to their brass. Three days ago, it sailed from Ningbo on the China Sea bound for the North Pacific on a test run for the HF3. You see what's left of it."

"What happened?" Bolan asked.

"Officially, an accident on board, cause unspecified."

"And unofficially?"

"Langley says they were hit. Lured off-course by a false distress signal, then smacked with some kind of thermobaric weapon—a fuel-air bomb—likely delivered by an aircraft. Took out the bridge and the defensive batteries. The *Shenyang* was dead in the water within a matter of seconds."

"And the HF3s?" Bolan asked.

"There's the rub," Brognola said. "*Officially* they were destroyed by fire. No detonation of the warheads, since they weren't armed at the time. The Company says otherwise. Its eyes and ears in Ningbo claim the ship was stormed by pirates while it burned—decked out in fire-retardant suits and hoods, air tanks, the whole nine yards. Somehow, says Langley, they retrieved two HF3s, transferred them to another ship at sea and sailed away to who knows where."

"Suspects?" Bolan asked.

"There's no shortage," Brognola replied. "The China Sea's crawling with pirates, most of them Malaysian. It doesn't get the airtime CNN spends on Somalia, but the situation's pretty much the same. They'll rip off anything that moves on water, ransom back the ships and cargo—or, with special lots, auction their booty to the highest bidder."

"Beijing's got the case to buy its missiles back," Bolan suggested.

"Not an option, I'm afraid," Brognola said. "Seems this deal was commissioned by another party, with an eye toward private usage of the cruiser-killers. And if Langley has it straight this time, our Navy is the target."

SIXTY MINUTES LATER, in his room upstairs, Bolan reviewed the detailed file Brognola had compiled for him on CD-ROM. It started with depictions of the Hsiung Feng III on parade in Beijing, and in test-fire action on some anonymous seascape. The target ship, light-cruiser size, went down in something close to record time. Bolan supposed a carrier would last a little longer on the surface, but not much. The extra time afloat wouldn't mean much to pilots in the air and suddenly deprived of any place to land their jets on hostile seas, when they were half a world away from home.

The rest of the report included speculation—any terrorist on earth who had the wherewithal to float a ship would gladly bid on missiles capable of taking out a U.S. aircraft carrier—but more specific thoughts on suspects for the lift. His sources named one Khoo Kay Sundaram as being dominant among the several pirate "admirals" who fought for turf along Malaysia's coast, and noted Sundaram's occasional involvement with the Chinese triads. How that played into a theft of missiles would be anybody's guess, but Bolan knew the triads would sell anything to anyone, as long as they received their asking price.

What would they ask for two hot HF3s?

According to the CIA's best estimate, each missile cost the Chinese government around five million dollars fresh off the assembly line. That price would be inflated for illicit sale to criminals, and if a bidding war got started, it could double, even triple or quadruple.

That would mean a hefty profit margin for whoever snatched the merchandise, and tragedy beyond financial calculation if and when the warheads found their mark.

Bolan's mind explored the problem's several permutations. First, there was no guarantee that one militant group would buy both missiles. They were easily divisible for sale, one at a time. Likewise, the fact that HF3s were labeled "ship-to-ship" ballistic missiles didn't rule out adaptation to a different role.

Say a boat on Lake Michigan fired an HF3 into Chicago's O'Hare International Airport. Or took a cruise on Manhattan's East River for a shot at United Nations headquarters. How about a ride on the Potomac, with a list of targets including the White House and Congress. Or lying offshore from Miami, New Orleans, Los Angeles, San Francisco—the possibilities were literally endless. Taking it further afield, most major capitals of Europe were accessible by water: London on the Thames and Dublin on the Liffey, Paris on the Seine, Berlin on the Rhine, Vienna and Budapest on the Danube, Prague on the Vltava. The list went on and on.

Bolan knew he couldn't chase the missiles willy-nilly around the world. The only feasible approach would be for him to find the thieves and nail them down before the merchandise was transferred to a buyer. And if he could take the would-be users down at the same time, so much the better.

But he wouldn't count on it.

He had a red-eye flight booked out of Dulles International in Wonderland, leaving at half-past midnight. Nineteen hours in the air, if there were no delays—fat chance—plus downtime on the ground at LAX and Honolulu International before his feet touched down in

Kuala Lumpur. From that point on he would be winging it without a plane, acquiring wheels and hardware in Malaysia's capital, proceeding overland on lousy roads to reach the eastern coast of the peninsula, acquiring means to reach Tioman Island....

And then fighting for his life until the smoke cleared, with his mission rated either as a victory or Bolan's last hurrah.

A muffled rapping at his door distracted him. Bolan closed his laptop, went to answer it. He found Barbara Price in the hallway, smiling up at him, the zipper on her jumpsuit two strategic inches lower than it had been in the War Room.

"How's it going?" she inquired.

"Getting better by the minute," Bolan said, and stood aside to let her in. He didn't bother checking out the hallway, conscious that their on-and-off relationship was public knowledge at Stony Man HQ.

"You're leaving...when?" she asked, as Bolan closed the door.

He didn't have to check his watch. "Three hours, give or take. I'm packed already."

"Do you ever *un*pack?"

"I've been living on the road so long it feels like home," he answered. "There's a point where what you do becomes the same as who you are."

"That must be grim," Price said.

"Depends on how you look at it. I sleep all right." No point in mentioning the ghosts who sometimes visited his dreams.

"You sleepy now?" she asked.

"I catch up in the air," he said. "I've got the best part of a day to rest before it's time to rock and roll."

"Or we could rock and roll right now," she said, and stepped into his arms. "If you don't mind."

His smile was perfectly relaxed now, as he said, "I thought you'd never ask."

CHAPTER THREE

Tioman Island, Malaysia

Bolan heard the racket made by their pursuers as the mob drew closer to the mangrove swamp. Whatever self-restraint the pirates exercised on any given day, it had been stripped away from them by his surprise attack and unexpected rescue of their hostage. He couldn't understand a word they shouted back and forth to one another in the darkness, but their voices had the manic tone of rioters or lynchers.

They were out for payback, and it had to be in blood.

No problem. Bolan meant to see that it was theirs.

He checked the woman crouching ten yards to his left, recalling that he'd given her a name but had never got hers in return. No matter. If they managed to survive the next few minutes, there'd be time enough to chat.

If not, it wouldn't matter, anyway.

A flashlight swept the darkness, seeking Bolan's trail. He hadn't tried to hide it—couldn't, with the woman on his heels—but he had no idea how good the pirates were at tracking human prey on land. They knew he wasn't heading inland, which propelled them toward the swamp and cove beyond.

Toward waiting death.

Bolan had swapped out magazines for his HK416, stowing the one that he'd half emptied in the pirate camp and feeding the rifle a fresh one. Thirty rounds ready and waiting, each with a spitzer projectile designed to tumble and fragment inside soft tissue. He had the weapon's fire-selector switch set for 3-round bursts, improving chances of a kill in murky darkness, but he couldn't guarantee it would be clean. In fact, "clean" kills were rare in combat, where the norm was blood and suffering and screams.

Bolan wished there had been time to do a proper head count of his enemies in camp, but he was used to flying in the face of killer odds without specific information on the numbers ranged against him. "Shock and awe" had been a Bolan trademark years before it turned into a buzz phrase tossed around on CNN, and it was still effective.

Hit the enemy with stunning force. Drive through them like a runaway bulldozer, mangling anyone who stood and fought. No quarter asked or offered in the heat of battle, where the only currency was sudden death.

It was a tactic that the pirates had employed in their attack on the *Shenyang*. Now they would be on the receiving end, getting a taste of what they usually dished out.

There'd been no time or opportunity in camp to judge the woman's capability. She'd fired her pistol on their run for cover, which was something. Bolan couldn't say if she'd hit anyone, but at the moment it had hardly mattered. Now, after her ordeal and their mad dash through to the mangrove swamp, he guessed that she'd be shaky in the face of further mayhem, maybe crashing as fatigue and nerves kicked in. He would be satisfied if she stayed out of sight, without distracting him. Whatever she contributed beyond that would be gravy, if she didn't accidentally shoot him.

And, then again, she might surprise him.

Bolan harbored no illusions with respect to female warriors. Going back to Viking days, if not beyond, there had been women who bore arms beside their men and left their mark on history. In Bolan's own campaigns he had known several who fought as hard and well as any man—better than most, in fact. If this one measured up to that standard, she'd be an asset in the fight to come.

And either way, he hoped there'd be a chance to find out why the pirates had detained her for interrogation at their camp.

A wedge, perhaps, to help him peer inside their world. Before he started tearing it apart.

The voices on his trail were louder now, approaching swiftly. Bolan crouched behind his weapon, waiting for a target to reveal itself.

TIONG KRISHNAN WAS worried that his men were rushing forward too precipitously, but he shared their anger and their sense of urgency. He dared not try to call them back, knowing that it would be a waste of time, one more voice added to the clamor they were raising as they ran on through the midnight forest.

Racing into danger? He had every reason to believe so, but the risk was necessary. Taking time to creep along in silence only gave the woman and her rescuer more time in which to slip beyond their grasp, and that meant punishment for Krishnan when the news reached Khoo Kay Sundaram. Better to lose a few more men and stop the runners than to let them get away.

Full speed ahead, then, while he trailed the pack. No reason why the leader should be the first to fall.

Krishnan stumbled on a root, cursing, but caught

himself before he sprawled headlong into the dirt. It cost him seconds, but he lurched back to his feet, palms stinging where they'd scuffed the earth, and snatched his submachine gun from the ground. Embarrassment mixed with his anger drove Krishnan on in greater haste.

He'd nearly caught up with the pack again, when someone in the front ranks started firing. Krishnan glimpsed the muzzle-flashes, wondered if his men had actually spied a target, then he heard one of them crying out as if in pain. It struck him then that the shots were being fired by someone else. His men had run into an ambush and were dropping now, returning fire without direction as they fell or dived for cover.

Krishnan ducked behind the stout trunk of a kapur tree that loomed above him, forty meters or more. His ears ringing with the sounds of combat, he took time to sniff the night air, picking out the scents of gunpowder and stagnant water. They were near the mangrove swamp that rimmed the nearby cove. Advancing farther meant wading knee- or hip-deep through the marsh until it cleared and they could see the beach.

But that wasn't their goal this night. The man and woman they'd pursued from camp had turned to fight. Were they alone, or had the rescuer brought reinforcements when he came to Tioman?

The only way to answer that was to press onward, face the guns and overrun them. Now, before his men could falter, Krishnan had to exert authority and drive them forward.

"Move ahead!" he shouted at them, without leaving cover.

It seemed to Krishnan that their counterfire became more concentrated then, perhaps with the location of a target. He received it as a hopeful sign and called out more encouragement.

"Attack! Kill them!" he commanded.

Slowly, by inches, the assault advanced.

MAIA LEE WAS CAREFUL not to waste her ammunition when the shooting started. Her weapon was a Browning Hi-Power standard model, and she had fired four rounds already while fleeing from her captors. That left ten shots, if the pistol had been fully loaded when she grabbed it from Syarif Hairuman's dead body, since there'd been one in the chamber and the magazine could hold thirteen. If he'd been careless with his loading, though, who knew how many rounds remained?

Make each one count, she thought. Sell your life dearly at the end.

Or better still, hope that the stranger who had rescued her—this man who called himself Matt Cooper—could kill the rest himself.

Maia had never been particularly violent, except where her profession had required it, but her ordeal in the pirate camp had stripped her of all mercy, even as it did her dignity. Hairuman would certainly have killed her soon, most likely after passing her around the camp to entertain his troops, and anything that happened to the bastards now was simply payback for the misery she'd suffered at their hands.

But if the stranger's plan fell through, she hoped to have a bullet ready for herself.

Maia's first target came in from her left, out of the darkness, having left his friends to try a one-man pincer movement. She glimpsed him first at the periphery of vision, swung around to meet him with the Browning gripped in both hands, elbows locked. The pirate had his rifle braced against a hip, prepared to fire it when she shot him one time in the chest and put him down.

It was a good hit. Even if he wasn't killed outright, the bullet should have struck his heart—or, at the very least, torn through the major arteries that pumped blood to the lungs, perhaps even the great aorta. Dead or dying, he wouldn't rejoin the fight.

Nine rounds remaining in the gun. She hoped.

Matt Cooper was firing short, controlled bursts from his automatic rifle, dropping targets left and right. Maia hadn't time to admire his method, but she felt a sense of gratitude and something that reminded her of hope. She'd given up on that when she was taken prisoner, convinced that she would soon be dead and that the end would be a sweet release from suffering.

But now…

If there was any hope at all of getting out alive, she'd go down fighting for it, tooth and nail.

The pirates, startled and disorganized when Cooper first started shooting at them from the darkness, had begun returning fire. Most of their shots were hasty, flying high and wide, but one came close to parting Maia's hair and made her duck back under cover of the nearest mangrove's roots. Waist-deep in brackish water, trying not to think about what might be squirming in the muck around her feet, she peered into the shadows lit by muzzle-flashes, searching for another target.

There! She saw a shadow-figure edging closer, letting others spend their ammunition while he closed the gap to bring Cooper within effective range. Her eyes were sharp, or she'd have missed him creeping forward like some kind of giant lizard, belly to the ground.

At first sight, he was too far off to risk wasting a pistol shot, but if she gave him time he just might solve that problem for her. In the meantime, Maia scanned the battleground for any nearer targets, then came back to focus on her chosen mark, ready to shoot despite the range, if it appeared he was about to fire at Cooper.

And was he aiming now? It seemed as if he might be peering down his rifle's barrel from a range of twenty yards or so. It was far from ideal, for handgun shooting in the dark, but Maia couldn't take the chance on having Cooper killed or disabled by a gunman he had overlooked in the chaotic swampland skirmish.

Aiming for the bulk that was her target's head and shoulders, praying that she didn't have her sights fixed on a dead log by mistake, Maia exhaled and squeezed the Browning's trigger. She felt it jolt against her palm and saw her target slump back out of sight.

A hit? A near miss that had spoiled his aim? If she had wounded him, was he disabled, even dying? Or would he recover from a simple graze to fight again?

A burst of automatic fire sprayed stagnant water into Maia's face. She fell back, sputtering, but kept her weapon pointed toward the enemy, ready for anything.

BOLAN SAW two opponents rise from cover on his right and charge toward his position. Maybe they were fed up with the waiting game, or angered by the losses that their side had taken in the ambush. Either way, it left them in the clear and he took full advantage of the moment.

Swinging toward the runners, Bolan took the closer of them first, a 3-round burst above the belt line, 5.56 mm manglers virtually disemboweling his mark. The pirate went down screaming, lost his weapon as he fell and started thrashing through the final agonizing moments of his wasted life.

The second gunman saw or heard his partner fall, thought better of his charge, but by the time he changed his mind it was too late to turn. Bolan had found him, framed him with the HK416's red-dot sight and sent three rounds downrange that nearly took his head off at the upper lip. Stone-dead before he fell, the pirate went down like a sack of dirty laundry falling from a second-story balcony.

How many left? The night prevented Bolan from determining a number, as the tents had back in camp. Presumably, he'd know that he'd run out of adversaries when their muzzle-flashes were eradicated and their slugs weren't swarming in the air like angry hornets.

Off to his left, the woman chose her targets carefully, conserving ammunition. Bolan gave her points for keeping her composure under fire, and wished he had more magazines to feed whatever kind of handgun she had taken from the pirate who'd been grilling her. No way to help that now, but he could always let her have his USP if they were stuck in place much longer.

It would be better, though, if he could break the stalemate soon, wipe out his enemies or send any survivors running back to camp, wounded and terrified.

With that in mind, Bolan unclipped one of his frag grenades and pulled its pin. It was an Austrian Arges HG 86 fragmentation grenade—the "Mini 86," weighing roughly six ounces but packing the same lethal punch as a larger grenade. Bolan pitched the bomb overhand, toward the spot where half a dozen weapons winked and clattered at him from the shadows, then ducked back to dodge the blast.

Its thunderclap was trailed by cries of pain, perhaps three voices, which told him the rest had been silenced. For good? Maybe not. But the blast had discouraged six snipers from peppering Bolan's location with full-auto fire, reducing the odds ranged against him.

The Executioner palmed a second grenade while the first's echo rang in his ears. He yanked the pin and side-armed the lethal egg toward another group of shooters, this time on his left. Another air-burst, spraying shrapnel at his enemies from overhead, and more guns stuttered into deathly silence.

It was time to go among them.

Bolan rose from cover and advanced into the killing ground.

TIONG KRISHNAN HUDDLED tight against a looming banyan tree and wished that he was somewhere else on the planet other than where he lay cringing and trembling, a heartbeat from hell. Around him, men were cursing, screaming, firing weapons at an enemy who seemed invisible, yet capable of striking them from darkness, wreaking havoc in the ranks.

He nearly panicked when a third grenade exploded, shrapnel hammering his banyan tree like hatchet blows. He nearly wet himself from fear, but clenched his muscles with a force of will, biting his lower lip until it bled. Sweat welded Krishnan's palms to his VB Berapi SMG, but he had yet to fire a shot in the engagement that was slaughtering his men.

How many shooters had been waiting for them on the border of the mangrove swamp? Krishnan had made no effort to count muzzle-flashes in the split second before he dropped and wriggled under cover, shouting imprecations to his men.

How many of his people still survived? From the return fire they were laying down, he guessed that at least half the men he'd followed out of camp were either dead, wounded or afraid to join the fight. An awful toll, and if some of the stunned survivors chose to slip away, evaporate into the darkness, who could blame them?

Khoo Kay Sundaram, for one. And he would blame their leader first, before he got around to punishing the small fry. Krishnan would be first to suffer on a list of charges that included losing an important prisoner, failing to guard against a raid upon his camp and leading—well, *pursuing*—his men into a disastrous ambush. There could only be one punishment for such malfeasance, but the manner of his death would be determined at his trial.

If he was still alive. If Sundaram could find him.

Realistically, he knew that there were many places in the world where Sundaram possessed no agents. Sadly, most of those were places where Krishnan himself would stand out to the dullest of inhabitants as strange. An alien. Still, any kind of life was better than the long and agonizing death that Sundaram might plot for him, considering the loss of life—and face—occasioned by his failure.

Time to run, then, if he meant to get away in the confusion. Screwing up the remnants of his courage, Krishnan bolted from the cover of his banyan tree just as another frag grenade exploded. Lifted by the shock wave, riddled by a score of fragments, he touched down with force enough to empty out his lungs and found he couldn't draw another breath.

So this is what it's like, he thought.

AFTER THE FOURTH GRENADE exploded, eerie quiet fell over the battlefield. Bolan didn't assume that all his enemies were dead, or even wounded. That required examination, confirmation, and he didn't feel like leaving active shooters at his back while he was trying to escape.

He gestured for the woman to remain in place. Whether she covered him was immaterial. He'd seen enough of her in action to be fairly confident she wouldn't shoot him in the back—at least, not by accident. It might have been a smart move to disarm her, but he'd trusted her this far and hadn't been let down. If nothing else, her hatred of the pirates who had caged and tortured her should keep him safe until they'd had a chance to talk.

Bolan began to work the field, pausing beside the bodies of his fallen adversaries, striking with the silent trench knife where he found a sign of life that might prove threatening. For those already obviously at death's door, he left them there to make the crossing in their own good time, first shifting any weapons well beyond their reach.

Of those he visited, only two men were strong enough to offer much resistance. One clutched at the knife as it descended, trembling hands intent on keeping it away from him, so Bolan drew his USP left-handed, thrust it underneath the straining pirate's chin and took him out that way.

The other, it appeared, hadn't been touched by either bullets or the shrapnel from grenades. Perhaps he had been stunned to immobility, or only terrified, but as the Executioner approached him he jumped up, clutching an AK-47, squeezing off a hasty burst that churned the soil in front of him. Before he could correct his aim, a double-tap from Bolan's sidearm dropped him sprawling on his back.

All done.

"It's clear," he told the woman. "If we're leaving, we should go."

She rose, looking around the swamp. "Go where?" she asked.

"Through there," he told her, pointing. "To the cove. I have a boat."

"And then the mainland?"

"That's my destination," Bolan said. "But if you'd rather stay on Tioman—"

"No!" she blurted emphatically. "I'll come with you, at least as far as land."

"Beats jumping in the water when we're halfway there," he answered, brushing past her, moving on a beeline toward the spot where he had left the Zodiac.

Splashing up beside him in the dark, the woman said, "It's later, yes? For talking?"

"If we keep it down," Bolan replied. "To hear if anyone's coming along behind us."

Lowering her voice to whisper level, she inquired, "Who sent you after me?"

"Nobody," Bolan said.

She blinked at that. "I don't understand."

"I came for them," he said, thumb cocked over his shoulder toward the killing ground they'd left behind. "You just happened to be there."

"You *didn't* come to rescue me?" He couldn't tell if she was angry now or on the verge of tears.

"Sorry," he said. "I'm glad it worked out, though."

She muttered something in her native language that he thought had to be a curse.

"As long as we're together and you know my name," he said, "do you mind sharing yours?"

"It's Maia Lee," she answered. Then, almost defiantly, she added, "I'm an agent of the Chinese Ministry of State Security."

CHAPTER FOUR

Johor Bahru, Peninsular Malaysia

Khoo Kay Sundaram replaced the satellite phone on his desk top with exaggerated care. It was an exercise he sometimes practiced, claiming self-control when he was overcome by blinding, homicidal rage. It helped him, he believed, to lead his men effectively—cool-headed in a crisis, though they all knew that his urge toward mayhem lingered just below the surface, ready to explode.

The news he had received was bad, and absolutely unexpected. A survivor of his garrison on Tioman Island had called in a panic, barely coherent until Sundaram calmed him with a promise that no punishment would be forthcoming. This time, he assured the caller—one Meor Noor, a name he didn't recognize—there would be no execution of the messenger.

By fits and starts, the story came. A stranger had appeared in camp, had freed the Chinese woman Syarif Hairuman was questioning, attempting to discern the reason for her interest in Sundaram's brotherhood of buccaneers. At last report, she had spilled nothing, but he'd trusted Hairuman to crack her. Now, the sneaking bitch was gone, along with her savior—described as "a tall man with guns"—and the bulk of Sundaram's unit on Tioman Island.

According to the caller, Hairuman was dead. So was

his second-in-command, Tiong Krishnan, and nearly all of the thirty-odd pirates whom they had commanded. Killed by a stranger—or several, if he believed Meor Noor—and by the woman herself.

Sundaram wasn't sure what it meant, except that he'd been dealt an unexpected and embarrassing defeat. It wouldn't please the big men who had hired him for the most important job of his career to date, and while he'd carried out that task successfully, part of the deal was making sure that no one traced the stolen merchandise through Sundaram to his employers. Failing to do that meant failure and disgrace across the board.

And probably, he thought, the end of life itself.

Sundaram was an accomplished thief and killer, but he knew when he was overmatched. It was a risk inherent when he dealt with leaders of the Chinese triads, but the money they had offered him was irresistible. He had considered every possibility of danger when he took their money and the job attached to it, convinced that he could pull it off. And so he had…up to a point.

The merchandise had been secured, the worst part put behind him with a stroke of daring and—why not admit it?—genius on his part. The men who'd hired him had received their cargo at the time and place appointed for delivery. They had been satisfied. Had paid in full.

But now…

A Chinese agent sniffing around Sundaram so soon after completion of his special task could only mean a breach in security. How and where the breach occurred were questions that remained unanswered, since the woman had escaped. Perhaps the leak had come from someone in the triad, but the leaders of that syndicate would certainly deny it. Without proof of some negligence on their part, Sundaram would bear the stigma of incompetence—or worse, deliberate betrayal.

Either one could put a price tag on his head, and there would be no shortage of contractors eager to collect the bounty. Some would kill him for the pleasure of it, or to settle an old score. Money would simply make the mission that much more attractive.

Khoo Kay Sundaram had no illusions about waging war against the triads and surviving. He had, what? Two hundred men at his disposal on a good day, while official estimates of triad membership ranged upward through the tens of thousands. They were everywhere, from Hong Kong and the Chinese mainland to Great Britain, Canada and the United States. To cross them was a suicidal act, and simply pleading that he *hadn't* crossed them wouldn't save his life.

What Sundaram required was proof, the vanished Chinese agent, preferably, still alive and talking. Or the stranger who had plucked her from Syarif Hairuman's clutches before he could force her to speak. Either might save him, if he found them soon enough.

But first, Sundaram had to be the bearer of bad news in his own right. He had to report his failure to Beijing, before the men who had employed him heard it elsewhere and surmised that he was keeping secrets from them.

That would never do.

Dreading the next few moments, Sundaram retrieved the sat phone, tapped in a number and waited while it rang through at the other end, three thousand miles away.

South China Sea

BOLAN MADE the best time he could manage, heading back from Tioman to the Malaysian mainland. Watching out for other craft along the way, particularly any boats that might pursue them from the island, he was still able to question Maia Lee.

"Do you mind my asking what you're doing in Malaysia with a gang of pirates?"

"I'm aware you saved my life," she said, "but still, my work is classified."

"Why blow your cover, then, and tell me who you work for?" Bolan asked.

She frowned at that. "Perhaps I was afraid you'd think I was some prostitute they picked up to amuse themselves."

"You asking me, or telling me? And either way, why would it matter to you what I thought?"

"You seem…most capable," she said. "If we speak honestly, until the day that I was kidnapped, I did not believe that I was making any progress on my task."

"Rough way to find out you were wrong," Bolan said. "When we get ashore, I'll try to find a doctor who—"

"That won't be necessary," Maia interrupted him. "My injuries are superficial. They were just beginning serious interrogation when you came, and…"

Bolan listened to her voice trail off, wondered how much he could afford to say. Considering the circumstances, he supposed there wasn't much to lose.

"All right," he said. "My job is classified, the same as yours, but here's the bottom line. Your country's lost a pair of missiles. Mine's afraid that we might be the target for whoever has them now, or plans to buy them from the hijackers. If you're working on something else, I'll drop you off ashore and wish you luck. But if we're on the same page—"

"Yes," she almost blurted out. "We are, as you say, on the same page."

"Right, then," Bolan said. "And both of us had information pointing us to Tioman."

"Not quite," Maia Lee replied. "I was investigating pirates in Johor Bahru, headquarters for the so-called brotherhood controlled by Khoo Kay Sundaram."

"I know the name," Bolan said, thinking back to Brognola's initial briefing and the CD he had scanned at Stony Man. "Top pirate in these parts."

"This week, at least," Maia replied. "He is the prime suspect. Before I could locate him, though, I was abducted. I believe that I alerted them with questions, then was too eager to meet with a supposed informant. Careless. Stupid."

"Hey, don't beat yourself up," he said. "That's someone else's job."

"And they were fairly thorough."

"About that doctor…"

"No. I won't let them delay me any longer," Maia said.

"You know best. What was the next move that you had in mind?"

"It's still the same," she said. "Find Sundaram and question him."

"That works for me," Bolan replied. "Between us, I imagine we can scare him up."

"I had three possible addresses when I reached Johor Bahru," she said. "Two of them yielded nothing. I was caught before I had a chance to check the third."

"Sounds like the place to start," he said. "One thing you ought to know, before we start. I'm not a prosecutor or policeman. I don't gather evidence. I don't take prisoners unless it serves a purpose."

"I've seen what you do," Maia said with a small half smile. "My service is not squeamish, as a rule."

"And what about the missiles?" Bolan asked her.

"If they cannot be retrieved," she said, "then they must be destroyed."

"Same page," Bolan confirmed. "I think we're good to go."

Jakarta, Indonesia

JIN AU-YO WAS just considering the possibility of sleep when his chief bodyguard, Ma Mingxia, approached him deferentially with news of an incoming phone call.

"Who?" Jin asked.

"Sundaram, sir."

The hour told Jin it could only be bad news. "I'll take it."

Ma produced a cordless phone and handed it to Jin. "Line one, sir," he said, then left the room on silent feet.

Jin waited for the door to close, then took the line off Hold and spoke his first lie of the long-distance exchange. "My friend."

"I apologize for the disturbance," Khoo Kay Sundaram replied. "If you were sleeping—"

"No. Proceed with your most urgent news, by all means."

A silent moment passed. Jin pictured Sundaram racking his brain in search of something positive to lead with. At last he said, "The merchandise is still intact."

"I hope so," Jin replied. "It would be most disturbing, otherwise. But since efficiency is what I pay you for, I doubt you've called me at this hour to confirm the status quo."

"No, sir. There have indeed been difficulties, but I wanted you to know—"

"Explain these difficulties."

"I informed you that a spy was captured by my men. Chinese. A woman."

"Yes, yes."

"Well…tonight, before they could complete interrogation, she was rescued by a stranger. Unidentified. A soldier with a painted face."

"A painted *face?*"

"For camouflage, sir."

"Ah, yes. I see. You say a soldier."

"Deadly," Sundaram replied. "He killed most of my men on Tioman. Sir, that's an island located—"

"I don't care where it is," Jin said, cutting him off. "You've lost the spy *and* all your men?"

"Not all. On Tioman only. Say thirty, more or less."

"Killed by a single man?"

"According to the lone survivor. I'm not sure I trust him, sir. He may have run away and hidden."

"Do you have him now?"

"I do," Sundaram said.

"Then wring him dry of answers. Verify his statements. If you need assistance…"

"No, sir. Thank you. We can manage."

"I hope so. And you say the merchandise is absolutely safe. Beyond all doubt?" Jin asked.

"Oh, yes, sir. In the morning, we begin transporting it."

"Why not start now?" Jin asked.

The question seemed to baffle Sundaram. When half a minute passed with no reply, Jin said, "Before the woman and her helper can resume the search."

"Oh, yes! Of course! That's brilliant, sir. We shall begin at once."

"And I suggest that you enhance security," Jin said.

"Remember, Khoo, your life depends on safe, timely delivery."

"Yes, sir. I won't forget."

"See that you don't, for all our sakes," Jin warned.

He cut the link before the Malay had a chance to grovel any more, switched off the cordless phone and set it on the low table in front of him.

A Chinese spy—if spy she was, in fact—could only mean the Ministry of State Security was now involved, as Jin had known it would be from the start. Initially, he'd thought that Sundaram was being paranoid about the woman, but her rescue proved the opposite.

Her rescue by a soldier capable of killing thirty pirates, all armed to the teeth, without sustaining any injury himself.

Not good.

Unless he had been sent specifically to find the female spy and that fulfilled his mission, Jin thought such a man would press ahead, use any means available to reach his goal. And what was that, if not the woman?

It could only be the merchandise Jin waited for, which his intended buyers lusted after in their single-minded dedication to *jihad.* Or, was it now *fatwa?* In truth, Jin neither knew nor cared what term was used for any zealot's madness of the moment. He concerned himself with cash, the nonnegotiable price he had arranged for the delivery of items ordered in a high-risk bargain.

Now, it was his loathsome task to call Beijing and tell the man who had assisted him in setting up the job that there was—no, *might be*—a problem.

Jin consulted his watch. It was one hour later in the Chinese capital, too early to rouse a sleeping man of great importance. But this day he had no choice.

It would be infinitely worse if he delayed the call

three hours and the whole deal turned into a steaming pile of feces while he stalled.

Scowling, he reached for the telephone.

Kampung Sedili Kechil, Johor, Malaysia

BOLAN HAD LAUNCHED his Tioman excursion from a cove on Malaysia's eastern coastline, near a small village. No one within the village knew his face, much less his business, and the time he'd chosen for departure guaranteed that most of the hardworking folk who occupied the hamlet were in bed, asleep. Returning three hours before the scheduled sunrise, Bolan killed his outboard when the Zodiac raft was still two hundred yards offshore and paddled in, with Maia Lee assisting him.

They beached the boat, dragged it inland and deflated it. The raft had served its purpose and was now expendable. Ten minutes hiking through dark woods brought them to Bolan's rented vehicle, a Chery Tiggo SUV produced in China for export to Asian markets. Boasting four-wheel drive, a five-speed manual transmission and a 1.6-liter engine, the Tiggo had taken Bolan where he had to go.

So far.

The drive to Johor Bahru first required doubling back northward to Kampung Sedili Besar, then picking up the expressway southbound to Johor's state capital, linked to neighboring Singapore by the Johor–Singapore Causeway. Altogether, call it eight miles and change before they motored onto Khoo Kay Sundaram's home turf.

More time to talk along the way.

Maia said she'd have to touch base with her people, which was understandable but still gave Bolan pause. There'd be no problem for him if they called her off, since she'd already shared the last address she had for Sundaram. If someone in the People's Republic of China got hinky, though, and ordered her to turn on Bolan in the interest of deniability, he'd have to make a choice between her life and moving forward with his mission.

Bottom line: no choice at all.

Bolan had dropped the hammer on a few females in his long and lonely war. One was a mercy kill; the others eliminated deadly adversaries. He hadn't enjoyed those killings, any more than he took pleasure in eradicating male opponents, but he didn't discriminate in combat, when the stakes were life or death.

He and Maia were heading in the same direction now, this moment, but he couldn't guarantee what the next hour or day might bring.

Who could?

She used his sat phone as they drove, speaking Chinese, although he couldn't say if it was Cantonese or Mandarin. Since Bolan spoke neither, it hardly mattered. He focused on her tone, noting the change in pitch as Maia seemed to disagree with something she'd been told, heat levels rising, then receding as she seemed to put her point across. The conversation lasted for five minutes, give or take, before she broke the link.

"So?" Bolan asked.

"They're pleased that I'm alive," she said. "Less pleased that you are an American."

"Surprise, surprise."

"I have approval to proceed with caution, bearing China's interest foremost in my mind."

"I would expect no less," Bolan replied.

She took the borrowed pistol from her belt and checked its magazine. "Before we start," she said, "I need more ammunition. And perhaps a bigger gun."

Beijing, People's Republic of China

FENG JINGWEI HELD the rank of commodore in the Chinese People's Liberation Army Navy. After thirty-seven years of service, he was now landlocked, commanding a desk at the Ministry of National Defense compound's August First Building. His greatest challenge in the past two years had been preparing speeches for his immediate superior, Rear Admiral Bai Zi'ang, to deliver before the Central Military Commission of the National People's Congress.

That was, until now.

At fifty-six years old, Commodore Feng had found himself susceptible to flattery and bribes, the promise of eventual retirement in a style that he could never hope to afford on his PLAN pension. Of course he felt that he deserved more, after keeping China safe from rebels and aggressors over the better part of three decades. And if the task he had to perform truly posed no threat to China's national security, why should it bother him?

The men who had approached him—bought him—only wanted information. Dates, locations, codes, passwords. What was the harm? If certain items vanished from the PLAN's inventory, they could be replaced. As long as none of them were used to injure the People's Republic, why should Feng care?

Then came the *Shenyang* attack, so many sailors dead and missing, and Feng could hardly confess his involvement at that point. Who benefited if he stood before a firing squad? Would any of the dead return to life? Would the Brave Wind missiles reappear, as if nothing had happened?

No.

The best thing Feng could do was watch and wait, hoping that nothing led investigators back to him. How long could he survive under interrogation at Qincheng Prison, in Beijing's Changping District? Feng guessed that he might last a few days, perhaps only hours, depending on the methods employed.

He barely slept these nights, since the *Shenyang* incident, and his days were an agony of waiting for military police to invade his office. Was it better to be questioned at the ministry, or dragged off in chains to a dungeon? Either way, it meant the end of life as Feng knew it.

The end of life itself.

And now, as if his own thoughts weren't enough to rob him of much-needed sleep, the bedside telephone was clamoring for his attention. Feng glanced at the clock beside it, groaned and lifted the receiver.

"What is it?"

"Commodore Feng, I must apologize for waking you at such an hour."

He recognized the voice at once. There could be no mistaking it.

"What do you want?" he asked.

"You trust this line?" Jin Au-Yo asked.

"I do." At least, as much as Feng could put his trust in anything these days.

"I'm calling to inform you of a…difficulty," Jin explained. "It seems a Chinese agent has begun investigating our associates. She was detained, but then escaped with aid from an associate who has not been identified."

Feng felt his stomach twist into a painful knot. "The woman's name?"

"If we believe her travel papers, it is Maia Lee."

"And her affiliation?"

"That, regrettably, is one of many things she did not share before parting company with our friends in Malaysia."

Our associates. *Our* friends. Feng hadn't met them and he never would. Jin chose his words to reinforce Feng's sense of guilt, as if reminders were required.

"What will you do?" Feng asked, shifting the onus back to Jin.

"We will pursue all avenues, of course, but you can help us."

"How?"

"Pay close attention at the ministry. Find out, if possible, whether an agent was dispatched to seek the missing merchandise."

"I would expect no less," Feng said. "But bear in mind, this agent may not represent *my* ministry. There's still—"

"The Ministry of State Security," Jin interrupted him. "We've thought of that. Steps will be taken to investigate that possibility. Meanwhile…"

"I'll find out what I can, of course," Feng said.

"No one could ask for more," Jin replied. "Good morning, Commodore."

The line went dead. Feng laid the phone aside and slumped back on his pillow. Any idle thought of sleep was banished now. Feng's waking nightmare had begun.

CHAPTER FIVE

Johor Bahru

Khoo Kay Sundaram was drinking earlier than usual—or was it later? Either way, he could deceive himself by thinking of the Asta peach-flavored vodka as fruit juice, something anyone might drink for breakfast in the morning. And it soothed him, which was all that Sundaram could ask.

Unfortunately, it didn't soothe him enough.

His mind was still in turmoil, and his stomach still rebelled, leaving a rank taste in his mouth that undercut the vodka's fruity flavor. Sundaram wondered if he had ulcers, then decided that it made no difference. Unless he could regain control of his domain and solve the problem that confronted him, the odds were good that he wouldn't survive to worry any further about transient stomach pains.

His men were searching for the woman and the soldier who had rescued her, but they were limited in fundamental ways. As pirates, many of them former fishers and smugglers, they knew little about seeking out informers in the city, much less tracking Chinese spies. The triad would be better suited to that task, and while he knew that they were working on it simultaneously, Sundaram couldn't afford to sit by idly, hoping someone else would do his work for him.

The best that he could hope for in that case would be a short trip to a shallow grave. Perhaps a burial at sea. Shark food. It was a fate suited to buccaneers, but Sundaram preferred to die of old age, in a harlot's arms.

Assuming that the choice was his.

His headquarters, appropriately, were located in Waterfront Lot No. 1, on Persiaran Tun Sri Lanang, a quarter-mile west of the Johor Causeway. From his third-floor window, Sundaram could see the lights of Singapore and watch them start to wink out as a new day dawned. Fatigue and alcohol combined to make his eyelids droop, but Sundaram shook off his torpor, drained his glass and went to make a pot of strong black coffee.

"Sleep when you're dead," he muttered to himself, nearly smiling.

Sundaram had sent all but three members of his headquarters staff to the streets, with orders not to return empty-handed. It sounded good in theory, but what could he really expect? Would the Chinese spy risk showing her face in Johor Bahru, even with a soldier to protect her? Sundaram thought it more likely that she'd run for home, but he couldn't be sure. He had to go through the motions. Look busy. Appear to be doing his part.

Meanwhile, his business suffered. He couldn't launch any further raids on merchant shipping while loose ends from the big job still remained to be tied up. It struck him now that even when the missiles were delivered to the triad, he might not receive the payment that was due to him until he satisfied the Chinese mobsters that his mess had been resolved.

What was the woman doing now, that very moment? Resting and recuperating from the pain she'd suffered at Syarif Hairuman's hands, perhaps. Or making a report to Beijing that would bring more heat down onto Sundaram. He wouldn't put it past them to abduct him, given half a chance.

Never mind, he thought. At the moment I'm safe here, at the very least.

"THIS IS THE PLACE," said Maia Lee.

Bolan drove slowly past Waterfront Lot No. 1, eastbound, and checked out the spread. Its road frontage was close to four hundred yards long, and the whole lot—a kind of rectangular pier packed with buildings—protruded something like two hundred feet into Johor Strait, the serpentine strip of seawater separating Singapore from the Malaysian mainland.

Access to the property was via a north-south road called Jalan Ayer Molek, which reached a dead end fifty feet past the southernmost edge of the waterfront lot, with a dock and crane designed for loading and unloading cargo ships. Bolan supposed it was ideal for dropping merchandise from raids at sea, although he doubted anyone was dumb enough to try off-loading two Chinese ballistic missiles there.

"Ready?" he asked Maia.

"Ready."

She'd known a place in Taman Daya township where hardware was available at need, had ducked in while he circled three times cautiously around the block and came out with a Chinese Type 85 submachine gun, the silenced version, plus spare magazines and extra 7.62 mm Tokarev ammunition. Bolan didn't ask, and Maia didn't tell.

To reach the address that was third and last on Maia's list, Bolan continued westward. Turning onto a one-way street, he drove a hundred yards, then turned right to reach the waterfront complex. No one was stirring on the property, as far as he could see, despite the first pale light of dawn breaking to Bolan's left.

The soldier couldn't read the signs posted on any of the buildings, but their numbers were clearly visible and he had no trouble finding 107A. There seemed to be no 107B, but Bolan wasted no time puzzling over that anomaly. He motored past the address Maia had recorded as a possible hideout for Khoo Kay Sundaram and found a place nearby to park his SUV.

"We don't know what we're walking into," he told Maia, as he pulled the HK416 into his lap and double-checked its magazine. "If Sundaram's inside there, he could have a couple of dozen bodyguards, or none at all."

"He never sleeps or travels by himself," Maia replied. "There will be guards. As to how many, I don't know."

"And if he's not at home?"

She shrugged. "We find another way to locate him. Pick up one of his men for questioning. Keep on until we find one who can help us."

"Right," Bolan agreed, pleased with her go-to attitude. "I'll know him from his photographs if he's inside."

They left the SUV and Bolan locked it, then walked back the twenty yards or so to number 107A. Maia checked out the sign above its door and translated. "Floating Dragon Enterprises," she told Bolan. "It's a front for smuggling, I believe."

No great surprise, considering the tenant's stock-in-trade.

Bolan ignored the front door, found a narrow passageway between the prefab building and its neighbor to the east and reached its rear approach in seconds flat. The door back there was locked, but Bolan checked for any sign of wiring for alarms, found none and went to work with picks while Maia covered him.

The lock yielded a moment later, and the door swung inward at his touch.

MAIA FOLLOWED COOPER through the doorway with her submachine gun at the ready, muzzle-heavy with its sound suppressor and folded stock. Beyond the blacked-out entryway, a dim light beckoned from the second-story landing of a staircase just ahead. Beyond it lay closed doors flanking a silent corridor, no light leaking from under them.

If Sundaram was here, according to her information, they would find him on the top floor, number three, a suite of offices with windows facing south. There'd been no time for Maia to assess that information prior to being captured in Johor Bahru, but at the first two places she had checked, there had at least been signs of Sundaram's associates residing on the premises.

But if they missed him here…

Her companion started up the stairs, his eyes and automatic rifle raised to cover the landing above them. If trouble found them now, his body would block Maia's line of fire, but there was nothing she could do about it on the narrow staircase. Keeping to one side, placing each foot in turn with care, she tried to keep the stairs from creaking as she climbed. No sign of bodyguards so far, but if a trap was waiting for them—

Cooper froze on the stairs above her, half a dozen steps below the landing. Maia heard the floor groan then, a sound of footsteps moving closer, and she moved to reach the American, touched him on the shoulder, edging past him with her silenced weapon as he moved aside.

The Type 85 submachine gun used two different grades of 7.62 mm Tokarev ammunition. Type 64 rounds optimized performance for the silenced version, with their smaller powder charge and heavier subsonic bullets, while standard Type 51 rounds made more noise and added fifty yards to the gun's effective range. Maia had picked Type 64 to suit her weapon when she chose it from the covert armory her ministry maintained in Taman Daya township, and was glad now for her choice.

Ten long seconds passed before the shuffling man appeared before her, on the second-story landing. Maia hesitated long enough to see his shoulder-slung Ka-lashnikov, then stitched a silent 3-round burst across his chest and spilled him headfirst down the stairwell. As he tumbled past her, Maia rushed the landing, let her companion dodge the falling body in his own good time and had the next hallway covered by the time he joined her.

No one was there to greet them, with the first lookout eliminated. Six closed doors, three on a side, and nothing to suggest that any of the rooms were occupied. She could be wrong, of course. It was a risk to move ahead without clearing the rooms, but Maia felt time bearing down like an oppressive weight across her shoulders.

"One more flight," she whispered, and received a nod in answer.

He let Maia take the lead, whether impressed by her performance with the first guard or preferring silence if the need to kill arose again, she couldn't say. So far, the strike reminded Maia of her training with the Bei-jing Military Region Special Forces Unit, which was mandatory for field agents of her ministry. It might have been a graduation exercise inside the "killing house," except that there was real blood on the stairs, and more yet to be spilled.

Should she feel something for the man whom she had slain?

Maia remembered the indignity and pain she'd suffered in captivity, letting the chill of hatred guide her toward the final flight of stairs.

KHOO KAY SUNDARAM was halfway through another cup of coffee and felt his stomach simmering in protest. This would be his last. Enough caffeine was coursing through his system now to keep him wide-awake for several hours, he supposed, and there was nothing to be gained from artificially inducing nausea.

He rose to pace the smallish office, checked the view with dawn's pale light advancing eastward, gradually turning off the lights of Singapore across the water, and decided that it might help if he went to check in with his men. Aside from exercise to keep him on alert, there was an outside chance that he might catch one of them dozing and amuse himself by chastising the sluggard.

Not that he really expected to find any of them sleeping on the job. They knew what had befallen their comrades on Tioman Island and would be fearful of an enemy who could surprise and slaughter thirty men. Granted, the odds of that same enemy appearing on their doorstep in Johor Bahru seemed slight, but while the threat existed, Sundaram's defenders would be on their toes.

And so should he.

To set the proper tone, he drew a pistol from his belt. It was a 9 mm Vektor SP1 from South Africa, one of the several handguns issued to Malaysian troops as standard sidearms. Sundaram checked the magazine, confirming a full load of fifteen rounds, and eased back the slide to see one in the chamber.

All set.

Returning the piece to his waistband, he gulped the last of his coffee and stifled a belch, then crossed to the exit and stepped from his office. As the door closed behind him, Sundaram thought that he heard a muffled ripping sound from somewhere to his left, in the direction of the staircase.

Someone sneezing? No, that wasn't right. Nor had it been a shuffling footstep.

Possibly a rat at large, prowling for scraps before full daylight drove it into hiding.

Why not ask his men? With that in mind, Sundaram set off toward the stairs, lamenting once again that he had rented quarters in a building with no elevator.

Never mind. At least the climbing up and down was beneficial exercise.

Sundaram was halfway to the staircase when a sound of whispered voices reached his ears. He paused in mid-stride, frowning, tried to think of any reason why his men should have to whisper, when they had the whole damned building to themselves. Perhaps complaining of their duty overnight? If he could catch them at it, there would be another chance to rail at them, venting his anger and frustration on convenient targets.

He moved, more cautiously this time, in the direction of the stairs. It would be nice to take them by surprise, loom over them, glaring, demanding that they voice their grievances directly to his face. And watch them wither in the face of his disgust at men who couldn't do the simplest job without stopping to whine about it.

Sundaram was almost at the landing, had his first

line framed in mind, when he heard footsteps coming up to meet him.

He was reaching for his pistol when two strangers, male and female, suddenly rose into view.

Each held an automatic weapon pointed at his face.

IT SEEMED to be a toss-up in the pirate's mind, whether to go down blazing or surrender. Bolan watched him with the HK416 rock-steady on his center of mass, his index finger on the rifle's trigger fresh out of slack. If Sundaram twitched, he was dead. And he had to have known it.

When they hadn't killed him after six or seven seconds, he asked, "Who are you? What do you want?"

English. No great surprise, since Malaysia had been a British colony through the late 1950s, and English remained the country's second official language. Sundaram had obviously sized them up, processed the fact that neither one of them was Malay and took his best shot.

"First thing," Bolan replied, "you need to lose the gun and any other weapons that you're carrying."

"You will not shoot me?"

"If that's what we wanted, you'd be dead right now," Bolan assured him.

Cautiously, like an arthritic man reaching for an object he'd dropped, Sundaram set his submachine gun on the floor, then nudged it away with his foot. A wicked-looking switchblade followed, snapping open as it hit the floor. That done, Sundaram stood erect and raised his empty hands.

Bolan let Maia search him, covering the pirate chief while she lifted the loose tail of his baggy shirt, turned his pockets inside out and lifted the cuffs of his trou-

sers. Done with that, she took his SMG and knife, retreating to the sidelines.

"Where's your office?" Bolan asked.

As if afraid to point, Sundaram cocked his head to
the left and behind him. "Back there."

"We'll talk in there," Bolan said. "Lead the way as
if your life depended on it."

Which, in fact, it did.

Sundaram played it straight, no bolting for the open
office doorway, waiting on the threshold until both of
them caught up with him, then entering with measured
steps, keeping his hands in view. Bolan went next and
scanned the room for weapons, seeing none. Desk drawers could hide a multitude of sins, though, and he mo-
tioned Sundaram to take a chair standing alone, off to
their right, beside a coat rack.

When their prisoner had settled in his seat, Bolan
informed him, "We don't have much time, so here's the
rule. We ask, you answer. If it feels like you're evading,
playing games or stringing us along, you die. Got it?"

"I understand," Sundaram said. Bolan supposed he'd
played this game before, as the inquisitor, with someone else stuck in the hot seat.

Maia spoke up, saying, "Your men attacked the
Shenyang and removed two missiles from the ship."

No question there, but Sundaram read Maia's face
and answered with a nod.

"Where are they?" Maia asked him.

"Presently in transit," he replied. "Delivery is scheduled to occur—" he checked a flashy watch "—in four
hours."

"Delivery to whom?" Bolan inquired.

"The buyers," Sundaram replied. "To members of
the Flying Ax Triad."

"They are the second strongest triad," Maia told Bolan, "after 14K. An estimated twenty thousand members. Their godfather—the 'mountain master'—is Wu Guchan. He has headquarters in Beijing."

"I've never spoken to the top man," Sundaram advised them. "All my dealings were with Jin Au-Yo."

"The triad's 'vanguard,'" Maia said. "He is the operations officer, equivalent to a vice president—or underboss, if we were speaking of the Mafia."

"Four hours," Bolan said. "And where does the delivery take place?"

"At sea," Sundaram replied. "One of our ships proceeds from Kuala Terengganu toward the Spratly Islands. While en route, the other vessel radios the rendezvous coordinates. The chances of a trap are minimal."

And Bolan couldn't call ahead for anyone to intercept the missiles. They were screwed, unless...

"Ballistic missiles have no value to the triads," he told Sundaram. "We need an ID for the end users."

"I asked that question," Sundaram replied. "Jin told me that the less I know, the more he trusts me."

Need to know. The bottom line.

"So, you have no idea who plans to take delivery and use the FH3s?"

A shrug from Sundaram. "It could be anyone," he said. "I'd tell you if I knew, but—"

Maia's weapon coughed a nearly silent round, and Sundaram spilled from his chair, a crimson keyhole gaping in the middle of his forehead.

"Useless," Maia said.

"At least we have another target," Bolan stated.

"The Flying Ax Triad."

"We're out of time," he said. "Let's hit the road. I need to make some calls."

CHAPTER SIX

Washington, D.C.

Hal Brognola almost made it. He was at his office door, hand on the knob, pulling it open, when his private phone line warbled at him, pleading for attention.

"Every time I think I'm out," he muttered in his best Pacino, "they pull me back in."

He shut the door, retreated and picked up the phone on its third ring. "Hello?"

"How's yesterday going for you," Bolan asked him, calling from half a world away, on the far side of the International Date Line.

"Could be worse," Brognola granted. "How's tomorrow?"

"Could be better," Bolan said.

"What's up?"

"We've dealt with Sundaram," Bolan said, knowing that the big Fed's private line was scrambled and secure, swept time and time again for taps throughout the day.

"Who's *we?*"

"At my first stop," Bolan said, "I found his people torturing a woman. Turns out she's an agent from the Chinese Ministry of State Security."

"After the cargo for her own side," Brognola surmised.

"That's it. We're trying to collaborate, so far."

"And how's that working for you?"

"We have the same goal, more or less. Retrieval or elimination."

"I suspect she's got a different take on the retrieval part," Brognola said.

"We'll talk about it if we get that far," Bolan replied.

"Okay. What did you learn from Sundaram?"

"His people definitely bagged the items, on commission for one of the triads. Flying Ax, specifically. They have a buyer, but they didn't share details with Sundaram. Delivery is set for—" Bolan paused, as if to check his watch "—three hours and change. They're handing off at sea."

"Which sea?" Brognola asked.

"South China," Bolan said. "No prearranged coordinates. They sail east, waiting for radio contact, then head for the meet."

The big Fed swore eloquently, then said, "So, we're too late. Nothing we've got's close enough to intercept them, even if we had the right coordinates." Another curse, with feeling.

"But we're not too late," Bolan advised him. "That's a hand-off to the Flying Ax, not to the end users. With a little luck, I should be able to extract more information from the triads."

"Just a little luck?" Brognola asked, sounding skeptical.

"I'll be persuasive," Bolan answered. "Maia—that's Beijing player Maia Lee, or so she says—tells me the nearest captain for the Flying Ax does business from Jakarta, so we're heading over there ASAP."

"We don't have anybody in Jakarta," Hal told Bolan. Meaning Stony Man had no one. "I could ask the Company."

"Let's not rush into that," Bolan requested. "Right now, I'm just touching base. If we need anything, you'll hear from me."

"Nothing against the lady, sight unseen," Brognola answered, "but I'd watch that *we* if I were you."

"I'm watching everything," Bolan assured him. "Later."

And the line went dead.

Jakarta and the goddamned triads. The big Fed knew Bolan's capabilities—and frankly hadn't seen his limits yet, regardless of the odds arrayed against him—but the latest setup worried him. It couldn't hurt to contact Stony Man and see what Aaron Kurtzman's cyber-heads could dig up on the Indonesian triad scene.

He cursed again, directed at himself this time. He hadn't thought to ask if Bolan knew the local triad leader's name, Jakarta address, anything about him. For the hundredth time that week, Brognola asked himself if he was slipping, then dismissed the thought.

Some miles left on me yet, he told himself. I'll know when I've run out of gas.

And hoped Bolan would be around for his retirement party, when the time came.

Not buried halfway around the planet in a shallow grave.

Changi International Airport, Singapore

FLYING SOUTH to Jakarta meant ditching the guns, ammunition, grenades and the rest of their gear. Bolan and Maia had discussed hiring a boat to keep their arsenal intact, but flight time was one hour and eight minutes, versus fifteen hours on the water, even if they found a boat that could maintain a constant speed of thirty knots.

No contest.

They would use some of the time they saved in flight to find new hardware in Jakarta. Maia mentioned having contacts there, and Bolan took her at her word.

They'd driven across the Johor Causeway into Singapore, since Johor Bahru's Senai International Airport was international in name only, its flights, in fact, restricted to southern and western Malaysia. The drive didn't cost them much time, and bookings were easily obtained with Batavia Air, a Jakarta-based airline flying out of Terminal 2 at Changi International.

An hour in the air wasn't much time for planning a life-or-death campaign, but they'd talked on the drive into Singapore and continued at the airport, sitting behind magazines they didn't read—couldn't, in Bolan's case—and speaking at whisper level.

The scheme they finally devised was relatively simple, if everything went according to plan. Of course, as Bolan knew from grim experience, that was the huge *if* that began every venture in life. Once plans moved into action, though, a thousand different things were likely to go wrong, whether the target was a simple Sunday drive or launching an amphibious invasion of a hostile shore.

The plan that he had hatched with Maia fell somewhere between the two extremes, closer to D-Day than a picnic in the countryside. They had no reason to believe that anybody would be watching for them at Jakarta's international airport, but they would still exercise the appropriate caution. Once on the ground and on wheels—Bolan had a car booked in advance—

they would touch base with Maia's contact and rearm themselves on Bolan's dime.

Which posed the first great risk of the Jakarta blitz, in Bolan's mind. Hal Brognola was suspicious of Maia sight unseen, reacting from a lifetime of distrust for Red China that lingered, with good reason, to the present day. Bolan, for his part, couldn't see why she would go to the trouble of setting him up for a hit in Jakarta, when she could have simply phoned the Chinese embassy in Kuala Lumpur for reinforcements.

There were two other risks while buying black-market weapons in a foreign country: the police and local gangsters. Maia could be leading them into a trap without knowing it, either exposing them to police surveillance and capture, or tipping some local syndicate—even the triads—that strangers were in town buying heavy-duty implements of destruction. From there, it was a short step to pursuit and trouble Bolan didn't need while he was trying to retrieve a pair of stolen missiles.

Tough it out, he thought, as a disembodied voice called boarding for their flight.

There seemed to be no other choice.

Pondok Indah, South Jakarta

ONCE AGAIN, the news from Johor Bahru was bad. Jin Au-Yo listened silently, letting the caller impart all the information that he possessed, then asked two questions. Both were answered in the negative. Jin cut the link without goodbyes, which he regarded as a waste of breath and energy.

So Khoo Kay Sundaram was dead, along with three more of his men. The flunkies didn't interest Jin. And, in fact, since his business with Sundaram would be completed with collection of the Chinese missiles in another hour and forty-odd minutes, Jin hardly cared about the pirate captain's death. He had no further use for Sundaram, and there were always other thieves.

It was the nature of the world.

Two things, however, had bothered Jin Au-Yo about the trouble in Malaysia. Since he had no faith in coincidence, he took for granted that the incidents were both connected—and, in turn, that they involved his business deal with Sundaram. First, the appearance of a Chinese agent in Johor Bahru, which Sundaram supposedly had resolved with her detention and interrogation. Next, the agent's getaway, assisted by an unknown soldier who had sliced his way through Sundaram's "elite" force like a heated blade through butter. Now, finally, there was the death of Sundaram himself.

But *was* it final?

That was Jin's next, and by far the most important, concern. He didn't really care if all the pirates in Malaysia were assassinated overnight. More would arise to take their place before a day had passed. His true concern was that the killers—and the Chinese agent he assumed had to be directing them—wouldn't be satisfied with the annihilation in Johor. Beijing would seek retrieval of the stolen missiles, which in turn would lead the hunters back to Jin Au-Yo.

If Sundaram had talked.

Jin had a comfortable life in Pondok Indah, South Jakarta's most affluent neighborhood, on par with California's Beverly Hills or London's Belgravia district. Three-quarters of the neighborhood's inhabitants were rich expatriates, many with children enrolled at Jakarta International School. Jin himself was childless and unmarried, but he did enjoy spending his free time at the Pondok Indah Golf and Country Club, once venue of the Golf World Cup.

Jin's wealth and status flowed from long, hard work on behalf of the Flying Ax Triad. He had joined the triad as a lowly "forty-niner" in the rank and file. With diligence and raw ferocity he had advanced to hold the rank of "red pole," or enforcer. More years spent in that position, shedding blood for those above him, ultimately led to Jin's promotion as the "vanguard" in charge of the triad's operations in Malaysia and Indonesia. His present coup, if it succeeded, would leave Jin ideally placed to lead the triad when its present "mountain master" died.

And that could be arranged.

But if he failed to consummate the deal, his prospects would be blighted. Either that, or Khoo Kay Sundaram's assassins might collect his head before the triad got around to meting out whatever punishment it deemed appropriate.

Jin planned to be prepared. And that meant reaching out to warn a colleague in Beijing.

Aboard Batavia Air Flight 436

MAIA LEE WAS TIRED but couldn't sleep. She'd tried, even before they started taxiing for takeoff, but her mind was racing and the knowledge that she'd only have an hour in the air prevented her from dozing off. Instead, she tried to read one of the in-flight magazines, but nothing held her interest.

Maia couldn't stop thinking of the grim events that had consumed her past two days, and those that lay ahead. More blood would be spilled, she had no doubt of that. And some of it might be her own.

The Chinese agent had understood the risks before she joined the Ministry of State Security. She had performed her duties expeditiously on prior assignments, but the present task trumped anything she had been asked to do before. It might be an exaggeration to suggest that world peace depended upon her success. Then again, it might not.

Certainly, hundreds of thousands of lives depended on finding the two stolen missiles and neutralizing their threat. What was Maia's survival compared to that goal? Beijing would only deem her death significant if it prevented Maia from completing her assignment. Otherwise, she was a resource to be used. A tool employed until it broke, then to be cast aside.

She had reported to the ministry, briefly described her capture and escape, the death of Sundaram and her intention of pursuing Jin Au-Yo. Maia hadn't informed her masters of another player's entry to the game. Matt Cooper would be her secret, and their victory—assuming they prevailed—would be reported to Beijing as hers alone.

Why not? It would enhance her reputation and her pay grade, possibly lift Maia to a rank where she wasn't dispatched to filthy corners of the world in search of evil men. Perhaps she'd have a desk and office of her own, from which she issued orders to people underneath her. Let them catch the red-eye flights on half an hour's notice. Let them dodge the bullets, take the beatings, face the alligator clips attached to hand-crank generators.

Or would she miss the action if removed from it? Her answer, at that moment, would have been a most emphatic negative. But if Maia was honest with herself, she didn't crave a stationary job devoid of all adventure. She would miss the cachet that accompanied the tough assignments, facing danger, carrying a gun on hostile foreign streets.

Romantic? Hardly. Still, there *was* an element of raw adventure that had drawn her to the job initially, hoping to serve her country, see more of the world and have a certain measure of excitement in her life. Which brought to mind an ancient Chinese curse: may you find what you are looking for.

Maia had done that. It had nearly killed her—would have killed her, but for Matt Cooper's accidental intervention—and now she was going back for more. Pressing her luck. Racing against the clock and flying in the face of danger.

If she failed, the blame would fall on her alone.

The good news: Maia probably wouldn't be living to experience the shame.

Ministry of State Security Headquarters, Beijing

DEPUTY ASSISTANT MINISTER Chou Hua Tian glanced up from the boring report he was reading, distracted by the purring of his private phone line. Frowning in surprise, he opened the upper-left drawer of his desk and extracted the telephone he kept inside. The phone wasn't secret, of course, since keeping secrets at the Ministry of State Security was an exercise in futility. The line was scrambled, though, and access to it was restricted.

"Yes?" he spoke into the mouthpiece.

"Are you free to speak?" a familiar voice asked.

"Briefly," Chou answered, as his frown deepened.

"We have difficulties," Jin Au-Yo informed him, speaking softly but with urgency.

"Explain."

"An agent, likely from your ministry, has been investigating our transaction," Jin replied.

Chou felt a chill seep through his bowels. He glanced around his office, as if worried someone might be crouched down in a corner, eavesdropping. "How do you know this?" he demanded.

"She was caught," Jin said. "Detained for questioning, but then escaped."

"Escaped? How could you—"

"Not from me," the triad spokesman interrupted. "Our employees in Malaysia."

Stressing *our,* making the point with Chou. "Can they retrieve her?" Chou asked Jin.

"Unlikely, since they're dead. Her rescuer, whomever he may be, is an efficient killer."

Lowering his voice almost to a whisper, Chou said, "Dead? Who's dead? How many?"

"Numbers aren't important," Jin replied. "One of them, I must tell you, was my contact and the leader of the rest. There is no way to know whether he was compelled to speak before he died."

The chill became a cramp, wringing a hiss of startled pain from Chou's throat as he clutched the telephone in a death grip. "What could he tell?" he asked Jin. "Theoretically?"

"My name, of course. The timing of delivery. Not much."

"Not much? How can you say—"

"He could not give a place for the delivery, which should occur within the hour. Sharing my name with his killers may direct them here. In which case, they will die."

"But if these people wiped out all the others—"

"Not all," Jin corrected him. "Twenty or thirty, I suppose, with their commander."

"So—"

"The men who've died so far were peasants. Most of them were probably illiterate. No one will miss them. If their killers come to me, they must confront the Flying Ax."

Hating to ask, Chou knew he was required to speak. "What can I do to help?" he asked.

"No doubt your agency was mobilized to find the Brave Winds after they went missing, eh?"

"Of course."

"Find out which agents were assigned to seek them in Malaysia. Check for women first, but get a full list of the names."

Another cramp. "If I—"

Jin cut him off. "You are a deputy assistant minister. Who will object to answering your questions? Who would dare?"

"All right. Yes. I will do it."

"Do it quickly," Jin amended. "There's no time to waste."

Chou listened to the dial tone buzzing in his ear and shuddered as his bowels cramped once again. The pain propelled him from his chair, across the office to his private lavatory, which he barely reached in time.

Scared shitless, as the crude Americans might say.

And thinking, even now, of ways to save himself. Distance himself from Jin, the Flying Ax Triad, and all of it. But first, before he chose a path that might lead him to ruin, even death, he would attempt to do what Jin demanded of him.

Find a name or names. Betray the patriots to shield himself from shame, trial, execution.

Yes, Chou thought. He could do that.

Soekarno–Hatta International Airport, Jakarta

BOLAN DISEMBARKED with Maia at Gate D3, in Terminal 2. He took it as a good sign that no uniforms were waiting to receive them, and no grim-faced types in plain clothes showing bulges underneath their shirts or jackets. Posted signs at Immigration separated them by nationality, and Bolan showed his passport in the name of Matthew Cooper, a California resident. The passport—one of many forged by Stony Man from blanks provided by the State Department—was in all respects immaculate. He passed inspection after answering the normal questions, and dawdled at a newspaper shop while waiting for Maia to catch up.

Indonesia had suspended diplomatic relations with Red China for a quarter century following the xenophobic upheaval and massacres of 1965. Civil communication was resumed in 1990, but tourists from the PRC were still viewed with suspicion as potential spies in some quarters. With that in mind, Maia had brought along a passport from Taiwan, aka the Republic of China, occupied by descendants of Kuomintang supporters who had fled the mainland in 1949, when Mao Zedong's Communist Party won the nation's long and bloody civil war.

It passed inspection, and she joined Bolan moments later, catching him with a foreign edition of *People* in hand. Scanning the headline of the article he'd been perusing, she remarked, "I can't believe they keep adopting all those children."

Bolan's contribution to the human gene pool had, so far, consisted solely of removing dismal specimens. He frowned, shrugged, laid the magazine aside. "At least they can afford it," he replied. "Ready?"

They passed along the concourse to the Avis booth, where Bolan had a car reserved under his Cooper identity. Their vehicle was a Toyota Fortuner, a midsize SUV. Like its three neighboring countries—Malaysia, East Timor and Papua New Guinea—Indonesia had left-handed traffic, a holdover from old-time British influence. Bolan was used to it by now, from this and other missions overseas. With Maia navigating, translating the posted signs, he found the airport exit and was on his way.

"Guns next," he said, when they were clear.

"Guns, definitely," Maia said.

The contact they were seeking ran an import shop in Jagakarsa, South Jakarta. His name was Ruslan Bakrie, and while he wasn't expecting them—it would have been too easy to prepare a trap—Maia told Bolan that he always kept a backroom inventory suited to the needs of gangsters, paramilitary types, or one-off killers with a private ax to grind. Bakrie judged no one, took no sides. All customers were welcome if they came with cash in hand.

And he would be acquainted with the local triad operators, certainly.

That could be good or bad, depending how it played. Even if Bakrie sold them out after the fact, it might provide a point of contact between Bolan and the Flying Ax Triad.

And if he played his cards right, one contact could be enough.

CHAPTER SEVEN

Bolan drove south along Jalan Lenteng Agung Timur, pacing the one-way traffic flow, until he reached Jalan Jagakarsa and turned west. Another eighth of a mile brought him to Ruslan Bakrie's shop, under a sign that read Impor Murah.

"Bargain Imports," Maia translated. "I don't suppose we'll get a merchandise we're looking for."

"I wouldn't count on it," said Bolan, "but it's my treat."

"Ah. A rich American."

"Let's say it came to me as a bequest."

He still recalled the Pennsylvania mobster's final words. *Hey, take the money, pal. Who needs it, anyhow? It's yours!*

"A relative?" she asked.

"The kind you don't invite to babysit your kids," Bolan replied.

He found a place to park, locked the Toyota, and they walked back to the shop. Inside, the atmosphere was rank with incense. Tinkling bells announced their entry, and a man of middle age came out to greet them. He had black hair streaked with gray, blue eyes at odds with his olive complexion, and a rolling walk that could have indicated either years at sea or maybe stiffness in his hips.

At sight of Bolan he tried English first. "Good morning, sir and madam. Welcome to my humble enterprise. How may I serve you?"

"Ruslan Bakrie?" Bolan asked him, making sure.

"Indeed, the very same." He was all smiles, showing a gold incisor.

Maia took the lead then, telling him, "We've come for special merchandise."

The smile slipped. Bakrie told her, "I would like to think that all my merchandise is special."

Maia clucked her tongue and said, "We were referred to you by Jin Au-Yo. You understand?"

"Ah," Bakrie said. "Of course. The *extra*-special merchandise." He edged past Bolan, locked the shop's front door, reversed a dangling sign to indicate the place was closed. "If you would kindly follow me…"

A basement, air-conditioned to prevent humidity from breeding rust. Bakrie had guns and then some racked along three walls, with more displayed on tables in the middle of the room. Around the tables, crates of ammunition and explosives had been stacked thigh-high.

"This is my standing inventory," Bakrie said. "For *very* extra-special items placed on order, there may be a brief delay."

"You should have everything we need right here," Bolan remarked, as he began to browse.

He chose a Pindad SS2 assault rifle, standard issue for the Indonesian army, chambered in 5.56 mm. It had a folding stock and wore a Pindad SPG1 grenade launcher mounted below its barrel—an Indonesian knock-off of the American M-203 in 40 mm. As a sidearm, Bolan picked another local standard, the SIG-Sauer P-226 chambered in 9 mm Parabellum, fed from 15-round mags. The SIG's muzzle was threaded for a sound suppressor, and Bolan added that to his shopping list, along with a Tanto dagger for hand-to-hand work.

Maia followed Bolan's lead on the SIG-Sauer autoloader, but passed on a rifle in favor of a Pindad PM2 submachine gun with suppressor. The PM2 was modeled on Bolan's SS2 rifle, but chambered for 9 mm Parabellum and loading 30-round box magazines. Almost as an afterthought, she chose what Bolan took to be a knuckle-duster at first glance—until she pressed a button at the top to bear a curved blade like a puma's claw.

"A small surprise, eh?" she remarked.

"I'd say that's right," Bolan replied, and went to pay their bill while Maia packed the gear in matching duffel bags.

Pondok Indah, South Jakarta

"You know who this is?" the caller asked.

"Certainly, old friend," Jin Au-Yo said.

The triad vanguard's memory was excellent for voices, faces, names—all things, in fact, that might determine whether he remained at liberty. Whether he lived or died. The voice of Ruslan Bakrie was no challenge to him, even though they hadn't spoken personally for the past six months or more. It helped, also, that Ma Mingxia had tipped him in advance.

"I've had two customers for special merchandise," Bakrie informed him. "I thought you should know. They used your name."

"Did they?"

"Yes, sir."

"Describe them for me."

"A white man and Chinese woman," Bakrie said. "I would say the man is an American. Six feet, perhaps.

Dark hair, an ordinary face, clean-shaved. He has a killer's eyes. The woman is of average size. Her hair comes to the shoulder and is parted in the middle. Nothing to set her apart, if you saw her alone on the street."

"What did they purchase?"

"One rifle, one submachine gun, two sidearms, two knives. Assorted ammunition for the weapons."

"Thank you, Ruslan. I'm familiar with them. Rest assured your vigilance will be rewarded."

"Thank you, sir."

"You're welcome, and good day to you."

So Sundaram *had* talked, and now the people who had killed him were intent on making use of what he'd told them. At the very least, he'd spilled Jin's name, which presupposed some mention of his rank within the Flying Ax Triad. It was as well for Sundaram that they had slain him. Jin Au-Yo would have been forced to punish such betrayal with a bitter and protracted death.

But the Malay pirate was beyond his reach forever now, and Jin had other problems to concern him. Could he trust that only two opponents had been sent to stalk him? While that number coincided with the spotty information he'd been given from Malaysia, it seemed ludicrous to Jin that anyone who knew a thing about the Flying Ax would send two lonely fighters—one of them a woman—to contest the triad's power in Jakarta.

Ludicrous and fatal.

They were armed, but what of it? Jin had a hundred men at his immediate disposal, and no shortage of weapons. Khoo Kay Sundaram's death and the decimation of his so-called soldiers was a cautionary tale, but Jin couldn't compare a pack of fishermen-turned-pirates with the troops he kept on hand. The lowest forty-niner of the Flying Ax Triad was skilled in martial arts and

marksmanship, each man a proven killer. There would
be no repetition of the obvious mistakes that had led to
Sundaram's demise.

Jin wouldn't underestimate his enemies, but neither
would he *over*estimate them. Every soldier serving him
had sworn an oath in blood before an altar dedicated
to Guan Yu, a deified third-century general of the Han
Dynasty. The oath included thirty-six specific promises
of loyalty, with violation of any aspect subjecting the
recruit to death by thunderbolts or a myriad of swords.
Personally, Jin preferred a red-hot poker and a cleaver,
for the images they left with cringing witnesses.

In short, his soldiers wouldn't fail him. To a man,
he knew that they would rather die in battle with the
enemy than under Jin's own hand. That some of them
might die this day, he took for granted. But his enemies
would die, as well.

Die screaming for his entertainment, as he sent them
off to hell.

South China Sea

Aboard the freighter *Tiger Shark,* Captain Fahri Navis
smoked and waited for the signal. They were close now,
had to be. There'd been no message canceling the rendezvous at sea, using the prearranged code word *vol-
cano.*

If he called off the meeting without proper orders
from headquarters, Navis knew there would be an erup-
tion, all right, and he would be the one feeling its heat.
The last thing that he ever felt in life, no doubt, and he
could well imagine praying for the end to be a swift one.

But the order hadn't come, and so his venerable cargo
ship plowed on eastward, theoretically bound for Sand

Cay in the Spratly Islands, prior to visiting Manila. If, for any reason, Navis wasn't signaled for the rendezvous before his lookout saw the westernmost of the Spratlys, his backup orders were specific and concise: dump the cargo at sea, off Fiery Cross Reef, and let the tardy buyers salvage it as best they could.

Both sides, presumably, had ratified that option, for all that it mattered to Navis. He took orders only from his master in Johor Bahru, and silence on the radio told him nothing had changed. The *Tiger Shark* would continue on its way, and he would see what happened next.

Five minutes later, as the captain lit another cigarette, his radioman chirped out, "Incoming message, sir!"

Navis said nothing in reply, stood waiting, trying to appear cool and relaxed. A moment later, the communications officer announced, "It is the *Flying Fish*."

So far, all was in order, Navis mused.

"Confirm contact," he ordered.

"Aye, Captain. Confirming."

Navis waited for the confirmation to be sent and then demanded, "The coordinates?"

"Receiving, sir. Eight degrees, thirty-two minutes, fourteen seconds north…by one hundred and eleven degrees, fifty-four minutes, nine seconds east."

Navis found the spot on his nautical chart, confirming safe distance from land, then repeated the coordinates to his helmsman, who instantly acknowledged and changed course. They had about two miles to travel, call it five minutes at the *Tiger Shark*'s normal cruising speed of ten knots. Anticipation brought the faintest tremor to his hands, and Navis hid them in the pockets of his khaki trousers.

He would wait until they met the *Flying Fish* before he ordered preparation for the transfer. It was always possible—though unlikely—that security had somehow been breached, a trap laid for his ship and its cargo. In that event, Navis had more explicit orders from Johor Bahru.

Destroy the *Tiger Shark*. Send it to the bottom with its cargo.

As for the crew, it would be each man for himself.

Six minutes after ordering their change of course, Navis heard confirmation of a sighting from his lookout at the *Tiger Shark*'s bow. Raising his binoculars, he spied the *Flying Fish,* a vessel slightly larger than his own, and marked the cargo crane amidships that would make the transfer from his hold to the receiving vessel. No cash would change hands at this point, payment for the cargo being prearranged between the men in charge.

No conversation was exchanged by radio as they approached the *Flying Fish*. Both captains knew why they were meeting, and it was no one else's business. Navis hoped the transfer would go smoothly, so he could return to Johor Bahru with a good report, collect his pay and put the business out of mind. If he heard no more of the cargo in his hold for the remainder of his life, he thought that it would be too soon.

Jakarta

"THE MISSILES SHOULD HAVE BEEN transferred by now," Maia told Bolan, scowling at her watch. "We may already be too late."

"It's not too late until they pull the trigger," he replied. "And even *if* that happens, we're not done."

"My people are ambiguous about revenge," Maia observed. "We practice it, of course, yet all our ancient proverbs counsel otherwise. You've heard it said that he who seeks revenge should dig two graves?"

"One for the enemy, one for himself," Bolan finished the thought.

"Confucius," Maia said. "Another says, 'A man need never revenge himself, the body of his enemy will be brought to his own door.'"

"But when?" Bolan asked. "Me, I'd rather do the job myself and get it over with."

In truth, while he had killed men for revenge—the mobsters who had pushed his father to the razor's edge of murder-suicide, some others who had slain or tortured Bolan's friends over the years—he seldom pulled the trigger as an act of vengeance on his own behalf. Removing human predators from circulation was, to him, a form of execution. Those he killed had judged themselves, condemned themselves, by virtue of their actions, by the evil in their hearts and minds. Bolan was simply helping victims yet undamaged.

Taking out the trash.

His mission, this time, was to intercept the stolen Chinese missiles before either one was fired in anger. Failing that, however, he would do his best to punish those responsible for whatever atrocity ensued. And make damned certain that they never had another chance to spill innocent blood.

"I wish we had a home address for Jin Au-Yo," said Maia. "Unfortunately—"

"Never mind," he tried to reassure her. "We'll find something when we start to rattle cages with the targets that we *do* have."

"Even so," she answered, "finding him is one thing. Getting him to talk…"

"We'll manage. Trust me."

She made no reply to that, and Bolan let it go. Their first stop on a driving tour of Jakarta, spotting targets in advance of any action, was in Karet Kuningan, the fastest-growing district in Jakarta's "Golden Triangle." Its street scenes featured embassies and shopping malls, exclusive office buildings and luxury residential towers. Its centerpiece, the Plaza Setiabudi complex, offered corporate and legal offices side by side with stylish restaurants and cozy cafés, travel agencies, a fitness center and a multiscreen theater where hits from Hollywood and Bollywood competed for box-office gold. The neighborhood also harbored multiple cybercafés, which Maia described as popular fronts for casinos, banned under Indonesian law derived from the Koran.

Specifically, she steered him to a joint called Jaring Dunia, which translated to *Web World.* The logo in its window was a spiderweb, in which a smiley-faced tarantula was working on a laptop.

"Cute," Bolan said.

"In the back room," Maia said, "they play mahjong, pai gow, sic bo, also pachinko, slot machines and blackjack, take your pick. The Flying Ax Triad owns many of these operations outright, and collects a license fee or house percentage from the so-called independent operators. In a month, we estimate their income to be around two million renminbi. Say three hundred thirteen thousand U.S. dollars."

Close to four million per year. "Is that the total for Jakarta, or for Indonesia overall?" he asked.

"Jakarta only," she replied. "The same or slightly less for Bandung, Denpasar, Bekasi and Bandar Lampung. Half that much for other major cities nationwide, depending on their population."

"We do it right, a visit ought to shake them up," he said.

Bolan had no personal ax to grind where gambling was concerned, on moral grounds or any other. He was a libertarian in most respects, believing people should be free to do whatever pleased them on their own, or with other consenting adults, as long as no third party's rights were violated in the process. But experience had taught him that the predators he hunted earned the bulk of their infernal revenue from human weakness and addiction—to drugs, liquor, gambling, pornography, whatever—and until that corrupting influence was eradicated absolutely, there was no such thing as a victimless crime.

Mob money—call it triad, Mafia, Yakuza, pick your poison—was *always* tainted, one hundred percent of the time. You couldn't launder it enough to lose the stains of blood and misery it carried as it passed from hand to filthy hand.

And hitting human monsters where it hurt them most, most of the time meant striking at their wallets. Meant shutting down the flow of cash that let them buy protection while they lived the high life, courtesy of ordinary men and women whose weaknesses kept the underworld afloat.

"Looks like as good a place to start as any," Bolan said. "Shall we?"

Pondok Indah, South Jakarta

AT LAST, GOOD NEWS. The call had been relayed to Jin Au-Yo through Johor Bahru, from the *Mengantuk Naga* at sea. Transfer of the missiles was completed, and the buyers had professed their satisfaction with the merchandise. Transfer of the agreed-upon final payment would now proceed, via computer, from a bank in the

United Arab Emirates to yet another in Hong Kong. What happened after that was none of Jin's concern.

And yet, he *was* concerned. Not for the triad's money, since Hong Kong's legal system—based on British common law—and the strict security of its financial institutions remained sacrosanct, despite transfer of sovereignty from the United Kingdom to the People's Republic of China in 1997. By that time, Beijing's masters had long recognized the wisdom of lucrative commercial contacts with the West and luring capital from foreign lands to Chinese soil. Of course, the ruling party's bosses got their taste, as had the British overlords from 1839 until the tail end of the last century.

What else could any businessman expect?

No, Jin's concern focused on the opponents who had liquidated Khoo Kay Sundaram along with many of his men. Opponents who, Jin now had reason to believe, were in Jakarta, armed and stalking him. They might not know that he had passed the stolen Chinese missiles on to others who had commissioned their theft. And in fact, the stalkers might not care. They would require names for the buyers, and would seek them first from Jin Au-Yo, unless they found another source.

To stop them, end the threat once and for all, Jin had already mobilized his private army in Jakarta and its suburbs, searching for the hunters who were seeking him. It was a race against the clock, now, and the vanguard of the Flying Ax Triad believed that he would win.

Why not? He'd always won before. The proof was that he lived to fight another day.

Karet Kuningan, Central Jakarta

WEB WORLD SERVED customers around the clock, like any serious cybercafé or casino. Window-shopping at boutiques and travel agencies across the street, Bolan and Maia had a chance to watch the flow of customers who came and went over the course of half an hour. Maybe ten percent checked in to buy computer time, the rest passing a beefy skinhead at the register to enter a back room. During the thirty minutes they'd been watching, half the web-surfers had come and gone, but no one had emerged from the back room.

"A lot of gamblers here," Bolan said.

"It's a mania with many Asians," Maia told him. "I believe you have the same in the United States."

"You're right," he answered, thinking of the sights he'd seen in Vegas and Atlantic City. Seniors wearing leather work gloves as they worked the slots nonstop, until push-button models made them switch to thimbles. Blisters were a bitch. Tales circulated far and wide about crap-shooters who collapsed unnoticed from a stroke or heart attack, responding cops and EMTs compelled to push other gamblers aside before they could check vital signs or start CPR.

"Ready to spoil the party?" Maia asked him.

"Always ready," Bolan said, feeling the loaded SIG-Sauer's two pounds and change beneath his left arm, in its fast-draw rig. Spare magazines under his right armpit gave Bolan forty-six shots with the pistol, but he hoped things wouldn't go that far.

Maia, for her part, wasn't taking any chances. She'd put on a light raincoat, in deference to the Jakarta drizzle, and it helped conceal her silenced Pindad PM2. She also had her own SIG holstered, just in case the whole thing went to hell and thirty Parabellum manglers weren't enough to settle it.

"You had a good idea about the money," she acknowledged, as they spotted traffic and crossed the street with only minor bleats from hostile drivers' horns.

"We'll put ourselves on Jin's radar, just showing up and asking where he is," Bolan replied. "Tapping his till should drive the message home."

"Money is what he understands," Maia agreed, as if that settled everything.

But Bolan reckoned their opponent understood some other things, as well. Survival of the fittest, for example, in a world where "dog eat dog" was sometimes taken literally. Unless born to triad royalty, he'd have clawed his way up from the gutter, spilling blood along the way to prove himself and more to hold the post he'd finally attained. He might have plans for rising higher, gaining more authority, and dull wits wouldn't get it done.

Expect the worst. That way, you'd always be prepared, and any disappointment was a sweet surprise.

They made it to the east side of the street and entered Web World, breezing past the email junkies, toward the steely-eyed cashier. He saw them coming, didn't like it, and was reaching underneath the counter when they let him see their guns.

"Speak English?" Bolan asked him.

He got a brief nod back in reply.

"Okay," the Executioner commanded. "Show us where the action is."

CHAPTER EIGHT

South China Sea

The stolen Hsiung Feng III missiles didn't remain aboard the *Flying Fish* for long. A second rendezvous occurred as soon as the freighter's captain lost visual contact with the *Tiger Shark*. The new arrival was a larger vessel, overhauled before this voyage and rechristened as the *Thunderbolt*.

Nasir al-Jarrah watched from the *Thunderbolt*'s flying bridge as the missiles were off-loaded and secured belowdecks. The Saudi had forgotten how to smile long years ago, but would have said, if asked, that he was happy at that moment. Soon vengeance would be within his grasp for all that he had lost—his wives, children, his homeland—and he would be pleased to strike a telling blow against the infidels he hated, in the Sword of Allah's name.

Beside Nasir al-Jarrah stood the Sword of Allah's field marshal for Indonesia, Usmar Malik. It was he who had conceived the present operation and coordinated its fulfillment, working through the mercenary triads and Malaysian pirates to present al-Jarrah and the movement with the greatest weapons they had thus far managed to secure. And more than simple weaponry: a chance to punish the Great Satan for its stubborn opposition to the Prophet's word.

"Our time is coming," Malik said.

"And none too soon," al-Jarrah answered.

For the task at hand, the *Thunderbolt* had been refitted, transformed from a simple cargo ship into a vessel altogether different and deadly. While no outward sign of its conversion was apparent at a glance, a hatch with double doors had been cut into the freighter's forward deck. Below that hatch, on a hydraulic lift, a launcher had been built with parts accumulated from the same Chungshan Institute of Science and Technology that had designed and fabricated the Brave Wind missiles. In Taiwan, a CIST foreman and his crew were richer now, the missing parts recorded as defective and discarded on the company's books. Upon Nasir al-Jarrah's order, the deck hatch would open, the launcher would rise, and a missile would fly to its target, as straight as an arrow from God's own bow.

Soon, now.

"Have you decided on a target for the test-fire?" Malik inquired.

"It hardly matters," al-Jarrah replied. "Something of substance, flying an infidel's flag. Once we have demonstrated our ability and willingness to strike, I trust even the devils at the Pentagon to honor our demands."

Malik was clearly skeptical. "They boast that they will not negotiate with so-called terrorists," he said.

"And there will be no sniveling negotiation," al-Jarrah reminded him. "Unless the nonbelievers bow to our demands in full, we take one of their precious aircraft carriers. They will not be advised of where or when the blow shall fall, but it *will* come. The Nimitz class, I think. Constructed at a cost of $4.5 billion, with eighty-five aircraft and nearly seven thousand personnel on board. More than double the Twin Towers losses, Usmar. Think of it! One blow will rock America to its foundation."

"And then what?" Malik asked quietly.

Al-Jarrah shrugged. "And then, the war goes on. Of course, we don't expect them to surrender or abandon Israel. Only God's might unleashed directly could effect those ends. We are mere mortal soldiers, but we can make history. And while they reel from one blow, we shall plan and wait to strike another. There is truly no rest for the wicked while the righteous still have strength and will to fight."

"God's will be done," Malik intoned.

"His will is always done," al-Jarrah said. "Our generation may not live to see it, but the victory shall come."

Al-Jarrah imagined men stripped to the waist belowdecks, gleaming with perspiration as they placed one Brave Wind missile in the launcher, checking and rechecking all its systems, making ready for the moment when it flew.

The Chinese, he supposed, would be as furious as the Great Satan. And what of it? He cared no more for a nation schooled in atheism and the heresy of Buddhism than for the Christian wasteland of America. If they became embroiled in battle, one against the other, it could only aid the Sword of Allah's cause by crippling both.

His will be done indeed.

Karet Kuningan, Central Jakarta

WEB WORLD'S CASHIER GLARED daggers at the Executioner but did as he was told. Once off the high stool he'd been seated on, he was a runt of five foot one or two, but broad across the chest and shoulders like a power lifter. Bolan stayed beyond the reach of his long, almost simian arms and trailed the guy through a rattling beaded curtain to a door farther along a narrow hallway.

The lookout raised a hand to knock, and Bolan warned him, "Any tricks, you're first to go."

After a moment's hesitation, maybe altering whatever strategy he'd had in mind, the guy knocked twice, then paused. One rap, another pause, then two more taps to finish it. A shadow blocked the door's peephole, the inside lookout following procedure. He'd see nothing, since Bolan and Maia held their guns behind their backs until the lock clicked and the door swung inward.

Showtime.

Maia moved to give the little guy a shove, but he was viper-fast, spinning to make a grab for her SMG's muzzle. Bolan shot him in the chest from ten feet out and charged the door, shouldered it hard into the lookout standing just behind it, and the watchdog went down in a sprawl. Maia was right behind him as he cleared the threshold, muttering what sounded like a string of curses in her native language.

Down at Bolan's feet, the Chinese lookout started reaching for a piece under his jacket, then decided it was probably a bad idea. Bolan relieved him of the weapon, tucked it underneath his belt in back and told the fallen man, "Show us the counting room."

Maia repeated it for emphasis.

The guy got up and moved then, seeing there was no percentage for himself in playing dumb. Their entry had already caused a stir among nearby pachinko players, and the ripples spread from there in nothing flat. Whether the gamblers understood exactly what was happening, or thought themselves caught up in a police raid, Bolan didn't know or care. Their stampede for the exits served his purpose as he trailed the disarmed guard toward the casino's bank.

It was a small room, and the door swung open as they reached it, two more Chinese shooters rolling through to find out what in hell was going on. They saw guns, went for theirs, and Maia zipped them both together with a 6- or 8-round burst across their chests. They dropped together, in a twitching heap, and Bolan's guide recoiled, croaking a protest that earned him a rap on the skull.

Inside the counting room, one final Chinese worker bee stood facing them across a table piled with Indonesian rupiah notes and coins. He tried for calm, asking, *"Ni xiang ganshenme?"*

"English!" Maia demanded.

"Certainly. What do you want?"

"Let's try your money or your life," Bolan replied.

"You're making a most serious mistake," their hostage said, bending to reach beneath the table.

"Easy," Bolan warned him.

"Just a satchel. There's too much for you to carry as it is."

"Go on, then," Bolan said.

Their prisoner—the club's accountant, possibly the manager—produced a spacious leather bag and started stuffing it with notes as if he'd done it countless times before. Which, Bolan thought, he likely had. When it was stuffed and latched, nothing but coins remaining on the table, Bolan told him, "One more thing."

"And that would be...?"

"We need a home address for Jin Au-Yo," Maia replied.

The captive's face went blank. "Then kill me now," he said. "Your guns are nothing next to what he will do if I betray him."

Bolan thought about it, index finger on the SIG-Sauer's trigger, and made up his mind. "Okay," he said. "Call Jin and brief him on what happened here. Tell him it's just the start. Until we get the stolen cargo back, he's going to be living in a world of hurt."

The hostage couldn't help but look relieved. He asked, "Cargo?"

"Tell him a brave wind's come to blow his house down," Bolan said. "And if he doesn't get it yet, he'll have a chance to work it out while we're dismantling everything he's built. It's payback time."

South China Sea

THE DUTCH CONTAINER SHIP *Eiland Koningin* held a steady seven knots as it proceeded southwestward toward Ho Chi Minh City. The ship's name translated to *Island Queen,* but she was a frowzy old dame and her age was showing—all forty-five years of it. Her rust-streaked hull needed paint, and her engines could have used an overhaul. Replacement would have been a better option, but she hadn't sprung a leak yet, so to hell with it.

The truth be told, Captain Cornelis Pieterszoon liked the old tramp just as she was. Nothing fancy, but faithful. She carried whatever he put in the hold or on deck and delivered it safely, more or less on time. She'd been his first command, and might well be his last.

Pieterszoon thought that he could have done worse. Many had, and he'd listened to eulogies spoken over empty caskets, representing merchant seamen swallowed by the deep. After a lifetime on the sea, the captain sometimes found himself surmising that it was the best way for a man to go. God knew that there were damned few left ashore to mourn him when his own time came. Why make a fuss about it with a pantomime of simulated grief?

Not that he planned to go down with his ship on *this* run. It was all routine, delivering a load of Filipino farm machinery to Vietnam, where he would find another cargo waiting for him, bound for Babar in the South Moluccas. Round and round it went, with layovers when Pieterszoon couldn't resist the urge to stretch his legs onshore. Never for long, though. The Pacific Ocean was his one true love.

The helmsman, Louis Kuyper, called out from his post, "Captain, we have a ship to port, at ten o'clock. She'll cross our bow soon."

"Speed?" Pieterszoon asked.

"About twelve knots, sir."

"She won't cause any problems for us, then," the captain said. "Maintain our present course and speed."

"Aye, sir."

They hadn't seen another ship so far this day. The *Island Queen* traveled by routes that saw light traffic at the worst of times. It minimized distractions, making work a leisurely affair for Pieterszoon, if not for all his crewmen. Working in the engine room would always be a noisy, dirty job, but someone had to do it. At the rates he could afford to pay, those "someones" were Malaysians, Filipinos and sometimes a Timorese.

Pieterszoon found his old binoculars and scanned the blue horizon, searching for the other ship. After a moment's effort he discovered it, focused the glasses, tried to read its name.

Chinese. No luck.

He was about to lower the binoculars when a brilliant flash of light erupted on the other freighter's deck, lancing his eyes. Pieterszoon tried to make out what it was—some kind of flash-fire or explosion?—and was stunned to find the light hurtling in his direction on a clear collision course.

"My God!" he blurted out, before the fireball filled his lenses and the *Island Queen* rocked underneath him, as if rammed amidships by a whale.

The explosion that immediately followed impact hurled Cornelis Pieterszoon skyward, a straw man wreathed in flames that bit into his flesh ferociously. He may have screamed—it was impossible to tell for certain, deafened as he was—before he hit the ocean's surface with a sizzling hiss and sank.

He tried to swim, couldn't coordinate the movement of his arms and legs no matter how he strained to make his body function. Somewhere close at hand, he felt rather than heard the suction of his dying vessel as it sank.

Another empty casket, the captain thought, as he closed his eyes.

Jakarta

THE SAT PHONE'S TRILLING SOUND surprised Bolan as he was driving west along Jalan Pramuka, past an elevated highway cloverleaf with treetops down below. He snagged it from the map pocket beside his seat, left-handed, keyed Transmit and told the caller, "Go ahead."

"Bad news," Brognola said, from half a world away.

"I'm listening."

"The merchandise has been transferred."

"You're sure of that?" Bolan asked.

"Sure as sure can be," Brognola said. "They've used one."

"What? Already?" Bolan felt a tight fist close around his heart.

"No question. There's confirmation of the incident, and there's a video online. The Sword of Allah's claiming credit."

"Okay, fill me in," Bolan said tersely.

"First, the good news, if you want to call it that," the Justice man said. "The target wasn't military, and it wasn't ours. They hit a Dutch container ship, the *Island Queen,* in the South China Sea. She's down, apparently with all hands. Which, in this case, means approximately forty sailors. They were traveling between the Philippines and Vietnam, a normal cargo run. We likely wouldn't know that anything had happened, but the bastards posted it themselves. Not wasting any time."

"What else?" Bolan asked.

"You know how the Sword of Allah operates. They have demands, all nonnegotiable. End all American support for Israel, stat. Withdraw all military forces from Afghanistan, Iraq and any other Muslim area immediately. Close Guantanamo today, with passage for the prisoners to any nation of their choosing. Oh, and hand the Sword one hundred billion dollars' worth of gold and diamonds, details of delivery to follow."

"That's billion, with a *b.*"

"You heard me right."

"Or else…what?" Bolan asked, fairly certain that he knew the answer.

"Or they launch the other one. No details of the target, but Beijing calls the Brave Wind a 'carrier killer.' That's got the Pentagon spooked, but the Man's cabinet has some other ideas. What if they hit a supertanker in a major harbor, for example? Or who says they can't aim it inland, see what it does to a nuclear power plant."

Bolan considered the latter possibility. The Hsiung Feng III was designated antiship, but it was still a guided missile, meaning that it possessed an inertial navigation system using a computer, motion and rotation sensors, plus terminal active radar homing. If it could strike a moving ship at sea, nothing prevented it from taking out a stationary target ashore, within the limits of its striking range. In his briefing, Brognola had placed that range between eighty and one hundred miles.

"Still there?" the big Fed asked.

"I'm here," Bolan replied. And he was spotting nuclear reactors on a mental map from memory. Five in the Carolinas he was sure of, two each in Maryland and New Jersey, five more in Pennsylvania, six in New York, two apiece in Connecticut and Massachusetts, one each in Maine, New Hampshire and Vermont. Twenty-seven prime targets on the eastern seaboard alone, and a hit on any one of them could give America a taste of the same hell Japan had suffered after a tsunami shattered the Fukushima nuke plant in 2011.

"So, how's it coming?" Brognola inquired, his voice intruding on apocalyptic visions.

"We've confirmed that the heist was commissioned by the Flying Ax Triad. We're still looking for their shot-caller here, a guy called Jin Au-Yo. Now you've identified the end user. Maybe this Jin can tell us how to find the Sword."

"A sword and an ax," Brognola said, "ready to chop us up. Jesus."

"We won't let it come to that," Bolan replied, projecting confidence he wasn't certain of.

"Let's hope not," said the man from Justice. "While you're hunting there, a naval presence has been authorized, for what it's worth. Fresh targets, if you ask me. No one did."

"I'm signing off now," Bolan said. "Places to go, people to see."

"Good luck," Brognola offered, and the line went dead.

Pondok Indah, South Jakarta

"Repeat that," Jin Au-Yo commanded.

Standing at attention in the space before his desk, the trembling manager of Web World, Li Huating, told Jin, "The white man said a brave wind comes to blow your house down, sir."

"Those were his exact words? A 'brave wind'?"

"Yes."

"And how much money did he take?" Jin asked.

Li swallowed hard, then said, "Four hundred and forty-three million rupiah, sir. That is—"

"Three hundred and thirty-two thousand renminbi," Jin interrupted, making the conversion automatically. "Or fifty-two thousand U.S. dollars."

"Correct, sir. I can only apologize for my failure and—"

"Enough! You were not meant to be a soldier. Had you fought, you would be dead now, rather than providing a description of the thieves."

"Yes, sir. The man was an American. I'm certain of it. He was six feet tall, approximately. As to weight, I estimate two hundred pounds. Dark hair. His face was unremarkable."

"But you would recognize him," Jin replied, not asking.

"Absolutely."

"And the woman?" Jin pressed on.

"Chinese, but not Chinese-American. She must be six or seven inches shorter than the man, and slender. But aggressive, sir. She had a machine gun, while the American used a pistol only."

"And did she use the weapon?" Jin inquired.

Li hesitated, finally replied, "I can't be sure, sir. The shootings…I did not observe them personally. Bao and Shen both left the office when the noise began in the casino. I remained to put the money in the safe."

"But failed," Jin said.

"It's true, sir. They were too swift for me."

"No more apologies," Jin ordered. "They're a waste of time. I have an artist on the way who sketches suspects for the Indonesian National Police. You will remain here and assist him in preparing pictures of the bandits. When they are of photographic quality, then you may leave."

"Thank you, sir."

"Don't thank me yet. I mean that you will leave Jakarta. Leave this country. Go directly back to Hong Kong and begin your search for new employment there. The Flying Ax has no more need of you."

Stricken, the ex-casino manager asked Jin, "What will I do, sir?"

"I've told you what to do, Li," Jin replied. "Beyond that, what becomes of you holds no more interest for me. If you're wise, you will not let me see your face again."

"I understand, sir. It shall be as you say."

As Li was turning toward the office door, slump-shouldered, Jin spoke to his back. "Before you go, show courtesy and thank me for your worthless life."

Li faced him, swallowed hard and said, "I am in your debt for sparing me, sir."

"Better," Jin acknowledged. "Now remove yourself, before I change my mind."

Alone once more, Jin focused on the bandits Li had just described to him. The woman, he surmised, could only be the spy who had escaped from Khoo Kay Sundaram the previous night. A Chinese agent, almost certainly a member of the Ministry of State Security. Why would an American extract her from a Malay pirate's den, much less proceed to travel with her, stalking Jin Au-Yo?

The missiles.

Washington would shake hands with the Devil if it meant averting a disaster that would threaten the careers of those in power. Jin himself had no interest in politics beyond supporting candidates who helped his triad thrive, but he was well versed in the mind-set of professional campaigners, those who lived for nothing but pursuing votes along the road to wealth and power. They weren't so different from Jin, though he would trust the lowest criminal in Beijing's Tangjialing slum before he put his faith in any politician.

No matter how or why the American and the Chinese agent had joined forces, Jin was bound to stop them in Jakarta.

And he meant to stop them dead.

CHAPTER NINE

Pluit, North Jakarta

Bolan drove north on Jalan Pluit Barat Raya, then cut to the west across a bridge spanning the Cengkareng Drain, a broad canal designed for flood control that spilled into the Java Sea at the capital's waterfront. Maia had told him that eighty percent of Pluit's residents were immigrant Chinese whose influence had modified the neighborhood's longtime profile as a district where anything goes. Sailors' dives and tattoo parlors still proliferated along the waterfront, along with relatively low-rent ladies of the evening, but residential streets took over a few blocks inland from the wharfs.

Not all the houses sheltered families, though.

The one Maia had marked for Bolan was supposed to be a drug house, where pure China white heroin imported from Thailand was cut and packaged for sale on the streets. She'd given him the address, on Jalan Niaga, and he found the east-west street on his first try. The house in question showed no outward signs of being occupied by narco-traffickers. Why would it? They weren't cooking drugs inside, simply diluting and repackaging a finished product to increase the profit margin.

Free enterprise at work.

But they were going out of business this morning.

The Executioner was bringing an eviction notice they couldn't ignore.

He thought of asking Maia whether she was sure about the address, but she'd nailed the Web World operation and he saw no reason to believe she'd be mistaken this time. If it turned out she *was* wrong, they'd exit with apologies and leave a bundle of the triad's money to assuage riled nerves.

He parked the Toyota Fortuner a half block west of their target and checked his Pindad SS2. Full magazine, stock folded, 40 mm high-explosive round loaded and ready to fly from the under-barrel launcher. Maia flicked off her submachine gun's safety and nodded to confirm her readiness.

A drizzling rain explained the coats they wore to hide their long guns as they crossed the street. The modest home's front windows all had drapes drawn tightly across them, shielding anyone inside from daylight or a neighbor's prying eyes. Bolan advanced directly to the front door, following a concrete pathway to the porch. No yards or gardens here, the houses lined up side by side and back to back. Whatever happened in the next few moments would alert adjacent families, if anyone was home.

So never mind the stealth.

He fired the SPG-1A from twenty feet out and the front door imploded with a *bang* that rattled windows on the houses to the left and right. Using the shock to his advantage, Bolan plunged into a swirling cloud of smoke, eyes slitted, feeling more than seeing Maia enter on his heels. Ahead of him, a babble of excited, frightened voices told him where to go.

They cut and bagged their product in the kitchen, teenage girls the workers, overseen by men with guns and hair that could have used an oil change several thousand miles ago. Three shooters were trying to recover from the HE blast when Bolan found them, one a little faster than his buddies, so he was the first to go. A 3-round burst from Bolan's gun stopped his heart and pitched him back into the kitchen sink.

The girls were screaming then, hightailing it for the back door, while the two remaining gunmen tried to earn their last paycheck. Bolan's next burst defaced the gunner on his left, then he depressed the Pindad's muzzle and his third burst buzz-sawed through the final soldier's knees. The last man standing went down screaming, thrashing in a pool of blood.

A heartbeat later, Bolan had the wounded gunman on his back, hands clamped across his mouth and nose until the keening stopped, dark eyes bulging from lack of air. When he released his grip, he asked the wounded mobster, "English?"

He got a spastic headshake in return.

"Translate," he ordered Maia, then asked, "Where can we find Jin Au-Yo?"

The wounded triad gangster babbled something. Maia said, "He doesn't know."

Another clamp-down on the breathing apparatus, then the same question and same reply. Fear on the mangled soldier's face told Bolan he was probably sincere.

"He's useless, then," Maia said, reaching for a dagger on her belt.

Washington, D.C.

ON DAYS LIKE THIS ONE, Hal Brognola wished he could turn back the clock—or better yet, the calendar. Advances in technology had made it difficult, if not impossible, to keep a secret in the modern age. With WikiLeaks, Anonymous and God knew who else breaking news before it got to UPI or CNN, the good old-fashioned coverup was turning into an endangered species.

"So it's everywhere," he said to Barbara Price, speaking over his private line to Stony Man Farm.

"The hit, at least," she said. "Nobody's posted a connection to the *Shenyang* or its missiles."

"Yet, you mean," Brognola groused. "If someone doesn't manage to connect the dots within the next few hours, I'll be pretty damned surprised."

"They've gone a different way, so far," she answered. "Two attacks on ships in the South China Sea is news, but no one's tumbled to the missile theft. Right now, the speculation's running toward a feud between the PRC and hostiles on Taiwan. One crackpot claims Beijing is gearing up to nuke the Netherlands."

"Morons," the big Fed muttered. "Striker's doing what he can to find the Flying Ax's honcho in Jakarta, looking for a way to link them with the Sword of Allah. Whether that will help us find the ship that's carrying the second missile…well, that's anybody's guess."

"On that," Price said, "the Company and NSA are working overtime on satellite surveillance. We have backdoor views of everything they're doing, but they're empty-handed at the moment. As it is, with their demands on record, there's no reason to suppose the missile ship will even stay in the Far East. Nobody knows exactly what they're looking for, and there's no way to check out every ship afloat. It could be anywhere, en route to somewhere else."

"Could be," he said, "but *are* they? Now that our Pacific Fleet is moving in, the targets will be headed their way. Why go anywhere?"

Something was nagging at his mind now, and he missed Price's answer. Brognola was on the verge of asking for a repetition, when the missing piece fell into place.

"Is there any reason why the Brave Wind couldn't launch from land?" he asked.

There was a moment's silence on the other end. The big Fed pictured Price frowning as she answered, "Not that I'm aware of, but I'd have to double-check on that. You're thinking—"

"That they've got us searching for a missile ship," he said. "What if the test-fire was a lure, to bring one of our carriers in range? While everybody's busy checking trawlers, junks and yachts, the shooters sit back on a spit of land somewhere and pick their time."

Price cursed, a most unladylike response, then said, "We're screwed, I guess. A couple of years ago, they found a thousand islands in the Indonesian chain nobody had ever mapped before. God only knows how many places there could be to set a launcher up between Jakarta and the Philippines."

"Worse than a needle in a haystack," Brognola allowed.

"I'm going back to work," she said, and cut the link.

The Justice man closed his eyes, envisioning a carrier in flames, then started tapping out a number for the Pentagon.

Rawamangun, East Jakarta

THEY'D TORCHED the Pluit drug house, Maia shouting warnings to the neighbors as they left. The next mark on their list was a triad social club, Silver Nights, whatever that was meant to signify beyond the obvious allusion to glitter balls and "hostesses" in glittery metallic costumes. Bolan had no reason to believe the club would be open for business at noon—or open at all, on this day when the Flying Ax troops had to be scrambling to play catch-up from his early hits in town—but Maia thought there was a chance they'd find the manager somewhere around the place.

And since he worked for Jin Au-Yo, he might know where to find the boss.

Rawamangun lay to the east of downtown Jakarta, accessed via Jalan Pramuka, then by way of Jalan Kaya Pubh Raya southbound. Rolling down the main drag, Bolan watched for cops, although he didn't think their vehicle had been identified so far. When a patrol car passed him, headed in the opposite direction, and the driver didn't spare a second glance, it put his mind at ease on that score, anyway.

Their luck was holding, but it wouldn't last forever. Daylight raids were always riskier than night moves, but he couldn't spend the afternoon in hiding while the Sword of Allah found a target for its second missile. Maia had been translating the news that came to them through the Toyota's radio: the Dutch ship lost with all hands, impossible demands on Washington, a U.S. Navy strike force steaming toward the South China Sea in response, warnings from mainland China that its territorial waters had to be respected.

A recipe for disaster.

He'd grown up in an age of brinksmanship, and therefore found it hard to picture any crisis blowing up into a nuclear exchange between two superpowers, but it didn't have to go that far to rate as a catastrophe. One aircraft carrier boasted a population larger than that of many small towns in the States. A loss on that scale would make 9/11 seem like a love tap. The hysteria that would inevitably follow such a blow, complete with calls for military action against any nation found to be involved, would set the stage for catastrophe.

Al Qaeda's strike in 2001 had embroiled America in more than a decade of war overseas, with no end in sight. What would result from a blow that doubled 9/11's body count?

The Executioner meant to avert that horror at any cost.

Even if it meant wading waist-deep in blood.

Pondok Indah, South Jakarta

STILL NOTHING. Jin Au-Yo felt his impatience simmering, imagined the thoughts that Wu Guchan had to have been entertaining, sitting in his Beijing penthouse, far removed from any danger. The leader of the Flying Ax Triad admired Jin's courage and determination. Why else had Jin been promoted to command the clan's business in Indonesia? Still, that admiration could turn sour overnight if Jin proved unable to control his territory and eliminate a threat posed by two enemies.

And one of them a woman!

It was an insult to the triad, to his very manhood. Nearly all his soldiers in Jakarta were combing the streets, each team carrying sketches of the two offenders. How hard could it be to find a tall blue-eyed American accompanied by a Chinese woman, after all?

And what of Chou Hua Tian? The Deputy Assistant Minister for State Security had promised to identify the agent Jin was tracking, but so far he had delivered nothing in the way of useful information. How long could it take to scan computer files? How many female agents had the ministry sent to Malaysia following the *Shenyang* hijacking?

Suspicion was an aspect of Jin's character that helped him stay alive. For all their oaths of loyalty, he understood the mind-set of his fellow triad members. They were only human, which, of course, meant they were treacherous, mendacious and responded more to fear than any show of kindness. Any one of Jin's subordinates would likely stab him in the back for self-advancement. Some might call his feeling paranoia, but it came from personal experience.

Jin had employed the same technique himself.

He wondered now if Wu Guchan was having second thoughts about their dealings with the Arabs. Granted, it was too late to reverse the deal, but Wu might reason that he could escape responsibility by isolating Jin, letting him take the fall alone. In that case, would he let the government dispose of Jin? And would he risk the losses in Jakarta that the Flying Ax had suffered since the agent and her soldier came to town?

Jin used the office intercom to summon Ma Mingxia. Ten seconds later, Ma was in the doorway, saying, "Yes, sir?"

"Reach out to each team on the street," Jin ordered. "Find out where they are and what they're doing. Tell them I want updates at fifteen-minute intervals from now on."

"Consider it done, sir."

Ma vanished as suddenly as he'd appeared, leaving Jin to his thoughts once again. The vanguard meant to solve his problem and emerge victorious, either surprise or disappoint the old men in Beijing. But it was also time to think of viable alternatives, an exit strategy that left him situated for a comfortable life under a new name, with his skin intact.

Jin Au-Yo had laid the groundwork for escape the day he joined the Flying Ax Triad. He'd known then what some of his fellow members never understood: that all the vows of brotherhood meant nothing when your world turned upside down. His numbered bank accounts in Switzerland and the Bahamas waited for him, fat and ripe. His rural home in Mexico was ready to receive him. Jin could leave at any time.

But only if he knew the game was lost. And he wouldn't concede that yet.

In fact, he'd just begun to play.

Pulo Gadung, East Jakarta

GOH CHOK SWEE WAS nervous. He'd been keeping up with the reports of raids on triad property around Jakarta and had processed the alerts from headquarters to be on guard. He'd asked for more security, but had been told that everyone available was on the street, hunting an agent from the Ministry of State Security who traveled with a white man, either British or American. The agent was a woman, but headquarters rated both of them as dangerous.

So here Goh sat, with three men to secure the triad's counterfeiting plant. They didn't deal in currency, but rather in designer labels that were placed on bootleg products for domestic sale—a racket that put four *billion* U.S. dollars in the triad's pocket every year. The bogus products processed by Goh's team included makeup and shampoo, insecticide and pharmaceuticals, shoes and clothing, automotive parts and office equipment, sunglasses and handbags, not to mention movies, music, video games and other such items mass-produced in the People's Republic for sale overseas. The list was virtually endless, and the profits were huge.

But now, Goh had a target on his back. He hadn't seen the trouble coming, still had no idea exactly why the Flying Ax was being singled out for these attacks. Not *his* end of the operation, anyway. At least, not yet. Family business was compartmentalized, thus limiting the damage any given individual could do if he decided to forsake his oath of loyalty and silence.

Not that Goh would ever be a damned informer and betray his brothers.

Not unless it was required to save his skin, that was.

He was prepared to make another circuit of the factory, observe the workers and let *them* observe him watching *them,* so that they did their jobs efficiently. The printers, for example, had a tendency to be a trifle lax unless they knew that Goh was breathing down their necks. Perhaps a touch of discipline would break that habit and relieve some of his nervous tension at the same time.

The blast jarred Goh, caused him to drop his clipboard with a clatter that was lost in the explosion's rumbling reverberation. Fine dust filtered down around him from the ceiling as he got his bearings, but it didn't mask the scent of smoke and high explosives.

There was nothing in the factory that should explode. The printing presses failed from time to time, but with a wheeze and clatter, not a blast that rocked the squat two-story plant. The rest was all assembly stations and rooms filled with products awaiting their labels. Nothing that should burn unless it had been doused with gasoline and set afire. And even then, the clothes, cosmetics, VCRs and other items had no blast potential.

Goh moved toward the sound, tracking the HE stench in the direction of the plant's broad loading bay out back. When he was halfway there, he heard gunshots and knew that he was in the wrong place at the wrong damned time.

Cursing, he turned and ran.

PULO GADUNG'S MAIN CLAIM to fame was Cipinang Penitentiary, a prison built during Dutch colonial days and still in use by Indonesia's current government, housing a mixture of felons, alleged terrorists and political dissidents. A recent survey of Cipinang inmates by Amnesty International had found eighty-one percent claiming that they had suffered torture or some other form of abuse at the hands of their jailers. Protests to the state, thus far, had fallen on deaf ears.

Bolan had driven past the prison on his way to the triad counterfeiting plant, third on the list of local targets Maia Lee had put together. The factory was on Jalan Bekasi Raya, with access to a loading bay behind it, and he'd chosen that approach to minimize attention from the street. The doors were locked back there, and Bolan used a 40 mm key to open them, in lieu of wasting time with lock picks.

Once inside, he heard the workers scrambling for cover, exits, anything, their feet on concrete sounding like a swarm of panicked rats. He wished them luck and hoped that they would stay the hell out of his way. As for the triad's watchdogs...

Maia tagged the first one, caught him coming from a hallway to their right and zipped him with her P2 SMG. The guy let out a squeal and dropped his weapon, sprawling on the floor beside it with his arms outflung, reaching for nothing they would ever grasp. She played

it safe and made a quick detour, kicked the gun away
from him, then followed Bolan down another corridor,
into the old plant's musty heart.

Two women met them, squealed, then spun and ran
the other way. Bolan kept moving, following the muzzle
of his Pindad SS2 deeper into the factory, past rooms
piled high with jeans and blouses, women's shoes and
purses, cardboard cartons filled with who knew what.
He thought they'd have a chance to torch the inventory
later, but the first order of business was pinning down
whatever guards remained—and seeking out the man
in charge.

The guards, as it turned out, were easy. Only two
were left, and they came out to fight without much
thought behind it, blasting from the hip before they
had a target in their sights. Bolan and Maia caught them
with a crisscross double stream of automatic fire and
rolled them up, no hits on their side as the triad shooters fell.

Still cautious, Bolan moved ahead, clearing the several rooms they passed, homing in on what could only
be an exit to the street. He got there just in time to find
a man trying to clear the double dead-bolts, fumbling in
his haste. Well-dressed, apparently unarmed, he looked
like management.

"That's far enough," Bolan said.

Maia echoed it in Chinese.

The man turned, raised his hands as if it were a mug-
ging, studied each of them in turn with jumpy eyes.
"You are the ones," he said at last.

"Which ones?" Bolan asked, confident that he already knew the answer.

"Who are being hunted," the man said.

"Funny," Bolan replied. "I thought we were the hunters."

"Killing me will gain you nothing."

"It's one less Flying Ax to deal with," Bolan told him.

"I am not a soldier."

"Management, I take it?" the Executioner asked, and got a curt nod in response.

"We want your leader," Maia interrupted, cutting through the chitchat. "Where is Jin Au-Yo?"

"If I betray him—"

"Thunderbolts and myriads of swords," Bolan said. "Yada yada."

There was something cagey in the man's attitude. "You only want an address?" he said. "Well, why not?"

CHAPTER TEN

Beiheyan Street, Beijing

Commodore Feng Jingwei was edgy as he left his chauffeured limousine and climbed the concrete steps outside the Ministry of State Security. No one enjoyed a summons from the agency that functioned, in effect, as China's KGB. Some who were called to answer questions here wound up in prison or in rural camps that practiced reform through labor. Others simply disappeared.

Feng felt all the worse because he knew why he'd been summoned. It was no relief to get the call from Chou Hua Tian's terse secretary, even though the Deputy Assistant Minister for State Security was Feng's accomplice in the crime that could result in both of them facing a military firing squad. Chou might be planning to off-load responsibility on Feng and thereby save himself.

But Chou might surprise him yet. And if their meeting realized the commodore's worst fears, he had a secret stash of evidence that would make life most uncomfortable for the deputy assistant minister.

Feng made his way past three sets of guards to reach Chou's fourth-floor office. The secretary who had telephoned him greeted Feng without a smile and checked his name off on a list, then led him past her desk and through a leather-padded door into Chou's private office. As she left him there and closed the door behind her, Chou turned from his window, smiling primly as he waved Feng toward a nearby chair.

When both of them were seated, Chou said, "I've identified the woman."

Momentarily confused, Feng echoed, "Woman?"

"In Malaysia. Well, now in Jakarta. From the ministry."

The commodore remembered now, felt foolish for his lapse. "Of course," he said. "So she *was* one of yours."

"Still is, apparently," Chou said. "Our comrades with the Flying Ax have been unable to locate her."

"And the man?" Feng asked.

"Still unidentified. Survivors who have seen him claim he is American, perhaps British."

"Your agency collaborates with the United States and England?" Feng inquired, surprised.

"On rare occasions," Chou admitted. "Not this time, I can assure you. Any interaction on this matter is unauthorized."

"About this woman…"

"Maia Lee. She holds a rank equivalent to a sergeant in the army."

From the rank, Feng knew that she wasn't an upstart rookie with the ministry.

"She's chosen to deceive you, then," he said.

"It would appear so," Chou acknowledged. "In the circumstances, I believe it may be best for all concerned if others deal with her. A trial for insubordination in this case might only highlight certain…lapses, shall we say?"

"You mean the Flying Ax."

"If they can manage it," Chou said. "If not, there are covert alternatives within the ministry itself."

Feng cleared his throat. "This incident with the Dutch freighter—"

"Goes unmentioned in Zhongnanhai," Chou said, referring to the sector of central Beijing, adjacent to the Forbidden City, where China's president and State Council conducted their daily business. "There is no proof of a link to us, and there will be none."

"Ah." The commodore knew that he should have felt relieved, but apprehension nagged at him. "Still," he persisted, "there have been demands."

"With no specific reference to any weapon," Chou replied. "As we demanded in advance."

"You place your trust in these fanatics?"

"To the point where they desire cooperation in the future," Chou explained. "And fear retaliation if they break their promises."

Feng thought that he would rather try hand-feeding a mad dog, but kept it to himself. The small, silent recorder in his pocket captured Chou's words for posterity. Another weapon he could use in self-defense—or, at the very least, to make sure that he didn't die alone.

Rawamangun, East Jakarta

"DO YOU TRUST HIM?" Maia asked, when they were half a mile beyond the counterfeiting plant, smoke showing in the sky behind them.

"What else do we have?" Bolan asked.

In the middle distance, sirens. Probably police, maybe the first fire trucks arriving.

"It could be a trap," Maia said.

"Sure it could," he answered. "But it's still the first lead that we've had on an address for Jin Au-Yo. Blowing it off without a look feels wrong to me."

"I understand," she said. "But if it *is* a trap?"

"We fight on through it," Bolan told her. "Try to grab one of the shooters. See if we can squeeze fresh information out of him."

She nodded, kept whatever she was thinking to herself. Bolan could see she wasn't sold on the idea. There were two ways to play it: win her over to the plan or cut her loose. In either case, when Bolan hit the door at the address they had been given, he had no use for a distracted backup second-guessing every move he made.

"All right," he said into the silence filling the Toyota. "It can only play two ways. Either the guy back there was lying to us or he played it straight. If he was lying, then we have two other options to consider. One, he fed us anything that he could think of, hoping it would save his life."

"Which didn't work," Maia said.

"No. We couldn't bring him with us, and we couldn't trust him not to warn his boss. His time was up, regardless."

"And the second option?" Maia asked.

"If he lied deliberately, knowing there's a trap in place, Jin must have put him up to it. That mean's he's thinking two, three moves ahead of us and knew that we'd be going to the factory instead of any other target we might pick. I'd hate to think that he's that smart— or we're that dumb."

"You're right," she said. "We have no choice."

"*I* have no choice," Bolan corrected her. "You're not obliged to tag along."

She shot a sidelong glare at him. "How do you say it in America? You're dumping me?"

"Your choice," he said, then asked, "What did you

tell your people when you checked in with the ministry?"

She hesitated for a moment, then replied, "I did not mention you. It seemed…too awkward. Why risk being summoned home for an interrogation, when we have a chance to finish the assignment?"

"And you haven't called since then?" Bolan asked.

"No. Same reason, and we've been too busy."

"That's better," he suggested, "if you want to drop out now. Just tell them that your leads played out. You can't find Jin."

"While you go on to find the missiles by yourself?" she challenged him.

"It's not a competition," Bolan told her.

"They belong to China!"

"One's already up in smoke," he said. "Smart money says the other one will have to go the same way, if and when we find it."

"I must be there," she insisted.

"Fine," he answered. "Just make sure your head is in the game."

Pondok Indah, South Jakarta

JIN AU-YO SNAPPED his cell phone shut and shouted through the open office door for Ma Mingxia. His bodyguard appeared as if he had been waiting just outside the door, expecting to be summoned.

"Yes, sir?"

"We're leaving," Jin informed him. "Now. Have Dewei bring the car around at once."

"What shall I pack, sir?" his faithful servant asked.

"Nothing. We have no time to waste."

Ma left without another word, as Jin turned toward

his wall safe, tucked behind a fifteenth-century painting. Setting the piece of art aside, Jin opened the safe and removed all he needed to flee in a rush. Passports in three names, none of them his own, all with supporting ID documents and credit cards. Traveler's checks. And a Norinco QSW-06 semiautomatic pistol with factory standard suppressor, chambered for 5.8 mm DAP92 armor-piercing ammunition. Its box magazine held twenty rounds, and Jin put three spares in his pockets.

He was ready—and beside himself with fury that he had to leave.

A contact from the Indonesian National Police had tipped him to the raid in Pulo Gadung. Goh Chok Swee and his three guards were dead, the workers scattered who knew where. That call had come mere seconds after Chou Hua Tian had phoned him from Beijing to speak a woman's name.

Jin's mortal enemy, although they'd never met.

He meant to keep it that way, until he could lay a trap for this infernal Maia Lee and her companion, seemingly American, who still remained anonymous.

And that meant running while he had the chance.

It went against the grain with Jin, but he wasn't foolhardy. While his enemies were scouring Jakarta for him, he could regroup at his secret place and lay the groundwork necessary to destroy them. If it happened that they fell into his hands alive, so much the better, but he wouldn't miss the opportunity to kill them outright if it came to him.

No, make that *when* it came. He had too much at stake to contemplate defeat.

"The car is waiting, sir," Ma Mingxia told him, from the doorway.

Jin followed him out and through the suite that he

had occupied for eighteen months, as much a home to him as any other place he'd known. He had no way of knowing whether he would ever see those rooms again, but they held nothing that couldn't be easily replaced. That was the simple part.

Survival might require a bit more ingenuity.

Four soldiers waited in the hallway outside Jin's apartment. They surrounded him, with Ma Mingxia leading, on the short walk to the elevator, waiting with their hands on holstered weapons as the empty car arrived. Downstairs, his driver waited with the Humvee, armor plating hidden underneath its jet-black paint.

When they were all inside the vehicle, Dewei turned in the driver's seat to ask, "Where shall we go, sir?"

"Banten," he said. "The country place."

No more description was required. Dewei faced forward, put the Humvee into gear and headed west.

MAIA LEE KEPT TRACK of urban landmarks as they rolled through sunbaked streets toward Pondok Indah, on the south side of Jakarta. Cooper made good time along Jalan Sultan Iskandar Muda, rolling past large auto dealerships and Club Aquarius. On Jalan Metro Pondok Indah, traffic flowed around them, some of it diverting to the giant Pondok Indah Mall, more to the sprawling Padang Golf Club on their left.

The man they sought might be a member of that club, but he didn't reside upon its grounds—at least, if they could trust the information gained at gunpoint from his lackey at the factory. Both that man and the building would be smoking ruins now, and they were forced to take his dying word or leave it, gambling their own lives on a hope that he'd been truthful.

If he had, Jin Au-Yo would be found beyond the golf

links, in a high-rise condominium on Jalan Metro Kencana 4. It stood to reason that he would be guarded, doubly so in light of their recent attacks on his turf, and that he wouldn't yield without a fight.

So be it.

Maia yearned to finish her assignment and go home. She had worn out her welcome in Malaysia and Jakarta, saw no entertainment value in remaining and had scratched both off her short list of potential holiday retreats. In fact, if she could make it through the next few hours, she would be happy with a desk job. Even with dismissal from her ministry position, if it came to that.

She had assumed the mission with a sense of pride at being chosen to defend her homeland. If, as she'd suspected, there were traitors to be rooted out along the way, so much the better. Maia recognized the problems China faced in dealing with the world at large and thought those difficulties were best mended from within, by people like herself, who placed the country's welfare first, above their own.

But was that true?

Why had she *really* kept the secret of her unexpected meeting with Matt Cooper, and their collaboration toward a common goal? Was she afraid of being called back to Beijing and chastised, even slated for "reeducation" by the ministry? Or had she hoped to find the missiles, save the day and claim all of the credit for herself?

A small voice in her head asked Maia why it mattered, if she got results. She knew the answer to that question, but had difficulty trying to articulate it. Something about duty, honor, sublimation of her own desires to China's greater need.

Which sounded like a steaming pile of crap when she spelled it out that way. Why should she *not* advance herself whenever possible, while following her orders from the ministry?

And if it all went wrong somehow—if she should fail, yet manage to survive against all odds, what then?

Blame the American, she thought, feeling a twinge of guilt. But just a twinge.

As far as Maia knew, Beijing had no idea that he existed, much less that they had joined forces to pursue the stolen Brave Wind missiles. If anything went wrong, who would contest her version of the facts, whatever that might be?

Maia focused on success, willing the gangster Jin Au-Yo to be at home when they came calling, trusting they could find a way to make him spill his secret knowledge of the madmen who had bought the missiles from him. Where they might be found, perhaps. Whatever Jin might wish to share.

Before they sent him to the hell that he deserved.

Beiheyan Street, Beijing

FANN LIEU EXAMINED his reflection in the men's-room mirror, wishing he had time to leave the ministry and have his hair trimmed. As it was, the urgent summons from the Deputy Assistant Minister for State Security had barely left him time enough to use the lavatory, wash his hands and now—an afterthought, but still important—straighten the knot of his necktie.

On his desk, two floors below the men's room, in the office space he shared with half a dozen other analysts, Fann had a tall stack of reports pertaining to recent guerrilla attacks on Chinese arms shipments to Sudan. He had been wading through the documents for two days now, with no end in sight, and Fann was no closer to identifying the persons responsible than he had been on day one.

Was that why he'd been summoned to the fourth floor? Was a reprimand—or worse—awaiting him?

Fann swallowed the lump of apprehension in his throat and left the restroom, moving briskly along the corridor to Chou Hua Tian's office. If there was trouble to be had, best face it quickly and be done with it.

Chou's secretary took Fann's name while barely glancing at his face, buzzed through on her desk intercom, then led him through a door behind her desk to meet the deputy assistant minister. Chou didn't rise from where he sat behind a spacious desk, much less offer to shake Fann's hand. As Chou's subordinate, Fann took the cue and did not extend his own hand, but ducked into the chair Chou indicated with a careless wave.

"You have been with the ministry for nine years," Chou announced, not making it a question.

Fann nearly answered, *Almost ten,* but swallowed the reply. He would gain nothing from correcting his superior. Instead he nodded, waiting.

"In that time," Chou continued, "you have done no active fieldwork."

Did that call for a response? An explanation or apology? Fann split the difference and answered, "No, sir."

"We have decided it is time for you to broaden your horizons," Chou announced. "There is a matter that requires attention in Jakarta, and we feel you are well suited to perform the task."

Fann caught his eyebrows on the rise and reeled them back. "Jakarta, sir?"

"Indonesia," Chou replied, as if addressing a slow-witted child.

"Yes, sir," Fann responded, careful not to snap at his superior. "If I may ask, what is the task?"

"You are acquainted with a field agent named Maia Lee," Chou said. Again, not asking.

"Yes, sir." Feeling the need to elaborate cautiously, Fann said, "We trained together at the University of International Relations."

"Where both of you excelled," Chou said. "Are you aware of the events surrounding an attack on the guided missile destroyer *Shenyang?*"

"In broad terms, sir. Only what has been reported in the media." Or whispered in the halls, Fann could have said, but rather added, "Nothing classified, of course."

"Your friend has been assigned to the investigation of those behind the attack," Chou revealed. "The area of her assignment was Malaysia and Jakarta."

Was? Fann felt a knot of apprehension forming in his stomach. Had something happened to her? He bit his tongue, waiting.

"It pains me," Chou said, pressing on, "to inform you that Maia Lee has become…unreliable. She has broken off communication with the ministry, and she's begun to act erratically. There have been incidents. Fatalities. We now have reason to believe that she's collaborating with an American agent toward some unknown end that may be detrimental to the PRC."

"An American agent, sir?" Fann was uncertain whether he could trust his ears.

"According to the information we've received," Chou said. "Your mission for the ministry is to locate your one-time friend and issue a direct order for her to contact headquarters at once."

"Of course, sir," Fann said, before the sheer enormity of it sank in. "But in Jakarta there must be, how many people?"

"Approximately 9.5 million," Chou replied. "Do not allow that fact to daunt you, Agent Fann. We have a plan. The first thing you must do is…"

Pondok Indah, South Jakarta

"IT'S CLEAR," Maia Lee said, hissing a curse between clenched teeth. "There's no one here."

Bolan emerged from one of three large bedrooms, carrying his Pinda SS2 with its twin muzzles pointed toward the deep shag carpet underfoot.

"Jin bailed," he said. "And from the looks of things, it wasn't long ago."

"You think someone alerted him?" Maia asked.

The soldier frowned, then answered, "I don't see how they could. We left nobody at the factory to make a call."

Maia moved toward the nearest window, peering through rain-speckled glass as if the answer to the riddle lay somewhere outside. It likely did, in fact, but Bolan knew they wouldn't pick it out by staring at the city skyline.

They could toss the place, but Bolan didn't think they'd find a note from Jin Au-Yo directing them to wherever he'd gone. And there was passing time to be considered. Someone might have seen them entering the building, possibly a triad lookout, though their quarry had left no one in the condo to secure it.

"Well, at least we know it is Jin's place," Maia said, turning from the window now and staring at a wall of photographs depicting Jin Au-Yo with people Bolan didn't recognize. Some of them wore sports gear, others looked like celebrities, though none he knew by sight. Some of the backdrops were Jakartan, others looked Chinese.

"He left his memories," Bolan said.

"And his clothes," Maia replied. "He was definitely in a hurry."

So are we, Bolan thought and said, "We should get out of here."

Tucking their weapons under still-damp slickers, they retreated from the condominium, walked toward the service elevator.

"Stairs," Bolan directed, as they reached it. "Just in case."

Twelve flights to reach the street, but it was all down-hill. They had the staircase to themselves, no one else coming or going as they made it down to street level. The last steel fire door had a little window in it, double panes of safety glass making a sandwich out of wire mesh in between. Bolan peered through the window, left and right, then risked a look outside.

"All clear," he said, and led the way.

A moment later they were in the alley, hustling past a line of garbage bins to their waiting vehicle. As Maia settled in the shotgun seat she asked him, "So? What now?"

"Jin's gone somewhere to hide out," Bolan said. "We need to find one of his people who can put us on the trail and squeeze him till he cracks."

CHAPTER ELEVEN

Kebayoran Baru, South Jakarta

Maia suggested that Jin's lawyer was their next best bet for pinning down the triad vanguard's whereabouts. In fact, he used a firm—Meng, Shangguan and Firdasari—the last-named partner being Indonesian and the other two Chinese—known for representing gangland clients and an ever-growing list of multinational concerns.

"If Jin was taken into custody," she said, "Syamsir Firdasari would be representing him on any criminal indictments. The others work primarily with contracts and investments, the financial side."

"So, one-stop shopping," Bolan said, as he drove west.

"Full service," she assured him. "We will find their office on Jilan Wiyaya 1."

Bolan stayed on course and started counting off the blocks until they reached their destination.

"I'll take whoever's in the office," Bolan said, "but say we start with Firdasari. Have you researched him at all?"

"Only enough to locate him at need," Maia replied.

"I guess we'll have to test his dedication to attorney-client privilege," Bolan suggested.

"Indonesia does not honor all your rules from the

United States," Maia explained. "There is no rule protecting anyone from self-incrimination and no guarantee of confidentiality for legal documents."

As if it matters, Bolan thought. He didn't plan on serving a subpoena at the law firm, wouldn't fawn and beg them for the information he required. The Executioner was all for civil liberties in theory, but he had no patience for the human predators who violated every law, then tried to hide behind the same laws, shirking punishment. Likewise, while Bolan never criticized a lawyer for defending scumbags in the courtroom, those who helped their clients prey on innocents behind the scenes were fair game in his neverending war.

"Let's wait and see how it plays out," he said, as the Toyota plowed into another rolling sheet of rain.

"No matter what they tell us," Maia said, "their next move will be warning Jin."

"It *would* be," Bolan said, "if they had any other moves."

Same story as their other interviews. When bargaining with killers and the people who supported them, Bolan had no compunction about lying, building up false hopes that they could walk away unscathed by ratting out their bosses, friends, associates—even blood relatives. Whatever made the critical intelligence available, he'd use those tools to maximum advantage.

And the end result would always be the same.

Bolan couldn't trust a squealer not to turn around and rat *him* out, after his target of the moment was betrayed. It was a fact of human nature, as immutable as drawing breath. But when the breathing stopped, so did betrayal.

Dead canaries didn't sing.

And no dead mouthpiece ever squawked.

Beijing Capital International Airport

FANN LIEU SHIFTED in his stiff, uncomfortable plastic chair, watching the monitor that streamed departure times for flights out of Terminal 3E. His Air China flight to Jakarta should have been boarding by now, but it was delayed by unspecified "maintenance procedures." A restless flier at the best of times, Fann hoped that didn't mean one of the aircraft's wings had fallen off.

Or *should* he wish for that? If circumstances stalled his takeoff long enough, perhaps the Deputy Assistant Minister for State Security would change his mind, recall Fann from this mission which—at least, in Fann's view—was preposterous.

He was a friend of Maia Lee's. So what? It had been six or seven months since they had seen each other in passing in a hallway at the ministry. They'd barely said hello to each other at the time and, as for socializing, they hadn't been out to lunch or dinner in at least five years. Even on that occasion, they were joined by other former classmates from the University of International Relations where they'd trained for duties at the ministry, a kind of class reunion without bunting or the need to rent a meeting hall.

Now Chou Hua Tian supposed that Fann could locate Maia in a teeming city of Jakarta's size *and* somehow ensure that she "came to her senses," as Chou spelled it out. The whole thing had a fishy smell about it, Fann surmised. Even supplied with Maia's cell phone number and a coded phrase that Chou presumed would lure her to meet with Fann in person, how could Fann persuade an agent Chou described as traitorous to change her ways, returning to the fold? *Why* would she change? And what awaited her if she agreed?

Despite his total lack of operational experience, Fann knew the reputation of his ministry where turncoats were concerned. Reform through labor would have been a pleasure cruise compared to the reprisals meted out to double agents and defectors. Maia would be lucky, Fann supposed, merely to face a firing squad at dawn. Of course, that wouldn't be the half of it. Before her trial, if such it could be called, interrogation would be necessary to discover how and why she had gone wrong.

Fann felt his small lunch curdle in his stomach at the thought of what Maia would suffer during that interrogation. He would happily have spared her from it, even knowing that she had betrayed her homeland and the ministry, but if he tried to shield her, then the ax would fall on *him*. And justly so, according to the state, since Fann would have become a traitor in his own right.

No.

He would fly south as ordered, do as he was told upon arrival in Jakarta, and then see what happened next. If he was very lucky, Maia would have lost her phone or might decline to answer when he called. And if they spoke, she might refuse to meet him. Let him wait in vain until he was recalled, and if that meant a dead end where advancement was concerned, Fann thought that he could live with it.

Indeed, the job could have been worse. Chou could have ordered him to kill Maia on sight, though sending Fann on such an errand when the ministry had trained soldiers available would be the height of foolishness. Whatever Chou might be, he didn't strike Fann as a fool.

A disembodied voice announced the boarding for Fann's flight. He was among the first to board, since he was seated at the rear, where he could watch his fellow passengers line up to use the lavatories. If Fann applied his mind to it, perhaps he could sleep through most of the six-and-a-half-hour flight to Jakarta, landing refreshed and with his wits about him.

He would need them on the ground, for all the good that it would do.

Kebayoran Baru, South Jakarta

THE FIRM OF MENG, Shangguan and Firdasari seemed to be thriving. Its suite of offices occupied half of the fifth floor in a fairly new building on Jilan Wiyaya 1, with views of a park to the southwest. The lobby was designed and decorated to impress new clients, and perhaps to reassure established ones. Each click of Maia's heels on marble flooring reinforced a sense of affluent success.

At least her shoes weren't *squishing* from the rain outside. Beside her, Cooper's soles squeaked a little, still moist from the sidewalk, and she might have found it humorous in other circumstances. Then again, who ever went to see expensive lawyers for a laugh?

The firm's receptionist was young, female, attractive, wearing a silk blouse in a dramatic shade of red that matched her lipstick. She watched Cooper and Maia cross the spacious lobby; Maia half imagined that she could see wheels turning in the younger woman's head. Dark eyes assessed an interracial couple with serious faces, no obvious romantic connection. Playing the odds, she started off in English.

"Welcome to Meng, Shangguan and Firdasari," she said to both of them at once, eyes giving each approximately equal time. "How may I help you?"

Five empty chairs behind them. No one waiting for a consultation.

Put another way: no witnesses.

"We need to see one of the partners," Maia answered. "Preferably Mr. Firdasari."

As efficient as she was attractive, the receptionist answered, "He normally sees clients by appointment only."

"This is an emergency," Cooper told her.

"I see." She was unflappable. "I'll check and see if Mr. Firdasari is available. Your names, please?"

"Sauer," Cooper replied, drawing his pistol, standing with its muzzle resting on the desk. "SIG-Sauer."

And she wasn't *quite* unflappable, Maia discovered to her pleasure, as the other woman's hand froze halfway to the telephone. Recovering some of her poise, she said, "We don't keep any money on the premises."

"It's not a holdup," Maia told her. "Is he in or not?"

Eyes flicked back and forth between them rapidly. "I'll have to check and—"

"No," Maia said, curtly interrupting the excuse and easing her raincoat back an inch to show the submachine gun slung beneath it. "There's no private elevator here. The partners pass your desk coming and going. *Is he in?*"

"Yes! Yes, he is."

"And what about the others?" Cooper inquired.

"Both out," the frightened woman said.

"Out where?" Maia asked.

"Mr. Meng should be in court," the receptionist said. "Mr. Shangguan's on holiday. New Zealand."

"Anybody else around?" Cooper asked.

"We have three associates. One is in court with Mr. Meng, the other two are at lunch."

"No time to waste, then," Maia said. "Take us to Mr. Firdasari's office."

Trembling slightly, trying not to show it, the receptionist rose from her chair and led them toward the nearest of three tall mahogany doors.

Banten Province, Java, Indonesia

THE COMPOUND STOOD nine miles southwest of Serang, in the midst of a tropical rain forest. There was no dry season here, although the rain lessened a bit in the latter weeks of October. Still far from that respite, the fickle sky drenched Jin Au-Yo's motorcade while simultaneously beaming sunshine down upon its vehicles. Outside the air-conditioned cars, steam rose from jungle foliage even as the rain came down.

The procession included five SUVs, two leading Jin's Humvee, and two more trailing it. Altogether, they carried twenty-six men and a fair assortment of weapons to join the troops already waiting at the triad vanguard's rural stronghold. Jin didn't enjoy retreating under fire, but he had long since learned that it was better to withdraw at times, survive and fight to win another day, than to present himself before his adversaries as a human sacrifice.

Dead men were worthless in this world, regardless of the wealth and power they accumulated while alive.

Two guards were waiting at the compound's gate, both dressed in hooded ponchos to protect them from the rain. Regardless of those garments, both turned dripping faces to the motorcade as it approached, with automatic weapons poking out from underneath their rubberized capes. The lead car slowed, its brake lights winking, and the others coasted in behind it while the riflemen approached on foot. Another moment, recognition made, and one of them fell back to roll the gate aside, while his companion stood and watched the cars edge past him, covering the road behind them.

Nothing left to chance.

Inside the compound's fence, squatting on thirty acres, stood a group of mobile homes that had been trucked in nine months earlier, mounted on cinder blocks and wired for power from the camp's own generator. A latrine stood off to one side of the tiny settlement, downhill from the mobile homes and the space set aside for tents when—as in the present case—Jin summoned reinforcements to the site. A satellite dish angled skyward from the roof of Jin's personal trailer, granting access to television, wireless internet links and sat phones. One mobile home served as a field kitchen and mess hall, though with forty troops in residence, some of the men would have to eat outside or scatter to their tents for cover from the rain.

The compound, Jin believed, would serve his purpose amply in the present circumstances. Though he wasn't far removed from the excitement in Jakarta, it was still another province and he saw no reason why his enemies—the cursed agent Maia Lee and her American companion—should come looking for him here. Aside from those who had accompanied Jin in flight from the capital, only a handful of acquaintances knew that the jungle camp existed, much less that he was in residence this day. Jin's soldiers in the city would continue hunting in his absence, keep him posted on their progress and alert him instantly if they secured their prey.

And if his enemies *should* find him in the forest somehow, well, perhaps so much the better. It was easier to deal with adversaries in a setting where police were few and far between. No nosy neighbors peering from behind their blinds and summoning authorities over a little wailing in the night.

The trap would soon be set, and no one who set foot inside it would emerge unscathed.

Kebayoran Baru, South Jakarta

THE BRIGHT BRASS nameplate on the lawyer's desk identified him as Syamsir Firdasari. He was startled by the unannounced appearance of three visitors, and his surprise turned into irritation as he turned to his receptionist.

"What are they doing here?" he challenged her.

"Mr. Firdasari, they are here to see you on an urgent matter."

Firdasari saw their guns then, and his face went blank for just a beat, before he managed to compose himself. "If you intend to rob us—"

"You don't keep any money on the premises," Maia said, finishing it for him.

The secretary edged back toward the exit. "If you have no further need of me—"

"Stay where you are," Maia directed, and the younger woman froze.

"We're after information," Bolan said. "Concerning Jin Au-Yo."

The lawyer frowned at that, put on a puzzled face. "I don't believe I know the—"

Bolan's pistol coughed at Firdasari and a crystal paperweight exploded on the lawyer's desk, spraying his face and stylish suit with jagged shards. The mouthpiece yelped and flapped his hands, smearing the blood from several tiny cuts across his cheeks and forehead.

"Wait!" he cried. "Don't shoot!"

"Don't lie," Bolan advised him. "We already know you represent Jin and your firm is on retainer from the Flying Ax Triad."

Cringing, the lawyer moaned, "Our files are confidential."

"And I likely couldn't read them anyway," Bolan said. "Listen up. Jin's not at home. We want directions to the place—or places—where he runs to hide from heat. You must know how to get in touch with him in an emergency."

"No, no!" said Firdasari. "*He* calls *me*. I don't—"

"Wrong answer," Bolan interrupted, leveling his pistol.

"Wait! Perhaps I've seen the place you're looking for, but there is no address."

"Explain," Bolan commanded.

"I was flown in once, by helicopter," Firdasari said. "It is a fortress in the countryside. You have no hope of entering."

"That's not your problem," Bolan said. "We want directions to this fortress."

"As I said, I only saw it from the air."

"Start with directions. Which way from Jakarta?" Bolan asked.

"West, to Banten Province."

Bolan shot a glance toward Maia and she nodded. "It's the farthest western part of Java. You would say it's next door to Jakarta."

"All right," Bolan said. "If you flew in by chopper, you saw the landscape. You can rough out a map."

"I'm not much of an artist."

"Get started," Bolan said, waving his pistol toward a pen and legal pad that lay near Firdasari's elbow.

"Yes, of course," the frightened lawyer said. "But you must understand—"

To Maia's left, the prim receptionist exploded. Shouting, she leaped across her boss's desk, snatching a silver letter opener, and plunging it into the lawyer's throat. Maia, not quick enough to stop her, fired a 3-round burst into the woman's back that pitched her forward. Riding Firdasari to the floor, both of them drenched in spouting blood, the dying woman jerked and shuddered in a ghastly parody of sex.

Bolan was instantly beside them, dragging off the woman's body, shaking the lawyer, but his wound was fatal. Even if it hadn't been, the letter opener had ripped into his larynx, making any further speech impossible. In seconds he was dead.

Rising, Bolan asked Maia, "Could you make out what she said?"

"'You filthy traitor.' She belonged to Jin Au-Yo."

Bolan masked disappointment with activity. "We're out of here," he said, leading the way. "At least we have a pointer now."

"It's not enough," Maia said, as they neared the elevators. "Banten Province covers more than three thousand square miles, much of it rain forest."

"So," Bolan replied, "we keep on looking for a guide."

CHAPTER TWELVE

Java Sea

The *Thunderbolt* steamed eastward, passing north of Bali and continuing along its course into the Southeast Islands, better known since early European exploration as the Lesser Sundas. Yet another part of Indonesia, the Lesser and Greater Sundas together represented the visible part of a volcanic arc that ran for seven hundred miles or more from Bali to East Timor. Some of the smaller islets, first discovered in the present century with aid from satellite photography, were still unnamed and, to the best of any living human's knowledge, unexplored.

Nasir al-Jarrah stood on the freighter's foredeck, enjoying the tang of salt spray on his face, so different from the arid winds of his Saudi homeland. He thought about the scattered remnants of his family sometimes, but overall had no more longing for his birthplace than he did for the war-blighted hill country of Pakistan.

He heard footsteps behind him, didn't turn as Usmar Malik joined him at the forward railing.

"So?" al-Jarrah asked.

"We have received their answer," Malik said.

"And the United States does not negotiate with terrorists," al-Jarrah stated.

"As you predicted."

It hardly took a psychic to anticipate what Washington would say. The hard line was the only line—at least, in public, though it hadn't stopped the U.S. State Department from arming Iran in exchange for the return of captive embassy personnel. Of course, in those days, Tehran had been at war with Baghdad, battling another tyrant of America's creation who had run amok. It had served Washington's purposes to kill two birds with one stone.

As long as both birds were Muslim.

The Sword of Allah had no such influence over world affairs. It had no country, hence no oil or other natural resources ripe for picking. While its leaders were forever hunted, it couldn't be bombed, invaded or embargoed. With no government to shun, no populace to starve through sanctions, it was more or less invincible.

And it could strike at will, from anywhere on earth.

"What now, sir?" Malik asked.

"Now we proceed as planned," al-Jarrah said. "The island is...how far, again?"

"The captain said two hours when I spoke to him," Malik replied, checking his watch. "Ten minutes less now."

Al-Jarrah had the utmost confidence that they would be successful. While the navies of the world searched seas and oceans for their prey, he would be safe onshore, prepared to launch the second Brave Wind missile at the proper moment.

At the perfect target.

First he had to set the trap, then came the bait, all in good time.

"Your people in Jakarta are prepared?" he asked.

"Ready and waiting," the Indonesian answered. "As instructed."

"And there have been no slips yet?"

"If there had been, the Great Satan's navy would be waiting for us."

Of course. And since there were no warships yet on the horizon, or revealed by any of the *Thunderbolt*'s radar devices, al-Jarrah believed that they were safe. At least for now. After the trap was set and sprung, however, it would be a different story. Then, he thought, the choices would come down to swift escape or martyrdom.

And Nasir al-Jarrah wasn't prepared to be a martyr. No. Al-Jarrah knew that he must postpone martyrdom until his work was done on earth. Until he'd slain as many of the Great Satan's followers as was humanly possible.

Only then would he rest. Meanwhile...

"You have the speedboats standing by?" he asked Malik.

"Ready when you are."

Bogor, West Java

BOLAN WAS READY to expand his war. Since Jin Au-Yo had fled Jakarta proper, and the last-known source for his potential whereabouts was dead, the Executioner prepared to look farther afield. Greater Jakarta was a sprawling realm with nine administrative divisions, claiming some twenty-eight million inhabitants at the last census. Bogor, with nearly a million residents, lay forty miles south of Jakarta on the Jagorawi Toll Road. Nearly all of the city's Chinese lived in their insular community surrounding the Gunung Gadung cemetery, reserved for Chinese only.

"Jin will have his people there," Maia told Bolan, "if he hasn't drawn them all away to guard him in Banten."

"We just need one," Bolan said, "who can tell us where he's gone to ground."

"I know some of their operations in the area," Maia replied. "Still, it would be better if I had access to information from the ministry."

"Go on and try it, if you want to," Bolan said. And added, "But they may try homing in on your cell phone."

Maia seemed to think about it, phone in hand, flipping it open, then, as quickly, shutting it.

"We need the information," she said, as if talking to herself, "but I'm afraid of interference."

Or an order to stand down, Bolan surmised. Would she resist that order, if and when it came? And if Beijing commanded her to stop him, would she?

He heard the phone click open one more time, then hum softly as Maia turned it on.

"I have two messages," she said. "From Fann Lieu? Why would he be calling me? How would he know…?"

"Who's that?" Bolan asked.

"Someone that I trained with at the University of International Relations," she replied. "Preparing for assignment to the ministry."

"You work with him? Or her?"

"It's him. And no," Maia replied. "Not even in the same department. Other than a quick hello in passing through the halls, I haven't seen him in a year or more."

"And now he's calling you out of the blue. Today."

"Twice in as many hours," Maia said. "No message other than a phone number with a request to call him back."

"You know that's fishy," Bolan said.

"Suspicious, certainly," Maia agreed.

"You want to call him back and see what's happening?"

"I'll think about it," Maia said. "Let's tend to first things, first."

South China Sea

FANN LIEU HAD GIVEN UP on sleeping. Even though his Airbus A330 was fairly quiet, most of the three-hundred-odd souls aboard either sleeping, reading or watching in-flight television, the nonstop vibration from its twin Pratt & Whitney PW4000 jet engines mimicked and aggravated the tremors quaking Fann's own body.

You're frightened. Admit it, he chided himself. And why not?

His first field assignment, absolutely unexpected, would drop him in the middle of a foreign battleground where men were dying by the hour. Unarmed and unprepared, Fann was expected to find Maia Lee and persuade her to stop whatever it was she'd been doing—with some unknown American, no less—to cause so much havoc.

Fann didn't like his chances of succeeding, thought that it would be a victory of sorts simply to get back home alive. Or would it? Unprepared or otherwise, the Deputy Assistant Minister for State Security had given him a job to do. And if he failed, there would be consequences.

Fann *had* been provided with a cell phone number and had called it twice, leaving his name and number, asking Maia to call back as soon as possible, but there'd been no response so far. Which told him nothing. Fann thought it stood to reason that she'd have her phone turned off, to keep from being tracked by GPS.

Beyond that, he supposed she could have lost it, which would make contacting her impossible.

And Maia might be dead.

If she'd gone rogue, as Chou Hua Tian believed, and was involved in crimes of violence, that choice on her part might have been a fatal one. Fann had been warned against contacting Indonesian law enforcement, which made checking morgues for Maia's corpse a risky proposition. And he didn't fancy looking at a lot of bodies anyway.

It felt too much like tempting fate.

His basic plan was simple. After landing in Jakarta, Fann would find a hotel room, continue leaving messages for Maia on her cell phone, asking her to meet him at the Ancol Dreamland theme park on Jakarta's waterfront. After that, he'd make his way to the park and make himself available for contact while the place was open. Maia would reach out to him…or she wouldn't.

And if she didn't? Then what?

Chou Hua Tian had given Fann no deadline for completion of his task. For all Fann knew, he might be left to sit around Jakarta for a week, a month, the rest of his career. Perhaps returning empty-handed to Beijing was unacceptable.

Another reason not to sleep at thirty thousand feet above the sea, hurtling through space at five hundred miles per hour. In theory, Fann knew he was nearly as safe as he would be at home, on his own swaybacked sofa.

So, why did he feel like a man on his way to the gallows?

Bogor, West Java

"THIS IS IT," Maia Lee said. "The fourth storefront."

They were rolling along Gang Sepatu half a mile

an hour slower than the posted speed, Bolan checking out the target and its neighbors in this bland commercial district.

"What's the sign say?" he inquired.

"Triangle Enterprises," she read aloud.

"Subtle," Bolan replied. "And this is where Jin's number two hangs out?"

"His red pole for Bogor," Maia confirmed. "Cai Shu."

Passing the storefront office, Bolan observed, "He may have gone to ground with Jin."

"I'll call him and find out," she said, taking her cell phone from a pocket. Since she didn't have the Bogor number memorized, she also had to find her pocket notebook, thumbing through its pages to the proper leaf and reading off the coded entry.

Bolan drove past their target, toward the street's intersection with Jalan Cibalok, and prepared to turn north, slowly circling the block. Maia tapped out the number for Triangle Enterprises, waiting while it rang once, twice, three times...

"Yes?" a gruff male voice asked.

Responding in her native language, Maia told the man, "I need to speak with Cai Shu. Urgently."

"Who is this?" the stranger asked.

"Not on an open line," she answered. "Is he there, or not?"

The stranger thought about it for a moment, then replied, "Hold on."

She waited for the phone to drop, then cut the link instead. "He's there," she said to Bolan.

"Okay. Anything else from your old friend?"

"Not yet. I'll think about that later."

Bolan took them north on Jalan Cibalok, two blocks

as it turned out, to Jalan Sawo Jajar. A left turn there aimed the Toyota eastward two more blocks, to where the road turned south and brought them back to Gang Sepatu. He began to seek a parking place and found one half a block east of Triangle Enterprises.

"Plenty of pedestrians despite the rain," he noted, sounding less than pleased.

"We could go somewhere and wait for closing time," she said.

"Too long," Bolan said. "That's if they *do* close down, with all that's going on."

Maia observed that Cai Shu's office seemed to have no customers. Shoppers passed by, perhaps uncertain what the business was from its vague name alone. The broad front windows were no help, obscured with banners announcing New Management, giving no hint of the service or merchandise offered within.

"They don't invite much business," she remarked.

"That's something, anyway," Bolan said. "Whatever happens once we're through the door, we need to keep it off the sidewalk, if we can."

"Agreed," she said.

Tucking her silenced submachine gun underneath her rain slicker, she stepped out of the car.

TRIANGLE ENTERPRISES, right. Bolan had recognized the play on triad instantly, but also felt a deeper irony that Maia wouldn't. His one-man war against the Mafia had started after loan sharks hooked his father back in Massachusetts and destroyed the family, pushing the old man into murder-suicide before death broke their stranglehold.

The front name of their company had been Triangle Finance.

Déjà vu and then some for the Executioner.

They jogged through traffic crossing Gang Sepatu, reached the sidewalk two doors down from their target and slowed to a walk. The horns that had been blaring behind them didn't seem to matter, being more or less a constant racket on the busy street. Nothing particular to draw attention from the soldiers of the Flying Ax inside Triangle Enterprises.

"Careful going in," Bolan warned Maia. "They may have civilian employees."

"Unlikely," she replied. "Whoever tries to stop us is fair game."

Enjoying it too much? He couldn't tell behind the sunglasses she wore, despite the drizzling rain. Maybe a problem if he had to cover her, as well as any adversaries in the shop they were approaching.

The place had double push-through doors that let them enter side by side, showing their weapons to the staff first thing. Maia rattled off some orders in Chinese that froze a half dozen male twenty-somethings at first, then they scattered like mice, diving off in all directions toward their several desks, tugging at drawers.

Going for guns.

It came down to a triad turkey shoot. No human being could outrun a bullet, whether it's a 5.56 mm NATO or a 9 mm Parabellum. They could *try,* hope for the best and play a ducking game, but if they couldn't reach hardware in a hurry to defend themselves, they were history.

Six targets. Bolan caught the nearest of them as he dived across a cluttered desk, three rounds exploding through the young man's rib cage in a spray of crimson, ripping through his lungs before he had a chance to scream. The dying gangster kept on going, sliding on a blood slick, sodden papers going with him as he tumbled out of sight.

By then, Maia had tagged a second runner with her submachine gun, muffled sputtering instead of the reports from Bolan's SS2 assault rifle. Her target lurched and stumbled, fell face-forward, and his forehead struck another desk with force enough to break his neck, if it had mattered. Which it didn't anymore.

Bolan kept tracking, caught his second target with one hand inside an open desk drawer, snarling curses in defiance. It was as good a way to go as any, and the next burst out of Bolan's weapon didn't keep him waiting. Three hot tumblers ripped into his torso at center of mass, an inch or less below his racing heart, and stopped it with a blast of hydrostatic shock. Amazement trumped defiance in the last half second of the man's life, before he dropped from sight and out of Bolan's thoughts.

Maia's next target didn't bother going for a gun, unless he had it stashed somewhere in a back room. He was a sprinter, pretty fast, but physics taught him that he wasn't fast enough. Whether the lesson took, with Parabellum manglers smashing through his occipital bone and into his brain, was a question forever unanswered.

Two triad members remained, and they'd both reached weapons, but the pistols didn't do them any good. The shooter Bolan targeted was dropping by the time he fired a wasted round into the storefront's ceiling, puncturing one of the water-stained acoustic panels. Maia's guy was quick enough to point and fire, but pointing wasn't aiming, and his shot missed Maia by a yard or more, drilling the plate-glass window at her back. She greased him with a 3-round burst and followed Bolan toward a room set back some fifty paces from the entrance, searching for Cai Shu.

When they were halfway there, a voice called out to them in Chinese.

"What's that about?" Bolan asked.

Maia frowned and said, "He warns us to stay out. He has grenades."

CHAPTER THIRTEEN

Lesser Sunda Islands, Indonesia

The island had no name as far as Usmar Malik knew. It was located north of Flores, where a team of foreign scientists had unearthed the remains of tiny ape-like proto-humans several years earlier. There were no monkey-men in evidence, however, as his crewmen carefully removed the final Brave Wind missile and its launcher from the ship.

Malik gave Nasir al-Jarrah full credit for the brainstorm that would bring their ship-to-ship missile ashore. The Sword of Allah's field marshal had reasoned that their enemies, quite naturally, would be searching for a ship after the test-fire on the Dutch freighter. No one would think of planting the missile on land, but its custom-made launcher would work anywhere. Its guidance system would lock on a target from a hilltop or a cave's mouth as well as from the rolling deck of a vessel at sea.

Malik caught himself holding his breath as the Hsiung Feng III descended in its cradle, supported by a shipboard crane. Just under twenty feet in length, it weighed more than three thousand pounds. The flatbed truck that waited to receive it had been lifted ashore in identical fashion days earlier, when work began on the landlocked launch site. The truck was old and shabby-looking, but its suspension was sound and bore the new weight with only a token groan from its springs. Its engine rumbled and the truck began to pull away, nosing inland.

Next, Malik's mechanics would begin dismantling the missile launcher and removing it in pieces from the ship for reassembly at the chosen launch site. It would take some time, but they were in no hurry. Hours more would pass before the great American Pacific Fleet drew close enough for one of its aircraft carriers to serve as a target.

He wondered idly whether it would be the Third or Seventh Fleet that was dispatched to prowl through Indonesian waters. The only real difference lay in which carriers Malik and Nasir al-Jarrah would have the chance to destroy. The Third Fleet, Malik recalled, included the USS *Nimitz, Abraham Lincoln, Carl Vinson* and *John C. Stennis.* The Seventh Fleet's flattop included the USS *George Washington* and *Ronald Reagan.* Any one of them would make a worthy target when the time came, although Malik personally hoped that it would be the *Ronald Reagan.*

Symbolism mattered, after all.

A voice behind Malik surprised him. "How much longer?" Nasir al-Jarrah asked.

Malik turned and said, "A quarter of an hour for the missile to be set in place before the truck returns. Then transport of the launcher and its reassembly. Possibly two hours."

"You are taking all precautions to avoid an airborne search?" al-Jarrah asked.

"We are. Naturally, there is no defense against surveillance from a satellite in space or from high-flying planes. So far, no visible aircraft have passed the island."

If that news pleased al-Jarrah, his mood wasn't reflected on his face. Malik wondered why the Saudis always seemed to look so sour.

"They must certainly be seeking us by now," al-Jarrah said.

"Beginning where the Dutch ship sank," Malik said. "They cannot have the *Thunderbolt*'s description, much less our direction of travel."

"They will find us, nonetheless."

"And you are counting on it, eh?"

"Not until we are prepared to greet them with a rude surprise, Usmar. Make sure the beacon is not triggered prematurely."

"I've reserved that duty for myself," Malik said. "I shall be honored to perform it."

And to watch Great Satan's minions die by fire and water, screaming as their hope ran out.

Bogor, West Java

"WE'RE RUNNING OUT of time," Bolan told Maia Lee. "Somebody must have called the cops by now."

"Don't be too sure," she answered. "If they think it's triad business, they won't want to get involved."

Some gamble, Bolan thought. And if police rolled up while they were still inside, their exit through the back door was obstructed by a thug who might—or might not—have a stash of frag grenades.

What now?

They couldn't tell the local triad boss they only wanted information, after killing half a dozen of his soldiers. Could they?

Was that a siren wailing in the distance, faint and far? Impossible to tell, over the bleating horns and revving engines on the street outside. Still, even if the cops *weren't* coming, Bolan knew that it would be a grave mistake to linger where they were. Whether their final adversary had grenades or not, he *would* have access to a phone back there. He could have reinforcements on the way by now, to cut off their retreat and turn the shop into a death trap.

"Try asking him where Jin is," Bolan said, and shrugged when Maia blinked at him. "You never know, right?"

Maia rattled off the question in her native language. Got a cackle from their barricaded enemy before he shouted back to her.

"So?" Bolan asked.

Maia smiled and said, "It's anatomically impossible."

"Okay, then. Tell him that we don't believe he has grenades, but I'm about to give him one."

Maia relayed the message, wincing at the answer.

Bolan glanced at Maia. She told him, "Let's say he's not convinced."

"Time to convince him, then," the soldier replied.

He aimed high with his 40 mm SPG1 launcher, lofting its HE round toward a corner of the back room's barely visible ceiling. The round detonated on impact, filling the chamber with smoke, dust and pulverized plaster. When the triad red pole finished coughing, he called out to them in breathless tones.

"Why do they always bring their mothers into it?" Maia Lee asked.

"One more to shake him loose," Bolan said, as he fed another round into the launcher's breech. "And then we need to go, regardless."

Maia nodded.

He aimed lower this time, toward a bank of filing

cabinets barely visible beyond the back room's open doorway. The second blast mingled shards of metal from the cabinets and clouds of mutilated paper in the smoky atmosphere. Their adversary, coughing louder now, lurched into view and staggered toward the doorway. In his hands, something that could have been a paperweight—or a grenade.

"Watch out!" Bolan said, as the mobster drew one arm back for the pitch.

They fired together, Bolan's rifle making all the noise. Bullets from both guns toppled the animated scarecrow over backward. And a third blast followed seconds later, shrapnel mostly wasted on the walls and ceiling of the shattered office space.

"I guess he *did* have a grenade," said Bolan.

Maia muttered something.

"I'll take your word for it," said Bolan. "Time to run."

Banten Province, West Java

MA MINGXIA HELD the sat phone out to Jin Au-Yo and said, "A call from Bogor, sir."

"Who is it?" Jin asked, as he took the phone.

"A brother. I didn't recognize his name, but he knew all the signs."

Jin raised the phone and spoke. "Yes?"

"Xue Poon, sir. I am but a lowly forty-niner."

"Yet you call me rather than conversing with your liaison officer," Jin replied. "Why is that, brother?"

"Sir, this is an extreme emergency."

"Explain," Jin ordered.

"We have been attacked in Bogor. Cai Shu is dead, with six of our brothers."

"When did this occur?" Jin asked.

"Minutes ago. Our headquarters is destroyed."

"By whom?"

"A man and woman."

"You observed this?" Jin demanded.

Momentary silence on the line, before Xue Poon replied, "Yes, sir. Cai sent me out to get office supplies. When I returned…there was shooting. Explosions. I had come too late."

"And yet, you saw the pair responsible?"

Another hesitation. "Yes, sir. As they were leaving."

"Did you try to stop them?"

"No, sir. There were too many witnesses. Police were coming."

"You could not be bothered to avenge your red pole and your brothers?" Jin demanded.

"Sir, I was unarmed, having left my weapon in the office."

"Did you follow them at least, to find out where they went next?"

Jin could almost hear the young man gulp. "The first thing that I thought of was alerting you, sir. I'm sorry."

"Silence! To atone for your pathetic failure and *perhaps* escape the punishment you well deserve, find all the soldiers that you can and search the city. These two people seek us out, so watch our places closely. If you find them, do what must be done. Fail twice, and nothing but your worthless shadow shall remain."

Jin broke the link before his frightened soldier could apologize again. Ma Mingxia reached out for the phone, but Jin held on to it.

"I have more calls to make," he said. "See to the guards. Make certain they're on full alert. Our enemies have followed us as I predicted. Have the trap in readiness."

"It shall be done, sir," Ma said, and left.

Of course, a raid in Bogor didn't mean the hunters would locate Jin in his forest stronghold, but he *hoped* they would. He craved an opportunity to pay them back in kind for all the misery they'd caused him, and to find out, in the process, who supported them behind the scenes.

He knew that Maia Lee was from the Ministry of State Security, but what of the American? It was unheard-of for a Chinese covert agency to work in league with operatives from the States. Too many years of paranoia and hostility divided the respective services, no matter what was said in public by their leaders in Beijing and Washington.

Jin had to solve that mystery while time remained, to save himself and all that he had worked for, killed for, through the years.

Over Palau

Fann Lieu tried Maia's phone again, hoping for contact this time, and was shunted once again to voice mail. Rather than record a message, he logged off, then sent a text instead. It read: Arrive Jakarta 9:00 p.m. Meet me at Ancol Dreamland soonest.

Wasted effort? Possibly. Fann still had no idea if Maia checked her messages, if she still had the phone he kept contacting or if she was even still alive. Another possibility, besides her death, was that she'd been arrested in commission of some crime with her supposed American accomplice. In that case, would he be summoned home as soon as Beijing got the news?

Uncertainty gnawed at Fann's mind and set his nerves on edge. He peered out through his window toward a string of islands far below him. The Republic of Palau was peaceful now, a major tourist destination, but he knew that in the war against Japan it had seen brutal fighting on the island of Peleliu. All long before Fann's time, of course, but he enjoyed studying history. Learning from the mistakes of other generations—not that it made any difference to a cog in the machine who shaped no policy himself, made no decisions more exacting than a menu choice for lunch or supper.

Fann wished he had done more training for the field, but counselors had chosen those who fitted the bill for black ops after batteries of testing that included psychological exams. If truth be told, Fann was relieved on learning that he'd been selected for an office job instead of skulking through back alleys, breaking into buildings, risking injury.

It was coincidence and nothing more that marked him as the right man for his task. Fann thought the Deputy Assistant Minister for State Security might just as easily have sent a trained macaque, if it had known Maia in school. Too much was resting on their tenuous association, Fann believed, but who was he to question his superiors?

He wondered whether this was how it felt to be a soldier on the eve of battle, though he'd been assured no fighting was expected of him. Fann supposed that meant that others would be standing by to capture Maia if and when she met with him, rejecting Fann's proposal that she go home to Beijing. Who in her right mind would surrender in the circumstances, when capitulation was the same as suicide?

Or was it all a huge mistake? Could she explain her actions and relieve the dangerous anxiety they had inspired? Fann thought it was unlikely, but he'd seen enough while deskbound at the ministry to know that black was often white, and up was often down. Nothing was precisely as it seemed to be.

Fann had decided that he had to acquire a weapon once he landed in Jakarta. Having no idea how he would find and buy a gun, his thoughts had turned toward other implements. Surely, a range of knives would be available for sale. And if he kept his wits about him, played his cards correctly, perhaps he could do better.

At least he should be able to defend himself. But against Maia Lee? If she was truly a traitor to China and all Fann believed in, could he raise his hand against her?

Yes, Fann thought. Reluctantly, of course. But to preserve his life and honor, he could strike her down.

Bogor, West Java

"I HAVE ANOTHER message," Maia said, eyeing the cell phone in her hand as if it were a crouching scorpion.

"Same guy?" Bolan asked.

"Yes. He writes that he will be in Jakarta by nine o'clock. He asks me to meet him at the Ancol Dreamland tourist park."

"Dreamland is right," Bolan replied. "You show up there, they'll put you to sleep."

She paused a moment, staring through her window as they passed Bogor's botanical gardens, then said, "I want to go."

"Say what?"

"To meet him. He would not have come this far from home—"

"Unless somebody sent him," Bolan interrupted. "It's a trap. It *has* to be."

She nodded. "Yes. But we may still learn something from it."

Biting back a sigh of sheer exasperation, Bolan told her, "I'm all ears."

"First, I may learn if Fann Lieu has betrayed me of his own accord," Maia explained.

"Who cares? You said yourself, you haven't seen him in a year or more. It's not like you're inseparable friends."

"But we were comrades," Maia said. "If he's been duped, then he should know it. There's a chance that he could help us."

"How?" asked Bolan.

"He may be able to identify a traitor at the ministry, or more than one."

"Because…?"

"Because I was assigned to find the Brave Wind missiles and to punish those who took them. Now, someone within the ministry seeks to deter me."

"I'll buy that," Bolan agreed. As far as he knew, trusting Maia to be straight with him for the duration, there had been no other contacts from her ministry. Her supervisor hadn't called or texted her for updates on her progress. Nothing but this sometime friend appearing out of left field. Still…

"I think you've put the cart before the horse," he said. "We need to find the missiles first, then think about who set the whole thing up behind the scenes. You getting killed at an amusement park won't help, as far as I can see."

"But if I don't get killed," she said, half smiling now, "if you were there to watch my back, we might accomplish something."

"Right. Turning Jakarta's take on Disney World into a shooting gallery."

"To find out who inside the Ministry of State Security is working against China's interest," she said.

"You said he lands at nine?"

"Correct."

"Which means he'll likely get a room and put his things away before he heads off to the park."

"I would assume so," Maia granted.

"And there could be trouble if we try to meet his flight."

"It's likely."

"And we don't know where he's staying," Bolan added.

"No."

"So, if we turn around right now," he said, "we'll have to spend the best part of three hours doing nothing in Jakarta, while your friend clears Immigration and gets squared away."

"I would agree," Maia replied.

"So, why not go ahead with what we started here," he said. "If we get something at our next stop that will put us onto Jin Au-Yo, we follow up on that. If not, we'll keep your date."

"Yes," Maia said. "It's for the best."

Their latest strike was on the radio already. Maia had translated for Bolan one of the reports, filled with speculation about foreign gangsters fighting one another. Maia told him someone in the lower house of Indonesia's legislature had renewed demands for curbs on immigration, to prevent a further swarm of "Chinese cockroaches" from overrunning the country.

"That's the spirit," Bolan said. "Go overboard first chance you get."

Oppressed by thoughts of human frailty and hysteria, he navigated toward their second chosen target on the outskirts of Bogor.

Cikaret Utara, South Bogor

THAT TARGET STOOD on Jalan Pulo Empang, two blocks south of the Sukarna gong factory. Gong-making, as explained by Bolan's guidebook, was a dying art. He sympathized with those involved, but knew the best thing he could do for them was make sure no *artistes* were standing in the line of fire when he and Maia made their move.

The Chinese agent's second target in Bogor—the last one on her list for Banten Province—was a meth lab catering to Indonesian addicts. Bolan had a few statistics at his fingertips concerning Far East trafficking in crank, the poor man's poison. Last year alone, police in Southeast Asia had seized more than 130 million methamphetamine tablets from dealers, freely admitting that they'd only scratched the surface of their problem. Ninety-odd percent of the drug manufactured in black-market labs slipped past authorities each year and made its way to strung-out tweakers. Indonesians called it *shabu,* preferring its artificial excitement over the lassitude induced by *putauw*—heroin.

The good thing about *shabu,* from a trafficker's perspective, was that you could make it anywhere. Given a moderate degree of skill, the proper chemicals, a roof over your head, you could cook meth every day, all day, year-round. You didn't need a lot of acreage, never had to pray for rain or hire a crew at harvest time. If you could work with ether, hydrochloric acid and the rest of it without blowing yourself to kingdom come, your biggest worry would be counting money day and night.

The triads had been peddling meth for decades, with a new twist logged in recent years. Aside from feeding habits on the streets, the Chinese mobs were also trading crank-precursor chemicals to abalone poachers, shipping the endangered, legally protected shellfish off to gourmet restaurants in Hong Kong and the PRC. The going retail rate for abalone meat: $108 U.S. per pound.

Busting one meth lab wouldn't stop the traffic, but it was another blow against the Flying Ax Triad in Indonesia, and another opportunity to see if anyone on-site could point Bolan in the direction of their master's hideaway. They had it narrowed down by province, but that wasn't good enough. Not even close, when Banten Province spread over thirty-five hundred square miles, with close to eleven million inhabitants.

Bolan still hoped they'd find a source, and soon. He didn't like the thought of trailing Maia through the crowded avenues of Ancol Dreamland, waiting for the ax to fall, but a promise was a promise.

One way or another, there would be more blood.

CHAPTER FOURTEEN

Lesser Sunda Islands, Indonesia

The sun had dipped from sight behind the unnamed island's densely wooded spine of crags, but work continued on the Brave Wind missile's launcher. Nasir al-Jarrah had ordered camouflage tarpaulins spread over the site, concealing handheld lamps the workmen used from any kind of aerial surveillance. When the job was done, and only then, the crew would have hot food prepared inside a military surplus mess tent on the south edge of the clearing.

Then, it would become a waiting game. Al-Jarrah was accustomed to delays, postponements and procrastination in his war against the festering Great Satan and its allies. Nothing ever came easily to God's chosen warriors, an anomaly that al-Jarrah had finally resolved by treating each new setback as a test of faith. Only when he was purified by sacrifice and suffering would al-Jarrah be worthy of his own reward in Paradise.

But how much longer would he have to wait?

He muttered an apology to God. Even *thinking* such a question could be blasphemy. A true believer kept the stout doors of his mind and heart locked tight against insinuating and subversive doubt. To question was to falter, and to falter was to fail.

He saw Usmar Malik approaching, stood and waited for the Indonesian to approach.

"It is nearly finished," Malik stated.

"What progress with the fleet?" al-Jarrah asked.

"No sighting on our radar yet," Malik answered. "When they reach us, you will be the first to know."

The makeshift radar station sat atop their nameless island's highest peak, six hundred feet above sea level, well positioned for surveillance of the Bali Sea westward and the Flores Sea to the northeast. Neither were likely waters for investigation by the great U.S. Pacific Fleet, but al-Jarrah would make it happen. When reports from loyal coast-watchers told him any portion of the target fleet was visible, he would begin broadcasting exhortations to jihad from the *Thunderbolt,* already anchored well offshore. They would expect to find the second missile on a ship, would field aircraft against the *Thunderbolt* when efforts at communication failed.

And while their eyes were on the decoy, Nasir al-Jarrah would strike.

The carrier, whichever one they sent, was his primary target, but he would be more or less content with any fighting ship obliterated. Amphibious assault ships, smaller versions of an aircraft carrier, each had two thousand crew members aboard, on average, not counting their Marines, and cost three-quarters of a billion dollars to construct. A guided missile carrier, including armament, cost about one billion dollars, carrying some four hundred officers and crew. Destroyers cost about the same, including the expense of weapons systems, with an average complement of three hundred-odd sailors.

All worthy targets, but al-Jarrah wanted the biggest, most expensive ship available. He wanted to outclass

Osama bin Laden's great blow to the West, and while he knew that competition was unhealthy, it was still a part of human nature.

"If you don't mind," Malik spoke up, "I am hungry."

"I do not mind," al-Jarrah replied. "But you will wait until the work is finished, like the rest. Set an example for the ones who labor in our righteous cause."

"It shall be as you say."

"And while you're waiting," al-Jarrah said, "check the radar operator. Make sure he's awake and that he knows his life depends on making no mistakes."

Cikaret Utara, South Bogor

METH LABS HAD a smell all their own, ammonia and ether combining to produce a stench a person might expect if several hundred cats had urinated in a room filled wall-to-wall with rotten eggs. The cookers did their best to clear the air—and to keep the pent-up toxic fumes from killing them—which called for odd experiments in ventilation for the standard drug house. Blowers pumping fumes into the nearest sewer outlet was a classic, and the crew in Cikaret Utara had employed it, but a cat-urine smell still emanated from the house they'd purchased on the cheap and turned into their workshop.

"Smell it?" Maia asked, when they were half a block away.

"It's hard to miss," Bolan replied.

The neighbors weren't complaining, since the houses on each side of the meth factory were vacant, windows without drapes staring across Jalan Pulo Empang like blank eye sockets in a pair of skulls. Bolan supposed it would have been no problem for the Flying Ax Triad to buy the tenants out or chase them off, either before the lab went operational or when it started to produce complaints.

Bolan knew they could do the job two ways. The simple way: hang back and lob a 40 mm HE round or two in through the meth lab's windows, strike a fatal spark inside and watch it blow sky-high. The flames would likely be confined to the immediate vicinity, meaning the two abandoned homes on either side. That would eliminate the lab, its personnel and send another jolting message to the Flying Ax.

But it wouldn't provide Mack Bolan with the information he required: an address or coordinates to help him find the man in charge.

So they had chosen option number two: entry at risk. Bolan had left his automatic rifle in the car, bringing his SIG-Sauer pistol only, with its sound suppressor attached. This time around, the muzzle tube would serve as a flash suppressor, minimizing danger from a flash-fire in the lab. Same thing with Maia's PM2, quiet and more or less unlikely to ignite whatever fumes still lingered in the cookhouse.

It was a risky operation overall, made doubly so by poor advance intelligence. They didn't know how many people were inside, how heavily the crew was armed, or whether they'd been placed on high alert after the recent blowout with Cai Shu. All variables that could make a crucial difference when it came down to survival, but no battlefield intelligence was ever perfect. No fight went precisely as it had been planned, without surprises.

When they reached the empty house south of their goal, Bolan and Maia veered off the sidewalk and crossed a small yard rife with ankle-high weeds. The rear of the house was even worse, with grass up to their knees that rustled as they walked, bringing to mind a thought of snakes. Bolan ignored that primal tremor, focused on the serpents waiting for him in the house that lay ahead.

"Remember," Bolan said as they approached the target, "we want one of them alive."

"If they cooperate," Maia said. And he could have sworn she smiled.

Banten Province, West Java

JIN AU-YO WAS SICK and tired of telephones. It made him grimace when he saw Ma Mingxia coming toward him with the sat phone in his hand again, anticipating more grim news that would contribute to his sense that matters had begun to slip beyond his grasp, subverting his control. That feeling troubled Jin more than the actual events provoking it, since he had learned from adolescence to rely upon his own self-confidence. If that deserted him…

"Who is it this time?" he asked before he took the telephone in hand.

"Beijing," Ma said. "The deputy."

Not Wu Guchan, at least. Jin had deliberately stalled communication with his godfather, until he had news to report that wouldn't make him seem an abject failure. If Wu sensed the slightest weakness, he would waste no time dispatching someone to replace Jin—and to eliminate him for the damage that the Flying Ax Triad had suffered through his paucity of leadership.

"What news?" he said into the telephone.

Chou Hua Tian's familiar voice replied, "The man I mentioned to you is en route. He should be landing in Jakarta in—" a pause, presumably to check a time-piece "—two hours and twenty-odd minutes from now."

Jin frowned. How much more damage could his adversaries do within that time? Deciding not to think about it, he replied, "You're certain that he will be able to make contact?"

"I have every confidence," Chou said. "He was a good friend of the other operative."

Meaning that damned Maia Lee. A false note in Chou's voice alerted Jin.

"You say he *was,* or *is* a friend?"

"They trained together. That creates a bond," Chou said. "They've kept in touch despite assignment to different branches of service."

Jin clenched his teeth, thinking the whole thing sounded like a reeking pile of crap. "So they went to school together," he replied. "What makes you think she'd risk her life to meet him now, with all that's happened?"

"It's human nature," Chou replied. "She's dedicated to the service and must see now that she's lost her way. The opportunity to reconcile and be forgiven—"

"Are you serious?" Jin challenged Chou. "How stupid is she, to believe there'd be no retribution?"

"I prefer to call it hopeful."

"Hopeful?" Jin could barely stop himself from laughing. "She would have to be insane."

"Or desperate," Chou said. "Her friend will offer aid, a chance to put it all behind her. Anything she needs."

"All right," Jin said, determined not to let himself be bogged down in Chou's flight of lunacy. "Just tell me where to send my men."

"You know the tourist park called Dreamland?"

"Yes, of course. A strange choice, I must say."

Jin pictured Ancol Dreamland on Jakarta's waterfront, its Dunia Fantasi theme park, the SeaWorld aquarium, the Atlantis Water Adventure, the animal shows and 4D theater at Ocean Dream Samudra—all crowded with tourists, young lovers, hordes of squealing children.

A potential slaughterhouse.

"It all goes with the training," Chou explained. "Seek public places. Minimize the danger."

"Not this time," Jin said.

"I leave the matter to your sole discretion," Chou replied.

"And what about your man?"

Chou's shrug was almost audible. "He knows the risk involved in fieldwork. He's expendable."

"You're one cold bastard," Jin said, with something close to admiration.

"Cold? It's part of doing business," Chou reminded him. "But not a bastard. I have paperwork to prove it."

Jin did laugh then. Might have thanked Chou for relieving his foul mood, but there was no time as the line went dead.

Cikaret Utara, South Bogor

HU XIUQUAN MOVED through the meth house, checking on the cookers and the packagers, before proceeding to his own small office at the rear. It may have been a pantry once, was barely large enough for him to turn around in, but he had a small desk and a metal folding chair that made his rear ache until he went out and bought a cushion for it. Hardly the comforts of home, but at least the closed door gave him some privacy.

Cai Shu had placed Hu in charge of the lab as punishment for being drunk on duty two months earlier. Hu might have managed to escape the discipline, but drinking made him mean and he had pistol-whipped a rowdy player at the Bogor gambling club he'd been in charge of managing. How could Hu have known the little bastard was the son of a police captain in Lebak Regency who would insist on shutting down the club unless his bribes were doubled?

Hu still had another month to serve in meth-lab purgatory, breathing in the stench of chemicals that never left his clothing, before he would be freed for normal duty. What his new assignment might entail was anybody's guess, but Hu suspected that he wouldn't have another cushy job that let him skim a little something extra from the house each night.

He was considering revenge against the bastard who had riled him in the first place, knowing it would have to be a subtle, surreptitious action, but he hadn't settled on the proper payback yet. The worm *did* have a very pretty girlfriend. Hu could always visit her—disguised, of course—and leave a message for her boyfriend that wouldn't soon be forgotten.

A shout reached Hu's ears through the closed door of his tiny office, interrupting his latest revenge fantasy. He cocked his head, waiting to hear the sound repeated, wondering what could have happened to provoke a yelling match between the meth-lab workers. If there was no further noise—

Another shout, and then a woman's scream, immediately followed by a blast of gunfire rattling through the house. Hu rolled out from behind his desk and drew the Walther 99 pistol he wore in a holster at the small of his back. It was the .40-caliber model, twelve rounds in the mag and one in the chamber, but Hu hoped that he wouldn't have to use it in the house, where any errant spark could turn the place into a mini-holocaust.

Hu snagged his left foot on the desk's forward strut and kicked back viciously to free himself, sending a bolt of white-hot pain lancing between his shin and hip. Cursing and limping, Hu slammed through the doorway to a corridor outside his office, turned right and began to hobble toward the sounds of mayhem. More shots now, one of the women squealing, glass and God knew what crashing on impact with the floor.

MAIA HADN'T ABSOLUTELY planned on shooting anyone, although she knew it likely would be necessary. It was strange, even disturbing, how she'd taken to violence so naturally since her rescue from the pirate camp by Matthew Cooper. Was it some innate facet of her character that she had never recognized before, or just a natural reaction to the violence she'd suffered and the urgency of wrapping up her mission?

There was no time to consider weighty matters as they slipped into the meth house through a back door left unlocked. Perhaps ironically, the kitchen that they entered first bore few signs that meth or anything else had been cooked there. Its counters were spotless, from what she could see, an old refrigerator humming in one corner and a drippy faucet leaking water into the sink.

Her partner was proceeding toward the nearest door leading to the other rooms beyond the kitchen when a scrawny Filipino wandered in making a beeline for the fridge. He spotted them a heartbeat later, focused on their guns and squawked a warning cry that rang out through the house.

Maia shot him where he stood. Why not? For all she knew, his baggy shirt concealed a weapon, maybe several. Three bullets to the stranger's concave chest removed whatever threat he may have posed to them.

The American leaped across the fallen body, cleared the kitchen exit and recoiled immediately from a burst of gunfire aimed his way by someone to their left. The hostile weapon had no suppressor attached and sounded like some variant of a Kalashnikov. Its bullets, ripping through the nearby lathe-and-plaster wall, encouraged Maia to return fire, her 9 mm Parabellum bullets stitching holes across the same wall, just below a line of hanging cabinets.

Maia couldn't tell if she'd hit anyone or not, but when the next burst from the automatic rifle came, immediately after hers, its bullets buzz-sawed through the kitchen cabinets and etched a ragged pattern on the ceiling. Cooper was moving then, ducking around the doorjamb, nearly on the floor, and fired two muffled pistol shots that stopped the rifle fire.

"This way!" he snapped, and disappeared into the corridor. Maia ran after him, careful to check her right-hand side as she went through the kitchen's exit. Nothing but a dead end at a blank wall there, which meant she wouldn't have to watch her back as she went after Cooper.

There was chaos in the house now, since the Filipino's shout and burst of rifle fire had warned the lab crew of intruders on the premises. Maia picked out the rifleman that Cooper had dropped, his flowered shirt a mess of blood and other fluids that suggested half a dozen wounds. Another hit for Maia, then, and where she once might have expected to feel something like revulsion, there was nothing but relief and satisfaction with another job well done.

How many people still remained inside the house who might be armed and ready to defend the drug lab?

From the range of voices she could hear, Maia suspected six or seven individuals remaining, but she hoped that most of them were simple workers with no stake in dying for their boss.

ANOTHER BURST of automatic fire blazed at the far end of the corridor, its muzzle-flash an invitation to disaster in the meth lab's warren of rooms. The ventilation system might be drawing off the bulk of fumes, but Bolan knew it only took one bullet smashing through the wrong beakers or bottles to ignite a flash-fire that would sweep the house, incinerating anyone who wasn't blasted through a door or window by the shock wave.

Dangerous, but he couldn't advance without returning fire. He edged along the murky hallway, staying low, and waited for the next flash to reveal his enemy's position. When it came, Bolan responded with a nearly silent double-tap and heard the guy on the receiving end cry out in pain. It came down to a rush then, charging past some open doorways where, for all he knew, an enemy was hidden, waiting for him, but he reached the fallen, twitching soldier and disarmed him, crouched beside him, Maia closing up behind him, covering his back.

"Where is Jin Au-Yo?" Bolan asked.

"Qu ta ma de ziji," the wounded shooter rasped.

"Translation?" Bolan asked.

"You don't want to know," she said.

"You ask him," Bolan said. "An address for his life."

Another shot rang out, and Bolan lurched back as a bullet drilled the fallen gunman's face, painting the wall beside him with an abstract pattern, gray and crimson. Bolan spun to face the latest threat, as Maia swiveled with her SMG, both firing at a man who limped along the hallway toward them, lining up another pistol shot.

He went down in a heap with half a dozen bullets in him, shuddering. Maia relieved him of the weapon, Bolan leaning in to lift his head, repeat his question, but he saw the life-light flicker out behind dull eyes.

They backtracked, sweeping rooms, and found four of the lab rats huddled in a room where Bunsen burners sizzled under flasks of liquid and several devices resembling small moonshine stills simmered in a line on a cafeteria-style table. Bolan covered them while Maia asked the questions, getting headshakes and blank stares in return.

"Nothing," she said at last, stating the obvious.

"Do you believe them?" Bolan asked.

"I do," Maia replied. "They're only what you would call flunkies. They may know Jin's name, though not necessarily. No one from the Flying Ax would tell them where or how to find him."

"All right. We'll cut them loose, then torch the place."

"They can describe us," Maia protested.

"So much the better," Bolan answered. "If the word gets back to Jin, there'll be no doubt of who he's dealing with."

Frowning, Maia issued rapid-fire commands and Bolan watched the meth-lab drones bolt toward the hallway, still afraid to speak as they rushed out and toward the nearest exit to the street. Bolan and Maia double-checked the other rooms for stragglers, finding none, and went back to the lab. They stood in its doorway, facing ranks of bottles filled with liquid neatly shelved along one wall, more lined up on the floor against the room's north wall.

"You get a head start," Bolan said. "Don't dawdle. I'll be right behind you."

"Are you sure?" Maia asked.

"Positive. Get moving."

Maia moved, stepped off into a sprint back toward the kitchen where they'd entered. Bolan turned and aimed his pistol at a shelf of bottles nearest to one of the hissing Bunsen burners. His first shot was all it took, a jet of clear fluid igniting in midair, and then it was a race for life along the hallway, with the sound of multiplying thunderclaps behind him and the house in flames. A fireball chased him through the kitchen, out into the night.

CHAPTER FIFTEEN

Bohol Sea

Carrier Strike Group Eleven of the United States Pacific Fleet steamed westward through the Bohol Sea between the Philippine islands of Mindanao and Visayas. Dead ahead lay the Sulu Sea and Borneo, with the South China Sea beyond them. Leading the force of three ships was the USS *Carl Vinson,* a Nimitz-class supercarrier displacing one hundred thousand tons, powered by two Westinghouse A4W nuclear reactors. The great ship carried 90 aircraft and 5,680 personnel on board as it prowled the ocean.

Hunting.

No supercarrier was put out to sea alone. This day, the *Carl Vinson* was accompanied by two flankers. One, the USS *Princeton,* was a Ticonderoga-class guided missile cruiser capable of dealing death to any enemy afloat, on land or in the air at ranges up to fifteen hundred miles with its Tomahawk missiles. The *Vinson*'s other escort ship, the USS *Pinckney,* was an Arleigh Burke-class destroyer equipped with both missiles and artillery, the latter ranging in size from five-inch Mark 45 "lightweight" guns down to 25 mm M242 Bushmaster chain-fed cannons and 20 mm Phalanx CIWS antiship missile-defense guns. Six launching tubes for Mark 46 torpedoes completed the *Pinckney*'s arsenal, all of it on tap to protect the *Carl Vinson.*

On the *Vinson*'s flag bridge, Rear Admiral Harlan Bishop surveyed the vast expanse of blue-gray water surrounding his strike force, frowning at the islands off to north and south. He knew that any bay or inlet might conceal a ship armed with a missile capable of taking down his carrier or either of its escorts, manned by fanatics who lived for the sole purpose of obliterating their perceived enemies.

And Bishop *was* their enemy, no doubt about it. As a U.S. naval officer, he tried to carry out his duties without letting politics—much less race or religion—color his decisions, but there came a time when battle lines were drawn and warriors were forced to choose sides. Over the past decade and more, his homeland had been targeted for sneak attacks by groups and individuals whose version of religious fervor drove them to commit atrocities in the name of their chosen deity. Thousands of lives had been sacrificed worldwide, from Manhattan's twin towers to the backwaters of Africa and Asia. All for what? A vision of religious piety at odds with leading scholars of the faith in every corner of the world.

Such questions were beyond Bishop's pay grade, matters left to politicians. On the military cutting edge where steel met flesh, practical matters ruled the day. Bishop's orders were simple: find and destroy the persons who had hijacked the two Chinese missiles then used one to commit mass murder while threatening still worse to come. He knew the Hsiung Feng III missile's reputation as a "carrier killer," and Bishop was supremely conscious of the fact that nearly six thou-

sand lives hung in the balance, dependent on his skill
and wisdom to preserve them.

That was the name of the game, and there could be
no turning back unless the strike force was recalled by
the Pacific Fleet's commander. Until that happened, *if*
it happened, they were on the hunt and Bishop wouldn't
rest until he made the kill.

Jagorawi Toll Road

"So, WHAT'S THE PLAN?" Bolan asked, as they motored
eastward through the wilds of Banten Province, toward
Jakarta.

"No plan," Maia answered. "I will meet Fann Lieu
and find out what he wants."

"Assuming he wants anything."

"You think he's simply bait?" she asked.

"Don't you?"

"Perhaps. Yes, probably," she granted. "But if I refuse to meet him, I have burned my bridges, as you say.
The ministry will see it as rebellion."

Bolan understood Maia's predicament. Their difference in viewpoint, he surmised, came from her willingness—or wish—to trust the people who had sent her to
Malaysia in the first place.

"You know," he said, "the odds are good that someone in your government back home set up the missile
hijacking. It doesn't strike me as the kind of thing a
gang of local thugs could pull off on their own."

"I've thought of that," she said, not quite resentfully.

"It wouldn't be a stretch to think there may be ties
between the triads and your government," he said. "I've
seen the same thing in the States, in Russia, South
America and Africa."

"Of course there is corruption," Maia said. "In spite of all the propaganda, everyone in China knows the truth. Or some of it, at least."

"That doesn't mean your friend is part of it," Bolan said, treading lightly. "Let's assume that he's as straight and honest as the day is long. The brass can still use him against you, and he wouldn't even know it till the hammer drops."

"You think I will be careless?" Maia asked him.

"What I think," he answered, "is that you could stand to see a friendly face from home right now. They know that, at the ministry. And they can use it as a weapon, if you let them."

"I'll be ready when I meet Fann Lieu," she said. "Assuming that he's even there."

"Another possibility," Bolan added. "They could use his name alone to draw you in. The ministry must have your photograph on file. Whoever shows up at the park would recognize you in a second."

"You may be right," Maia replied. "But I believe Fann Lieu will be there."

"Has he narrowed down the field at all?" Bolan asked.

"Dunia Fantasi," Maia said. "Within that complex, the Fantasi Hikayat."

"A toga party," Bolan said, vaguely aware that the theme park's Legendary Fantasy section featured mock-ups of ancient Greek and Egyptian architecture.

"I won't be dressing up for the occasion," Maia told him. "But I *will* be armed."

"And I'll be covering your back," he said. "They may know your face, but they don't have mine on file."

"You're sure?" she asked.

"Trust me," he said. "It's not a problem."

Once, his face had been well-known around the world, his profile topping the Most Wanted lists of Interpol and countless other law-enforcement agencies on two continents. That was before the orchestrated death scene and Mack Bolan's disappearance from the public eye. The face he wore today was altogether different, and he could count the living enemies who'd seen it on the fingers of one hand. Security cameras and cell phones could cause grief, but he had people who deleted his likeness from databases if there was one on file.

"I have no cause to worry, then," Maia Lee said.

"There's always something," Bolan answered. "Nothing kills you quicker than a dose of overconfidence."

"In that case," Maia answered, with a small, sad smile, "I should be all right. Because I don't feel confident at all."

Banten Province, West Java

"THE METH LAB this time," Jin Au-Yo said, handing the sat phone back to Ma Mingxia. "Destroyed."

"The same two people?"

Jin expelled a long, slow breath, willing himself into a calm, deliberative state. "I can't be sure," he said at last. "One of the neighbors told police he saw a man and woman running from the scene. The woman was Chinese, he said. The man, perhaps American."

"They should be dead by now," Ma said. "Sir, let me take a group of soldiers and destroy them now, before they cause you any further aggravation."

"Old friend, your offer is appreciated, but I cannot spare you in my time of need."

Jin didn't tell Ma that he doubted whether anyone could track and kill his enemies at this point. They had proved, if not invincible, at least elusive to the point that Jin despaired of catching them through any effort of his own devising. His best hope now was that the agent from the Ministry of State Security would walk into the trap her own superiors had set for her at Ancol Dreamland, on Jakarta's waterfront. Jin's troops would be there, waiting, ready to annihilate her and the damned American on sight.

But for the trap to work, Jin realized, his enemies must both be *in* Jakarta when the fated hour struck. If they ignored the summons and continued targeting his operations in the rural provinces, all of that preparation would be wasted. In which case, how would he end the bloody stalemate?

How else, but by serving as bait?

Wherever they went, his foes left the same message. They wanted Jin, no doubt to question him concerning his involvement in the theft of Chinese missiles—more specifically, the whereabouts of those who took possession of the missiles from his underlings. Jin could have spared them all much time and energy by speaking the simple truth: he neither knew nor cared where Nasir al-Jarrah and his band of fanatics had taken the weapons, or where they would use the one missile remaining.

Jin's only interest in politics concerned enrichment of his triad and himself. Whichever party, office holder or potential candidate offered the best accommodation for the Flying Ax, that group or person had Jin's full support. He cared not whether they were Communist or Kuomintang, Democrat or Republican, Christian or Muslim. In Jin's world, ideology was just another mask concealing ravenous self-interest from the public eye.

The mask Jin wore at present was an air of confidence he didn't feel, in fact. To hold his place within the Flying Ax Triad, to keep his troops in line, Jin knew that he had to always come across as strong and self-assured. He may have suffered setbacks, but he wouldn't be defeated.

Not while he was still alive.

And if he wasn't, well, what did it matter? Jin didn't believe his ancestors were watching him, much less depending on him to preserve their reputation. All that mattered was the present, with an option on tomorrow held by those with strength and nerve enough to seize it. Weaklings suffered, as they should, and they deserved no sympathy.

"Is all in readiness for the surprise?" he asked.

"Yes, sir. It shall be as you wished. Your orders were delivered and confirmed."

Jin nodded, speaking through a frown. "Then let us hope they will be carried out. If not—" he turned to Ma, allowed his frown to shift, become a wistful smile "—we may be living in the end of days."

Jakarta Outer Ring Road

APPROACHING THE CAPITAL, Maia Lee imagined she could feel her nerves begin to tighten like piano wires. A part of her was anxious for the meeting with Fann Lieu, but common sense told her Matt Cooper was right. It had to be a trap of some kind, whether planned by her superiors, the Flying Ax Triad or an unholy collusion of both.

And she meant to be ready.

She supposed that Cooper misunderstood her past relationship with Fann. Perhaps he thought they had been lovers while they studied at the University of International Relations. Nothing of the sort had happened, though she thought Fann might have been attracted to

her in that way. But he had lacked the courage to proceed with what Americans would call "a pass." If forced
to hazard an opinion, Maia might have blamed that very
weakness for Fann's failure to become a ministry field
agent. The recruiters had to have seen that he was better suited to a desk, where his decisions wouldn't impact life and death.

What if he *had* plucked up the courage to assert himself more forcefully? Would Maia have succumbed to
his peculiar charm? And might their lives be any different today?

No matter, she told herself. None of that had happened, and their lives were intersecting now because
Fann had been sent by their superiors to speak with
her—or to arrange her death. It never crossed her mind
that he would be the trigger man. He simply didn't have
the stomach for it.

People change, Maia acknowledged, but she couldn't
see the shy boy she had known at school transformed
into a killer. Possibly, in self-defense, Fann Licu might
strike a lethal blow. But calculated murder was beyond
him, in her personal opinion.

Still, she thought, she could be wrong.

And in the situation she would soon be facing, one
mistake could be her last.

Fann's flight from Beijing should be landing within
the half hour, if it was on time. Air China was renowned
for punctuality, recognized as the world's single largest
carrier by market value and most profitable airline. She
had no reason to think that Fann Lieu would be late, although some lag time would occur between his landing
and his arrival at their meeting place.

There was some reason, she supposed, why he hadn't
asked her to meet with him at his hotel, instead of Ancol

Dreamland. Granting that the setup was a trap, Maia supposed the theme park made a better killing ground than some hotel, particularly one where Fann was registered and might be questioned by police.

A crowd of thousands, with the rides and other park distractions, made convenient cover for a killing if it was conducted properly. However, Fann and those who pulled his strings might not have reckoned with Matt Cooper—or Maia's own will to survive.

Watching the sun set on Jakarta, Maia hoped that she would have a chance to speak with Fann before the trouble started. She had missed him, in a way, although her daily life distracted her from memories of friends who'd fallen by the wayside. Maia hoped there would be time to ask Fann why he had betrayed her. Was he simply following an order? Was it payback for his unrequited lust at school? Did he even understand the game that he was playing?

Maia wondered whether she could kill him if it came to that, for his betrayal.

And decided that she could.

Lesser Sunda Islands, Indonesia

NASIR AL-JARRAH SURVEYED the launcher with its missile and was satisfied. Camouflage netting concealed it from airborne surveillance and could be removed within moments when he gave the order. Infrared was still a problem. He was aware that spy planes—even satellites in space—could note the presence of his people on the unnamed island, but the missile shouldn't register until its engine roared to life.

By which time, it would be too late.

Discovery, at this point, didn't trouble him. With

eighteen thousand islands in the Indonesian archipelago, a thousand of them first discovered in the last decade, no comprehensive search was possible. An overflight with infrared would show the major cities first—Jakarta with nine million bodies, Surabaya and Bandung with over two million, Depok and Semarang with more than a million each—and then move on to smaller towns and villages. No eye in the sky could distinguish Nasir al-Jarrah's small encampment from any other unless they could lock on the missile.

And just in case, his own technicians had gone over it in detail, seeking any kind of sensor, transmitter or homing device that might have been installed as a precaution. Just in case the end user was careless, even simple-minded, and couldn't recall where he had left a twenty-foot missile weighing a ton and a half.

They had found nothing. Al-Jarrah wasn't concerned.

His worries now included timing, accuracy and escape.

When al-Jarrah received word that the U.S. fleet was close enough, he'd bait the trap with automated broadcasts from the *Thunderbolt,* offshore. That would increase his risk, of course, as carrier-based aircraft were dispatched to find their prey. Once he had locked onto his target, al-Jarrah would say a prayer for Allah's help to speed the missile past their target's various defenses and deliver a death blow.

Then, the escape.

He had two speedboats standing by on the south side of the small island. A Jeep was waiting to convey him there, with Usmar Malik and two others, when the Brave Wind missile launched. Malik and his chosen pilot would depart in one boat, al-Jarrah and his driver in the other, breaking off in opposite directions, east and west. Unknown to Malik, there was a transmitter in the boat assigned to him that would, with any luck, draw fighter planes to him while al-Jarrah escaped.

For all his piety, the Sword of Allah's field marshal thought it better to survive and fight again another day than to lay down his life unnecessarily and leave the holy war to other, less capable hands. No intelligent person would mistake that dedication for cowardice.

No sane man would suggest it to his face.

Jakarta Inner Ring Road

BOLAN FOLLOWED the flow of traffic toward downtown Jakarta, listening while Maia read her guidebook's description of Fantasy World at the Ancol Dreamland waterfront park. It sounded like a nightmare for logistics, worse for the civilians who would flock there, unaware of peril to themselves.

"'The theme park is divided into separate regions,'" Maia read, reciting from the text in front of her. "'They include Jakarta, Asia, Africa, America, Europe and Legendary Fantasy. Features include innumerable restaurants, nightclubs, steam bath and massage parlors, a marina, a golf course, a drive-in theater, an artificial lagoon for fishing, swimming pools and sea and freshwater aquariums. Browse through the art market and linger through collections of paintings, Indonesian handicraft and souvenirs.'"

"We won't have time for lingering," he interjected.

"No," she said. "But listen—'Take a thrilling rollercoaster ride or for a less heart-stopping interlude, experience the Doll Palace that is a local version of Disney's It's a Small World.'"

"Heart-stopping," Bolan echoed. "Let's avoid that, if we can."

"But wait," she forged ahead. "'Groups from vibrant accommodations can enjoy the Niagara flume ride and relax at the Monkey Parody Theater show. Tourists can also go on the rainbow or the Ferris wheel and the swinging ship or have fun with the spinning-cups ride.'"

"Are you done with the commercial?"

"Yes," she said, and laid the book aside. Her tone changed as she said, "I wish we didn't have to do this."

"That's the point," Bolan reminded her. "We don't. Just stand him up, while we go on looking for Jin."

"If I do that," she said, "I'll never know what lay in store for me. Whether the ministry wished to communicate with me, or something else."

"It's not too late to call direct," he said. "We have the sat phone."

"No," she said. "It's better this way. If Fann Lieu has turned against me, I must deal with him."

"From what you've said, he doesn't sound like someone who would handle dirty work alone," Bolan replied.

"No. He'd need help."

"In which case, call it fifty-fifty whether that comes from your ministry or from the triad," Bolan said.

She frowned. "It makes no difference."

"Be sure, before you take that step," he cautioned. "When it's crunch time, going up against your own people may give you second thoughts. And that can get you killed."

"I will not hesitate," Maia said. "I've decided."

"Making the decision's one thing," Bolan said. "Acting on it is another."

"You speak from experience?" she asked.

"The only kind that counts," Bolan replied.

"I feel you have lost someone close to you," Maia said.

"More than one. You push past it, but it never goes away."

"If Fann has turned against me, I want to remember it," she said. "A lesson for the future."

"But it won't be him alone," Bolan said. "If the ministry's against you, you've got problems, win or lose."

"I have this mission," she replied. "Beyond that, we shall see."

"So, how about we hit the waterfront?" he said. "Check out the park. It's been forever since I took a roller-coaster ride."

CHAPTER SIXTEEN

Soekarno–Hatta International Airport, Jakarta

Fann Lieu had his passport and customs declaration ready as he disembarked in Terminal 2D. Despite the nervousness he felt, like insects burrowing beneath his skin, Fann took his time and kept pace with the other passengers arriving from Beijing, resisting his impulse to hurry past them, shouldering aside the babbling dozens who delayed him.

His first stop was the baggage carousel, more waiting with a mob of strangers until Klaxons sounded and the long conveyor belt began to turn. He watched the bags appear, one at a time, biting his tongue to keep from mouthing curses. It frustrated him to no end to fly this long and far on vital business for his government, and still be forced to wait in line with tourists for his suitcase.

Even whispering that thought among the party faithful back at home would earn him scornful glances. Still, Fann knew that leaders of the Central Committee loved their luxuries and privileges, the same as any mandarin who had preceded them in power. It was only human nature, after all, and no political ideal had changed that for the better throughout all of history.

His bag arrived at last, and Fann Lieu snatched it from the carousel, proceeding toward the immigration checkpoint where his passport and his customs declaration were examined. The officer who dealt with him was fat and had a pockmarked face with heavy jowls drooping around a thick mustache. Fann saw that his inquisitor had sweated through his short-sleeved khaki shirt despite the great room's air-conditioning, which made Fann wonder whether *he* was sweating. Would the officer see through his claim that he was traveling for pleasure, as a tourist? Would Fann's next stop be a cramped interrogation room?

Instead, the fat man stamped his passport, twitched his fleshy lips in what he might have meant to be a smile and said, "Enjoy your stay. Next, please."

Fann dragged his rolling bag behind him, toward the main concourse and taxi stands outside, still half expecting someone to run after him and clap a hard hand on his shoulder. Could it be that easy, entering another country on a covert mission? Suddenly, Fann wondered whether there were other spies aboard his flight. What secrets had his fellow fliers carried from Beijing?

Fann caught himself and thought, I'm not a spy. The ministry hadn't dispatched him in a quest for information. All he had to do was meet with Maia Lee and tell her that she'd been recalled. Her work was done. The Deputy Assistant Minister for State Security was puzzled by her failure to communicate and wished to speak with her before assigning her to some new task.

All perfectly routine—and false.

He couldn't mention Chou Hua Tian's judgment rating Maia as unreliable. If she knew the ministry had deemed her unreliable, there would be no incentive whatsoever for her to return. Better to run and seek a place to hide, Fann thought, than face whatever punishment might be in store for her.

Not for the first time, Fann Lieu wondered why he had accepted this assignment. Why had he agreed to be the Judas goat?

For personal advancement—and survival.

Keeping those two goals in mind, he stood in line and waited for the taxi that would carry him to his hotel.

Ancol Bay City, Jakarta

DRIVING WEST along Jalan Pantai Indah, Bolan scanned the theme park Maia's old friend had selected as their meeting place. A giant Ferris wheel spun lazily above the neon landscape, easily a hundred feet in height, and through his open window he could hear excited squealing from a roller coaster as it whipped through loops and spirals in the night. Thousands of people out for a good time, spending their hard-earned money on a few cheap thrills and greasy food.

How many killers in the crowd or on their way to join it?

"What's your take on how they'll play this?" he asked Maia, as they reached Jalan Marina, turning south and rolling past the pleasure craft moored there, with easy access into Ancol Bay.

"If the ministry was handling it alone," she answered, "Fann would have a weapon and there would be others waiting to support him. If his orders were to kill me, the support force would observe and only intervene if he should fail."

"And if they wanted to arrest you?" Bolan asked.

"In any case, they would not wish to cause a scene," Maia replied. "There are fast-acting sedatives. If I appeared to swoon, they could escort me from the premises."

Bolan couldn't recall the last time he'd heard anyone say *swoon*. It brought to mind romantic novels from a bygone age, nothing that fitted with Ancol Dreamland's garish skyline and the threat of gunmen lurking in the shadows down below.

"If Fann is unsupported and they leave it to the triads," Maia said, "they will want both of us."

That figured, sure. Bolan meant to grant that wish, though not precisely in the way his adversaries might desire.

Light rain was speckling the Toyota's windshield, not enough to rate using the wipers, nor to dampen the enthusiasm of the Ancol Dreamland crowds. Bolan supposed that they were used to it and dressed accordingly, as he and Maia would on entering the park.

Prepared for anything the triads or her ministry could throw at them.

"It's not too late to blow this off," he said.

She shook her head. "I need to find out why he would betray me. Whether it's simply doing as he's told, or something else."

"What difference does it make?" Bolan asked.

"If he was your friend, you'd understand," she said.

"Point taken," Bolan granted. "We can head in anytime and scout the best positions."

Maia had already called the airport to confirm arrival of the last Air China flight that evening, from Beijing. Security precluded confirmation of specific passengers on board, and Maia's former chum might not have flown under his own name, anyway, but if he'd made the flight, then he was in Jakarta and presumably en route to some hotel.

As if in answer to that thought, he heard a muted buzz from Maia's cell phone. With a glance at Bolan, she retrieved it from her handbag, opened it and quickly scanned the message it displayed.

"Fann's here," she said. "He hopes to reach Fantasy World by ten o'clock, ten-thirty at the latest."

Which seemed appropriate, under the circumstances.

"Confirm it," Bolan said. "We'll see what kind of fantasy he has in mind."

Beijing, People's Republic of China

COMMODORE FENG JINGWEI frowned at the trilling telephone, considered leaving it to ring unanswered, then released a weary sigh and lifted the receiver.

"Yes?"

"All is prepared," Chou Hua Tian said without preamble. "My man has arrived and will be in position soon."

No mention of a name or place, but none was necessary. Feng knew where Chou's agent had been sent, and why. The man's name was irrelevant, since he would soon be dead. Once he had done his job, betrayed his former friend, the agent was a liability to be excised. Eliminated.

"So, no difficulty?" Feng inquired. He had no interest in the details, but felt obligated to say something.

"None so far," Chou answered. "Our associates will handle all the details."

Meaning the triads. Feng supposed that he could take offense at being lumped together with a band of mercenary thugs, but what would be the point? He had accepted money from them and expected more to come. Whatever right he may have had to protest had been bartered off, along with any remnant of his self-respect.

"You have no apprehension, then," he said.

"None," said the Deputy Assistant Minister for State Security. "They understand the need for absolute discretion."

Feng supposed he should be satisfied with that. Indeed, what other choice was there? Chou had to deal with his disruptive agent in whatever way he chose, while Feng stood by and hoped that there would be no fallout from the housecleaning.

"What word from the Americans?" Chou asked, breaking the silence that had stretched between them.

"They will not negotiate, of course," the commodore replied. "They attach no formal blame to us, but there is agitation at the People's Liberation Army Navy," he continued. "Some fear that relations may be…jeopardized."

"These things are always settled amicably," Chou answered dismissively. "Our nations share too much in common for such things to separate them in the long term."

"But there may be repercussions here," Feng said.

"Perhaps, but we are well positioned to control them. If it comes to that, we sacrifice the Flying Ax."

"And they accept it?" Feng asked skeptically.

"They have no choice," Chou said. "They live and operate by sufferance of the state. Once that protection is withdrawn, they die like any other parasite."

Or kill the host, Feng thought, but didn't voice it. He was well aware of how the Chinese government responded to embarrassment by scandal. After the Sanlu Group was caught adulterating infant formula with deadly chemicals, two of its chief executives were shot, and a third was imprisoned for life. What would the state do to a naval commodore who had participated in the theft of guided missiles and their sale to terrorists?

"Are you still there?" Chou's voice reached Feng, as if from far away.

"Yes, yes," the commodore replied. "I hear you. Sacrifice the Flying Ax if anything goes wrong."

"Exactly. A united and courageous front between us," Chou declared.

"Good night, then," Feng said.

He broke the link, knowing the Deputy Assistant Minister for State Security would sacrifice *him* in a heartbeat, if it meant preserving his own position and avoiding punishment. But Feng didn't intend to serve the gloating bureaucrat as any kind of human sacrifice. If he went down, all of the dirty secrets he'd collected over time would be dragged out into the glaring light of day.

He wouldn't be the only person standing at the wall before a firing squad.

Banten Province, West Java

MA MINGXIA LOOKED apprehensive this time, as he moved toward Jin Au-Yo, holding the sat phone at his side as if to make it less conspicuous. Over the years, he'd learned to recognize Jin's moods and knew his master had to be close to snapping from the weight of trouble on his narrow shoulders.

"Who this time?" Jin asked, before Ma had a chance to speak.

"Huo Zhangke," Ma said. "He's calling from that place."

Meaning the Ancol Dreamland theme park in Jakarta, where Jin had dispatched him with a dozen of his top surviving soldiers.

"And he wants what?" Jin demanded.

Ma shrugged. "Words with you, sir," he said.

"Son of a bitch!" Jin reached out and took the phone from Ma, swallowed his irritation like a bitter, wriggling thing, and said, "What is it, Huo?"

"We're all in place," the man replied.

"I would expect no less," Jin said. "Why are you calling me?"

"The man we're looking for," Huo said. "There's no sign of him."

Jin closed his eyes and muttered, "Give me strength."

"What's that, sir?" Huo asked.

"I said give it time." Jin felt his anger building, threatening to choke him. "I've confirmed that he arrived on time at Soekarno–Hatta. He had to clear the airport, get to his hotel. It all takes time."

"We'll wait, then?" Huo suggested.

"Yes," Jin answered with exaggerated courtesy. "Until the park shuts down, if necessary. Understood?"

"Yes, sir." From his new tone, it was obvious that Huo knew he was on shaky ground. "Please accept my most abject apology. I did not mean—"

Jin cut him off, handing the sat phone back to Ma. "Don't put him through again unless he calls to say they've been arrested," he said.

"Yes, sir."

"No, wait. Not even then. *Especially* not then."

Ma smiled and nodded as he turned away, leaving his boss to gnaw on whatever was troubling him.

Jin naturally hoped the trap would work, solve all his problems in a single stroke, but he wasn't prepared to stake his life on that alone. Too many things could still go wrong, from intervention by police to pure bad luck. Jin knew that Chou Hua Tian was only helping him in order to protect himself, preserve his own position with the government and head off lethal punishment. It was the kind of attitude Jin understood from personal experience.

Despite the setbacks Jin had suffered in the past, he was convinced that he could turn the tide to his advantage. He would destroy the female agent and her damned American accomplice to restore his honor. And if Wu Guchan refused to grant that Jin had proved himself, well, no man was invincible. The mountain master could be toppled from his pinnacle more easily than Wu supposed. Jin had already taken the preliminary steps to that end, just in case.

Upon promotion to his present rank, Jin had sworn loyalty to the death. But Wu Guchan had never specified *whose* death. Let that be his surprise.

Wu had a birthday coming up next month. Perhaps his last.

Central Jakarta

FANN LIEU SURVEYED his room on the third floor of the Fiducia Hotel and pronounced it adequate. He'd chosen on the basis of economy, from several dozen hotels advertised in brochures at the airport, and was glad he would be reimbursed upon returning to Beijing. The air-conditioning wheezed at him, putting out a stream of tepid air, and while Fann would have liked a shower, he didn't have any time to spare.

The taxi ride had taken longer than he had imagined, and another lay before him. On the street below, his driver waited with the meter running, glad to sit and smoke his foul cigar while logging twenty thousand rupiah per minute. A hired car might have made things easier, but Fann had been intimidated by the rush of downtown traffic, and the hotel had no parking for its guests in any case. Better to bill the ministry for the extravagance—three U.S. dollars every time the minute hand moved on his watch—and know that he could reach the waterfront before his time ran out.

The Ancol Dreamland park shut down at midnight, if the guidebook on his nightstand was correct. Fann looked around his shabby room once more, searching for anything he might need at the park that had been overlooked, and found nothing.

What else would there be, except the clothes that he stood up in and the story he was meant to tell?

He was unarmed, of course. Airport security had seen to that, and while it made him feel uneasy, Fann Lieu knew his limitations. He wasn't a gunman, had done poorly in the basic self-defense courses he was required to take while training at the University of International Relations. Maia had been far superior in marksmanship, and she had regularly beaten him at unarmed combat, to the point that they had laughed about it over frugal meals and coffee in the cafeteria. It had not hurt Fann's feelings at the time—well, possibly a little—but he felt the lack of preparation most acutely now.

For he was walking into danger. There could be no doubt of that.

As Chou Hua Tian had spelled it out, Maia had been involved in "incidents." *Fatalities.* Fann didn't know precisely how she was involved, whether the deaths had been her doing or a by-product of what Chou called her unreliability. In any case, Fann understood that if he let his guard down, if he didn't watch himself, his name might be appended to the growing list of dead.

It was ironic, he supposed. He had applied for a position with the Ministry of State Security hoping to find adventure, possibly even romance. There'd been none of the latter, unless Fann counted a brief liaison with a secretary from the Personnel and Education Bureau. As for the adventure, that had been ruled out when Fann was placed in the Eighth Bureau. That was Research, masquerading for outsiders as the Institute of Contemporary International Relations. Fann was, in effect, paid to read foreign newspapers and troll the internet for any bits of information useful to the ministry. And having found them, after writing up a summary, he filed it all away.

Now, here he was in Indonesia, on his way to an amusement park to meet an old friend who might try to kill him. How was that for high adventure?

Fann Lieu barked a bitter laugh and locked the room behind him when he left.

Ancol Bay City, Jakarta

THE SPITTING RAIN HAD TURNED into a steady drizzle by the time Mack Bolan parked the SUV with several hundred other vehicles and killed its engine. Reaching down behind the driver's seat, he found his open gym bag and removed the Pindad SS2, lifting it up into his lap. The rain, darkness and the deserted parking lot provided adequate security as Bolan checked the autorifle's load, distributing spare magazines and 40 mm rounds in pockets of a light tactical vest. All hidden by the poncho once he'd pulled it on and drawn the hood over his head.

Maia Lee was working on a similar makeover in the passenger's seat, securing clips on the straight magazines of her PM2 submachine gun to minimize fumbling when it was time to reload. Bolan still hoped that the full-auto weapons might not be required inside the theme park, but he'd stayed alive this long by always being ready for the worst conceivable scenario.

In this case, that would be an ambush on the crowded midway of Fantasy World, with countless tourists in the line of fire. As skilled as Bolan was, some of his shots at moving targets still might go awry, or even ricochet after they sliced through human flesh. That left whole mobs of innocents in jeopardy, when all they'd banked on was a thrill ride on the Power Surge, the Meteor Attack, Tornado or one of the other rides designed to merge laughter with panic.

"Ready?" he asked Maia.

She frowned, then nodded. "I've packed everything that I can carry."

Bolan kept his fingers crossed, hoping she wouldn't ask him if the poncho made her look fat. She spared him that and climbed out of the SUV into the rain, remembering the hood too late and cursing softly as she raised it to protect wet hair.

"I'll catch a cold now, wait and see," she said.

Bolan turned toward the theme park's entry gates, hoping that neither of them caught a dose of sudden death.

CHAPTER SEVENTEEN

Ancol Dreamland, Jakarta

Huo Zhangke loitered near the entrance to Dunia Fantasi, his hair plastered to his scalp by rain, wishing that he could tune out the incessant noise from screaming roller-coaster riders, bleating children and their whining parents, plus discordant music echoing from half a dozen sources on the midway close at hand. He had a headache, which was rare unless he'd earned himself a hangover from drinking too much rum, and it was only getting worse with the assault upon his eardrums.

Make that *one* eardrum. The other ear—his right— was muffled by the wireless headset that allowed him to communicate with other members of his team spotted around the theme park. In some other time and place, the headgear might have made him stand out in the crowd, but variations on his own device appeared to be the norm for Ancol Dreamland visitors. It made them look a bit like aliens or perhaps attendees at some science-fiction gathering, especially the ones with cotton candy smeared across their faces in a range of garish colors. At any given moment, Huo thought half the babbling around him was comprised of people talking to themselves.

Which likely made them feel at home in Fantasy Land.

Huo's team consisted of a dozen men and one ferocious female—Lia Yin—whom he had brought along in case their female target ducked into a women's lavatory or used some other gender-specific ruse to dodge his shooters. All had viewed and memorized the target's photograph, emailed presumably from somewhere in Beijing. As for the female agent's cohort, this American no one still living could describe, Huo guessed that they would simply have to kill whoever came into the park with Maia Lee.

Simple.

Huo had no orders from his superior to make the killings look like accidents or heart attacks. A simple bullet to the brain would do it, and if any of the tourists who surrounded him felt a compelling urge to act as heroes, well, Huo had enough guns on the scene to deal with them, as well. A massacre wasn't what Jin Au-Yo had ordered, but he *had* been crystal-clear in stating that the targets could not be allowed to slip past Huo's soldiers.

At any cost to bystanders and property, they had to be stopped.

It was the kind of order Huo Zhangke preferred, no nit-picking or micromanagement from his superiors. His skill wasn't in question, neither was his leadership ability. Simply unleash him, let him do his bloody work and then reward him for a job well done.

Huo hoped that there would be no collateral damage, of course. The negative publicity was never welcome, was often bad for business in the short run. But he wouldn't lose a moment's sleep if some stupid person crossed his line of fire at a critical moment and paid with his life. Belonging to the Flying Ax Triad meant that such petty irritations were beneath him.

Huo was content to know that he would do his job and two people would die.

At least.

BOLAN AND MAIA didn't approach the Ancol Dreamland ticket gates together. Maia took the lead and put her money down, while Bolan got into a different line and waited several minutes longer for his turn. Each moment that he spent outside the revolving gate, no view of Maia after she'd passed through, nagged at him with the thought that she might walk into an ambush on her own, before he had a chance to cover her.

But no shots sounded from the park, and when his turn came to push through the gate, a full-height turnstile made of stainless steel, he had the brief sensation of confinement in a cage. The moment passed and he was through, instantly enveloped by the clamor of a giant fair. Alter the faces, and it could have been in Kansas, Rio de Janeiro, Cairo or Nairobi. People massed together by the hundreds, maybe thousands, challenging the elements to drown their quest for simple pleasures.

Most of them, at least.

One man, either inside the park already or arriving soon, was coming to betray a friend. Maia didn't regard him as a threat, given his personality and background, but the Executioner wasn't entirely sold on that analysis.

Whether the finger man came dressed to kill or not, he wouldn't be alone. The only question left in Bolan's mind was whether he and Maia would be facing triad guns, a team from Maia's Ministry of State Security or both. He didn't speculate about the numbers, since he couldn't pick a figure from thin air.

One edge they had already, going in: none of the hitters sent to back Fann Lieu, the point man, would have seen Bolan before. They'd likely know that he was white, perhaps American, but there were other round-eyed tourists in the Ancol Dreamland crowd, and Bolan's hooded poncho did a fair job of disguising him unless he met an enemy head-on.

Another edge: Bolan himself.

He wasn't arrogant, just realistic. Bolan knew what he could do, what he *had* done, and he had a fair idea of how he stacked up against triad soldiers. They were killers, sure, but more accustomed to compliant targets. The Executioner was betting everything he had that they had never faced someone like him before.

And never would again, after this night.

They would be in for a surprise with Maia Lee, as well, if they came at her with the expectation that a woman was an easy tag. She'd proved herself in battle, and despite some latent ambiguity about her former classmate, Bolan thought she was prepared to treat him as an enemy if that, in fact, turned out to be the case.

And what else could it be?

Passing the Jaya Bowling Center, Maia fifty yards ahead of him, Bolan wondered if she'd have any hesitancy about facing other agents from her ministry, if it came down to that. It didn't worry him tremendously, but Bolan understood that even fleeting hesitation could be fatal once the guns came out.

As for himself, spies didn't qualify as cops in Bolan's view, and so they weren't protected by the private limitation he imposed upon himself. Civilians were the worry, on this crowded killing field, and it would be a challenge not to kill or injure any when the heat came down.

Beginning any minute now.

FANN LIEU HAD CASH in hand as he approached the ticket booth. Ten thousand rupiah translated to roughly nine renminbi in Chinese currency, or a little more than one U.S. dollar. It was modest enough, though he'd cringed at the number initially, prior to conversion. From what he could see as he stepped from the taxi, the park had to be making a fortune for someone in the firm that owned it.

It pleased Fann, in a small way, to have secret business at the park. When he had filed his application with the Ministry of State Security, he had imagined learning secrets, knowing stories that would separate him from the mindless throng of ordinary office workers in Beijing. Of course, he knew that everyone had secrets, but the sort accessible to him were a special kind. And while he couldn't share them with another soul outside headquarters—and few within—Fann Lieu felt privately empowered by the covert knowledge he possessed.

That all seemed vaguely foolish, now that he was actually in the field and moving toward the culmination of a real-life secret mission. There was danger in the air, and while the prospect frightened him, while he was torn by guilty feelings with regard to Maia Lee, Fann's secret knowledge still made him feel special.

Special and intensely vulnerable now that he was actually on the scene, clearing the entrance to the park, following signs to Dunia Fantasi and, within it, Fantasi Hikayat. Toward his rendezvous with Maia on an errand of the utmost critical importance.

As he walked along the midway, Fann tried picking out the watchers who, he understood, would have been sent ahead to shadow him. He had no practical experience with tracking anyone, and his imagination quickly ran away with him. A smiling couple with their toddler in a stroller might be agents, the child a lifelike doll concealing weapons in its pram. The clown who passed him, looking weary underneath the painted smile from hours of compulsory hilarity, could be another watcher. When an older man bumped into Fann and muttered an apology, Fann quickly checked his pockets. Nothing missing, and no covert message passed to help him with the task that lay ahead.

He had gone through changes since receiving his assignment to Jakarta. First came guilt at being asked to use their friendship as a weapon against Maia Lee. Next came acceptance of the claim that she had somehow come to be unreliable for service to the ministry. With that in mind, Fann had experienced a sense of pride at being trusted with a delicate assignment.

Only later, airborne on his way to Indonesia, had the thought occurred to him that he was being used because he was a small cog in the great machine, and thus could be expendable.

Which changed nothing, of course. If Maia had betrayed their homeland and the ministry, she had to be stopped. And if Fann Lieu could play a part in stopping her, whatever his precise role, it would be a feather in his cap. A means of climbing through the ranks.

One of the first things every child learned in the People's Republic of China was loyalty. First to the state—or to the people, if you managed to believe the two things were identical. Next, to the family, if they were worthy citizens who did their part to help the PRC. Self didn't enter into the equation. No man born since Mao Zedong was indispensable.

But Fann Lieu didn't plan to die this night.

With any luck at all, he would survive and prosper. As for Maia, well, she'd made her choice, and she could live or die with it.

Fantasi Hikayat, Ancol Dreamland

DESPITE THE CRUSH of bodies that surrounded her, regardless of her hooded poncho and the rain that fell in gusts then vanished just as quickly, Maia Lee felt terribly conspicuous. It was her own mind playing tricks, she realized, but who on earth was able to escape from his or her own thoughts?

Maia imagined, for a start, that nearly everyone who passed her on the theme park's midway had to be able to discern her worry from her grim facial expression, made grotesque by neon lights. It seemed to her that nearly anyone could spot the submachine gun bulging underneath her rain-slick poncho, even though she clutched it tightly against her side. Perhaps the SIG-Sauer pistol tucked into the back of Maia's jeans protruded just enough for passersby to note the bulge.

And then what?

She had passed police in uniform already, strolling past, examining the crowd with baleful eyes. If anything was out of place with Maia, surely they would be the first to see and challenge her. Or were they just too lazy, lulled into a kind of apathy by their assignment to a playground? Would that change if one of the civilians streaming past them pointed Maia out, accusing her of—what?

The firearms that she carried were illegal for civilians, and her ministry credentials carried no weight in Jakarta. She would be detained for questioning, and if the guns were matched to bullets taken from the men she'd killed since coming to Jakarta with Matt Cooper, it meant murder charges. Indonesian law prescribed execution by firing squad for convicted murderers, terror-

ists and drug traffickers, which theoretically left her in
mortal jeopardy on two counts, if arrested.

But no one raised the hue and cry as Maia passed
among them, hoping Matt Cooper was somewhere behind her, or running along a parallel track to her left
or right. Maia's garb, in fact, betrayed nothing to anyone. The park employees dressed as ancient Greeks and
Egyptians, staked out at scale models of the Parthenon
and pyramids, looked more bedraggled from the rain
than most of the tourists around them. They weren't on
the lookout for fugitives, gunmen or spies.

Lucky for me, she thought.

She was supposed to meet Fann Lieu somewhere
around a looming plaster model of the sphinx. No more
specific details were available, likely because Fann
didn't know the park himself and had had no access to a
detailed set of photographs before he chose the spot. He
could have worked from pictures on the internet, or he
may have been instructed by a planner at the ministry.

Someone who wanted Maia neutralized.

Well, she would meet Fann Lieu, but Maia didn't
mean to play the game his way.

And if he tried to take her down himself, it might
just be his last mistake.

THEME PARKS WEREN'T the kind of recreation mode
that Bolan normally enjoyed, preferring as he did the
peace of solitude or easy moments spent with his surviving friends. He understood the urge to join a crowd,
of course—to run, scream, gobble greasy food then
squander money on a dizzy ride to bring it up again—
but all that struck him as a child's pursuit, something
that normal folk outgrew around the time they came to
terms with puberty.

The mob at Ancol Dreamland obviously disagreed.

Maybe the park provided a release from numbing office work or a welcome contrast to manual labor. Perhaps some parents hoped their children would be so exhausted by the park that they'd sleep through the night, despite sugar infusions that could keep an army marching strongly. No doubt a few young men—and women, too—used Ancol Dreamland as a precursor to pillow talk.

More power to them, Bolan thought. To him, it was a little slice of pseudo-happy hell on earth, complete with screams and flashing lights that simulated flames.

But it could still get worse.

When Bolan chose an urban battleground, his first thought was the risk to innocent civilians. He would fight wherever trouble found him, but if given time to lay a plan, he wouldn't choose a hospital, a shopping mall or a crowded theme park as his killing ground. This time, of course, the choice had *not* been his. He had to cover Maia while she met her former classmate, watching out for hunters in the crowd, among the booths and noisy rides—throughout the whole damned park, in fact.

Impossible. But he would do his best to keep her safe and deal with anyone who threatened her, leaving the so-called friend in Maia's hands.

Exactly what she hoped to learn from placing her head on the chopping block eluded Bolan. Part of it was personal, no doubt, maybe a hope that she would be proved wrong about Fann Lieu's betrayal. Bolan thought the odds of that occurring rested somewhere close to nil, but life could still surprise him every now and then.

But if Fann Lieu *was* playing straight, what then? Would he come bearing information that would help them find the missiles, even track down Jin Au-Yo? Bolan already knew Fann wasn't trained in fieldwork, and the last thing either of them needed at the moment was a desk jockey hanging around to cheer them on. Moral support was great with family and friends, but it was useless on the battlefield.

So far, he'd spotted no one who stood out as obviously dangerous, but scouting shooters in a mob like this was difficult at best. Toss in the countless hiding places that a theme park offered, and it was a nearly hopeless task. For all he knew, there could be snipers riding on the Ferris wheel, bushwhackers hiding in the men's room toilet stalls. Until they made an overt move, they were invisible.

And by that time, it might well be too late.

CHAPTER EIGHTEEN

Legendary Fantasy, Ancol Dreamland

Fann Lieu was standing near the Parthenon and looking for the sphinx of Egypt, feeling edgy and disoriented as the Indonesian rain soaked through his lightweight jacket. He had packed in haste, not thinking of the weather beyond vague notions of tropic heat, and there had been no opportunity to buy a raincoat after he checked in to his hotel. Some of the people rushing past him on the midway had cut holes in plastic garbage bags and pulled them on over their heads, reminding Fann of photos he had seen from Baghdad's Central Prison early in the U.S. war against Saddam Hussein.

Better soaked to the skin, he decided, than dressed like a hostage—or a giant leech from some low-budget horror film.

The park employees dressed in ancient costumes had evaporated as the rain grew stronger, no doubt seeking shelter for themselves. Fann didn't have the luxury of hiding out and killing time until the rain stopped. First, he didn't know if it *would* stop. And more importantly, he had a job to do—meeting with Maia Lee.

He'd wondered, on the taxi drive from his subpar hotel to Ancol Dreamland, whether she had gone so far beyond the pale that she would try to kill him when they met. It seemed irrational, but hints of paranoia had been tossed into his briefing by the Deputy Assistant Minister for State Security. Why would an agent in the field turn rogue, unless her mind had somehow grown unbalanced?

Wait and see, Fann told himself. Do not prejudge.

Sound counsel, but his nerves were twitching nonetheless.

Again, Fann wished he had a weapon, even though his skills had barely been rated adequate in training, and he'd had no practice in the years since then. On second thought, false confidence might prove more dangerous than traveling unarmed, particularly if a weapon prompted Maia to some act of violence against him.

Meet and talk, he thought. Explain the ministry's concern.

If she would listen.

And if not...?

He had been promised backup and would have to trust that promise. Otherwise, if Fann believed he was alone in this, he might have turned and run away. Instead, he fixed his eyes on Dunia Fantasi's version of the sphinx and moved in that direction, jostled on his way past running children and the parents who pursued them without much success.

He should be safe here, Fann decided, with so many eyes surrounding him. A public meeting, he recalled from training at Beijing's University of International Relations, was considered best if it was feasible, large open spaces being much preferred over sequestered spots with poor escape routes.

As if Fann Lieu needed to escape from Maia Lee. The notion almost made him smile, until he recalled Chou Hua Tian's remarks. *She has begun to act erratically. There have been...incidents. Fatalities.* But even so, surely she wouldn't try to harm Fann in the midst of an amusement park, surrounded by a mob of witnesses.

Shoes squelching on the rain-slick pavement, shoulders hunched and hands thrust deep into his trouser pockets, Fann drew closer to the sphinx. He started focusing on women in the crowd now, trying to spot Maia from a distance, wondering if she had seen him yet. Fann hoped she wouldn't change her mind at the last moment, slip away and leave him standing in the sphinx's shadow like a jilted lover.

When she tapped him on the shoulder from behind, Fann nearly yelped aloud. Spinning to face her, it required a force of will to shift from startled gaping to a smile.

"Hello, Lieu," Maia said. "You came alone?"

"He's found her," Huo Zhangke informed his team, using the wireless headset. "Verify positions!"

Lia Yin, first to respond, said, "I have target acquisition."

One by one, the others chimed in until he'd heard from all thirteen. They had the sphinx surrounded at a distance, Lia closest to the targets at a range of thirty yards, while some of Huo's gunmen hung back at sixty, eighty and one hundred yards. The trick was to construct a living cage without alerting Maia Lee or spooking Fann Lieu into hasty action that would give away the trap.

And meanwhile, they were on alert, all watching out for the American.

Huo had seen a number of white faces in the crowd, between the ticket gates and Dunia Fantasi, but they had been paired in couples, one of them with squalling children. If a lone white man was lurking in the neighborhood, Huo hadn't spied him yet. Which posed a problem if the hypothetical American was covering his female cohort, ready to assist her when the trap sprang shut.

Huo found himself in a dilemma. He could take the woman now, or stall until her partner was revealed, at which time it might be too late for a clean shot at Maia. His orders, clearly stated, were to bag *both* of the up-starts who had wreaked havoc on members of the Fly-ing Ax Triad, but would he be forgiven if he let one slip away while waiting for the other to reveal himself?

Unlikely.

Huo Zhangke edged closer to the target and her friend, both targets now, the man from Beijing rated as disposable. Reaching inside his raincoat, he clutched the grip of his Type 80 machine pistol. Although its sights were permanently fixed for fifty yards, Huo wanted to be closer before he opened fire.

"Move in as planned," he told the others, trying to speak without moving his lips. The last thing that Huo needed was some stupid tourist watching him and run-ning off to park security because he'd seen a crazy fel-low talking to himself.

The first shot would be his, although he knew that Lia Yin was chomping at the bit to make a kill. She frightened Huo sometimes, particularly on the two oc-casions when they'd shared a bed, Lia seeming to be-lieve that pain and pleasure were identical. She was a witch, that one, with lethal magic in her hands.

Huo didn't rush as he approached his targets. There was no great hurry, certainly no reason to alarm them, and he still hoped that one of his people might spot the American gunman, as well. If they didn't discover him before the shooting started, Huo's last hope lay with the American jumping in to help when his associate went down. If that didn't provoke him, if he chose to flee instead of fighting like a man, Huo would be left with only half a prize.

Forced to explain his failure, throw himself upon Jin's mercy to survive.

Which was another problem in itself, since Jin Au-Yo possessed no mercy. Those who failed him had a way of winding up their lives in misery and pain.

Perhaps the American would be a knight in shining armor, dying for his lady. As he drew his pistol, Huo Zhangke could only hope.

MAIA HAD STUDIED Fann and his surroundings thoroughly before approaching him. He seemed to be alone, no watchers visible from where she stood, but that proved nothing. Even now, she had the option of retreating, leaving him to wait in vain, but part of her had to know why he'd been sent so far from home to meet her in the rain, at a bizarre amusement park.

She waited till his back was turned before approaching him, then tapped him on the shoulder.

When he'd recovered from his momentary shock, Fann replied, "I am alone. As promised."

"No one followed you?" she asked.

He frowned at that, delaying long enough for Maia to suspect deception, then said, "I saw no one following."

She had to press the point. "And you made no arrangements to be met here?"

"Only by yourself," Fann said.

Not trusting him, she said, "All right. Let's walk."

She wondered where Matt Cooper was, whether he was covering her as she started off with Fann, passing the sphinx and moving toward a sized-down model of an ancient pyramid. In these surroundings, she would not have been surprised if they were ambushed by a walking mummy.

"So," she said, "what brings you to Jakarta?"

"I came to see you, as you know," he answered.

"But at whose request?"

"The Deputy Assistant Minister for State Security himself," Fann said.

"I doubt that I am so important," Maia said.

"This is a time of crisis," Fann replied. "You have a critical assignment, and he worries that you may be..."

"What?"

"Unreliable," he answered, clearly reluctant to say it.

"Chou thinks I would betray the ministry?"

"He said there had been incidents. Fatalities. He said you have been working with an American agent. Is it true, Maia?"

She answered him with silence.

"No one understands," Fann said at last. "You don't communicate with headquarters. On top of all that's happened with the Brave Wind missiles, it's too much."

"And they sent *you* to stop me?"

"As a friend, to speak with you," Fann said. "You have no cause to mock me."

"I'm surprised, that's all," she said. "Why send an officer with zero field experience into a situation with *fatalities* involved?"

"Perhaps because they thought that you would speak to me."

"And here we are. What is your message, Lieu?"

"The Deputy Assistant Minister—"

"Chou Hua Tian," she interrupted him. "I know his name. Go on."

"He wishes you to stop whatever you are doing.

Catch the next flight to Beijing. Explain yourself at headquarters."

"Face trial, you mean," she said.

"There was no mention of a trial."

"Perhaps they will dispense with it and send me to the wall directly," she replied. "Such things are known to happen."

"You may be able to redeem yourself," Fann said.

"And how might I do that?" she asked.

"Surrender your accomplice. The American."

BOLAN MUTTERED a curse as Maia and Fann Lieu began to walk away, leaving the sphinx behind. He understood her motivation. It was better to become a moving target than to stand still and make it easy on your would-be executioners, but Bolan hadn't spotted any shooters yet, and breaking cover cut both ways. If enemies were watching out for him, somewhere amid the midway crowd, he would be more conspicuous following Fann and Maia than if he remained in place.

It was too late to think about that now. He couldn't let the pair slip out of sight and range.

They had walked on for thirty yards or so when Bolan spotted one apparent follower. A Chinese woman, slight of build, with hair tied back under a camo bush hat, was keeping pace with Maia and her friend but staying well off to one side. She wore a large black plastic trash bag poncho-style, to keep her clothes dry, denim jeans and well-worn sneakers showing underneath its floppy hem.

The makeshift rain gear was a common feature in the crowd surrounding Bolan, but this woman stood out from the mob because she was alone and moved with more determination than the others, homing in on her targets. The trash bag hid her arms and anything she might be carrying, but she would have to clear it if she meant to aim and fire with any accuracy. Nearly certain of her plan, still Bolan waited for the confirmation he required to drop a woman on the midway, and while tracking her, he kept on watching for the backup that he knew had to be in place somewhere nearby.

Still walking, Maia and Fann were talking with their heads almost together in the rain, keeping their voices down so no one passing by could overhear them. Maia shook her head in negative response to something Fann was saying, whether contradicting him or simply answering a question, Bolan couldn't tell.

Their single follower cut glances to her left and right from time to time, as if watching for comrades on her flanks. As Bolan closed the gap between them, he made out the earpiece she was wearing, thought he saw her lips moving in profile for a second, just before she turned away. That gave him all the confirmation that he needed of a team in place, but a preemptive strike would only warn the others, maybe spur them into action prematurely. He hoped to spot them, before they moved on Fann and Maia.

It would help to know if they were going for a snatch or a kill, but Bolan had no way of learning that before the trap closed. It would be too late by then, if they were sniping from a distance, but that struck him as a risky move with so many civilians in the line of fire. Or would they risk a massacre to get the job done, after he and Maia had inflicted so much damage on the Flying Ax Triad?

Hang in a little longer, Bolan thought. Another minute, maybe two.

And pray it's not too late.

"I won't betray him," Maia said.

"Betray *him?* What about the ministry? Your country?" Fann challenged.

"Someone from the ministry could be involved in this," Maia replied.

"In what? The missile hijacking? Think what you're saying, Lee."

"I *have* thought about it. It's the only answer that makes sense."

Fann recognized that tone, the stubbornness that he remembered from their student days together, any time they disagreed on something. Looking for a way to crack that wall, he said, "You're sounding paranoid."

She cut an angry glance in his direction and replied, "It isn't paranoia if I'm right."

"And you prove that by running off to the Americans?"

"I haven't 'run off' anywhere," she snapped. "The man you speak of saved my life."

"And now he's placed your life in jeopardy," Fann said.

"The choice was mine," Maia replied.

"There's still time to reverse it," Fann replied. "If you won't give him up, at least come home with me."

"Not until we've found the second missile. Fann, you must know what's at stake here."

"Maia, listen to me! If you don't—"

Fann lost his thought then, as a child came out of nowhere, running full-tilt while looking back over his shoulder. He caromed off Fann's left hip with a squeal of surprise and collapsed on the pavement as Fann, stunned and cursing the pain, turned to snap at the brat. Before the words could form, he heard a muffled popping sound and felt another blow, this one beneath his arm, lancing his chest with agony.

Fann dropped to one knee, gasping, suddenly unable to draw breath. His mind was churning, trying to make sense of the event, as Maia called his name from miles away, her voice barely an echo in his head. A coughing spasm racked him, and his bleary eyes beheld the boy who'd slammed against him, gaping up at Fann now, with a dripping crimson face.

Whose blood? he tried to ask, but choked on salty warmth before he could articulate the words. The boy was scrambling backward, spider-walking on his hands and heels, keening in panic as Fann expelled another gout of crimson. Someone clutched him from behind, tried to prevent his toppling to the pavement, but he slithered through the helping hands and felt the asphalt slap his cheek.

Impossible, Fann thought. A silly accident. This can't be happening.

Then someone in the press of bodies shouted, "She has a gun!"

The last thing Fann heard was sudden thunder hammering the neon night.

BOLAN HAD SPOTTED one more shooter—thought he had, at least, off to his right and closing in—when Fann and Maia stopped dead in their tracks to face each other. Maia's face was hidden from him by her poncho's hood, but Fann seemed agitated. He was saying something Bolan couldn't hear and wouldn't have been able to translate, using his hands for emphasis, when someone's rowdy kid came plowing through the crowd and ran head-on into Fann's flank.

It couldn't be part of the setup, but it worked for Bolan's

adversaries, visible and otherwise. The woman he'd been tracking snaked an arm out from beneath her trash-bag cape and fired a silenced pistol from a range of thirty feet or less, its bullet striking Fann as he half turned to help or reprimand the bleating child. It was a lung shot, clearly, bringing blood up in a spurting rush, as Maia brought her submachine gun out of hiding, into action.

Bolan turned to face the second shooter—male, Chinese, mid-twenties, whipping back his raincoat to reveal a stubby shotgun—just as Maia zipped the woman who had shot her friend. A short burst sent ripples through the trash bag, taking down the target as the female hitter squeezed off two more silenced rounds into the crowd at large.

Screams then, of pain and panic. Bolan had his Pindad SS2 lined up and tracking as the second shooter racked his shotgun's slide, something he should have done before, to save time once the killing started. As it was, the wasted fraction of a second cost him everything, gave Bolan all the time he needed for a doubletap that spun the youngster like a dervish, triggering a blast of buckshot in the general direction of the looming Ferris wheel.

More screams. More tourists down and bleeding. Bolan shoved through the crowd toward Maia and her fallen classmate, when the trap closed and all hell broke loose.

He couldn't count the guns, could only estimate their number at a dozen, give or take. They were surrounded, more or less, and their attackers clearly weren't concerned about collateral damage. Muzzle-flashes winked in competition to the garish midway lights, none of the other weapons silenced. Outside the kill zone, some park visitors mistook the shots for fireworks, craning for a glimpse of sky beyond the part bleached out by Ancol Dreamland's lights. Too late for some, they realized that Death had come among them and was taking names.

Blood-spattered from a near miss that had dropped a passing clown, Bolan reached Maia, clutched her arm and snapped, "Come on!" He pulled her forcibly away from Fann's body, lifeless now, no longer spitting blood, and hauled her toward the meager shelter of the nearby pyramid. No muzzle-flashes seemed to come from that direction, making it as safe as anywhere along the midway while they took a moment to regroup.

"She killed him," Maia said, dull-voiced.

"I saw," Bolan replied.

"He was surprised, I think."

"Forget that," Bolan told her roughly. "If your head's not in the game right now, you won't get out of here alive."

She blinked and seemed to see him clearly now. "I know," she said. "We're trapped."

"Not quite," Bolan said. "But we will be, if we hang around here any longer."

Maia nodded, clutching her SMG with grim determination.

"This way," Bolan said, and turned to jog along the east side of the pyramid, while wasted shots rang out behind them.

How long since they'd passed a pair of uniformed patrolmen on the midway? Five, ten minutes. Would the cops rush in to find out what was happening, or would they take their time and call for backup? Either way, the last thing Bolan needed was to meet one of them now. He and Maia had to find an exit, get lost in the crowd if possible, while either shaking off or taking down their ambushers.

"My fault," Maia said, as she ran along behind him. "You were right."

"Forget that now," he said. "We're getting out of here."

"You think so?"

"If we don't," he told her, "it won't be for lack of trying."

CHAPTER NINETEEN

Huo Zhangke saw Lia Yin squeeze off her first shot, striking Maia Lee's companion. Whether she meant to shoot the man first or her aim was poor, he couldn't say, but Lia paid the price immediately. Their intended target raised an automatic weapon from beneath her poncho, gutting Lia with a muffled burst that meant the gun was silenced.

Huo was grappling with his own weapon, still looking for the faceless American, when more shots sounded from his left. No silencer this time to mask the *pop-pop* sound of a light assault rifle. He spun to track the sound and saw another of his soldiers, Fei Haiping, reeling out of control, firing a wild round from his shotgun as he fell. By then, women were screaming up and down the midway, tourists running for their lives in all directions, and the rest of Huo's strike team had opened fire.

At whom?

Huo turned back toward the pyramid where he had seen the first shots fired. While it was difficult to pick out individuals in the stampede, he glimpsed a tall figure, dressed in a poncho matching Maia's, shoving past frightened runners with the skill of a footballer, closing on the spot where the traitor knelt with her wounded friend. Not one of Huo's men, obviously. Who else could it be except the American soldier he'd been ordered to eliminate?

Huo raised his pistol, steadied in both hands, and squeezed the trigger—just as one of the Dunia Fantasi employees ran between him and his target. The runner was dressed as a pharaoh of ancient Egypt, complete with a headdress depicting an asp, but his rain-soaked robe couldn't deflect bullets. The strange figure lurched, spun and fell, while Huo's target reached Maia and they bolted, dodging from view in the pyramid's shadow.

Huo cursed himself and anybody else he could think of. Biting back his fury, he barked into the headset, "After them! If they escape, we're all as good as dead!"

It was no idle threat, considering the urgency that Tan Sen Neo—underboss in charge since Jin Au-Yo had left Jakarta—had placed on bagging both the woman and her partner when he'd given Huo the job. During that briefing, Huo had thought it sounded like a plum assignment. Now, it seemed about to blow up in his face.

His pistol cleared a path before Huo as he ran after his vanished targets. All around him, the remainder of his team would be converging on the shooting scene, closing the trap on their intended prey. Of course, he hadn't stationed anyone *behind* the pyramid, since Fann Lieu was supposed to keep his old friend near the sphinx. Huo wasn't psychic, and it galled him that he might be punished for a failure to predict the unpredictable.

Better to kill the damned cockroaches and be done with it, eliminating any need to beg for mercy. All he needed was a clean shot, one chance to—

A voice behind him shouted out for him to stop and drop his gun.

Huo stopped but kept the pistol, judging distance and position for the voice. Before his challenger could speak again, Huo swiveled on his heels, dropped to a deep crouch as he turned and fired off half the contents of his pistol's magazine.

He caught the fat policeman by surprise, stitching a line of bloody holes across his khaki shirt. The cop fell, twitching on the pavement as the neurons in his dying brain misfired, then Huo Zhangke was running once again.

After his fleeing prey.

MACK BOLAN HADN'T BEEN to Egypt for a while, but he remembered it as nothing like the Ancol Dreamland version. For a start, there'd been no rain on that occasion, when he stalked a self-proclaimed "Eternal Pharaoh" who was raising hell among diverse religious sects. No Ferris wheel or roller coaster, either. No stampede of tourists panicked by a cross fire in the midst of an amusement park.

So much for fun and games.

He reached the northeast corner of the pyramid and hesitated long enough to get his bearings, Maia covering his back. They'd ducked their would-be slayers for a moment, but it wouldn't last. Based on the scattered sounds of gunfire, there were ample trackers to surround them if they dallied in one place too long, and precious little cover on the midway that wouldn't involve putting civilians in harm's way.

The theme park's one and only public exit was behind them, at the same point where they'd entered after paying for their tickets. Naturally, there were other ways to come and go from Ancol Dreamland—service entrances, emergency escape routes, access for employees only—and while he'd spotted some during their drive-around, before they'd parked and come inside, they'd

be exposed to hostile fire no matter which escape route
they selected.

As they were just standing there.

"This way," he said to Maia, turning left and picking
up his pace. When no one fired on them immediately,
Bolan hoped they'd got some breathing room.

He cast that hope aside a heartbeat later, when an
automatic weapon chattered from the shadows to their
right, strafing the pyramid and loosing streams of plaster dust from its facade. Bolan returned fire without
breaking stride, keeping the shooter's head down while
they gained some distance, seeking cover. Up ahead,
the Parthenon's stout pillars offered shelter, and they
ducked into the shadows there, putting its bulk between
them and the sniper.

One of them, at least.

Bolan had guessed a dozen guns were firing on the
midway after he and Maia had disposed of two hunters.
That meant ten or eleven unaccounted for, besides the
one who had driven them to ground inside the mock-up
of the Parthenon. How long before they had the custom-
built ruins surrounded and cut off? A minute? Two?
Three, at the most?

No time to waste, then.

Maia beat him to it, hissing at him from behind one
of the Doric columns, "We can't stay here."

"No," he granted, "but I need to buy some time."

He showed himself deliberately, ducking out and
back to draw fire from the shooter who had cornered
them. Marking the muzzle-flash, Bolan discovered that
the guy—or gal, whichever—had them staked out from
his place beside some kind of metal shed, most likely
maintenance equipment stored for use after the park
was shut down for the night. Bolan had seen no tourists

over there, and thought it should be safe to use one of his 40 mm rounds. That would surprise the gunner, and give his companions cause to rethink their approach.

This time, he ducked to his left, aimed, fired and got back under cover as the shooter sprayed the Parthenon with bullets. Seconds later, Bolan heard the HE blast, uncertain whether there had been a scream mixed in with it, not caring either way.

"Come on!" he snapped at Maia, while the blast still echoed.

And they ran.

MAIA HAD Fann Lieu's blood on her hands. She'd tried to wipe them on her rain-slick rubber poncho, but it didn't seem to help, just smeared the crimson stains around. The sleeves of her blouse had been smeared while she cradled his head in the moments before Cooper arrived and snatched her away.

Tears stung her eyes, and Maia let the rain sluice them away. It was ridiculous to weep for Fann; she'd hardly thought of him at all since their last fleeting conversation at the ministry, a year or more ago. She couldn't miss him in the normal sense, of someone loved and lost, since she had never loved him. It was stretching matters even to consider him a friend, since he had clearly set her up for execution.

Did he know? Did the surprise that she'd seen written on his dying face reflect amazement that he had been followed to their final meeting, or was Fann simply chagrined that *he'd* been shot, instead of Maia? Did it even matter now?

He had betrayed her and had paid the price. Maia hadn't been forced to kill him, which was something in her favor. Now, if she could just survive and punish those who'd sprung the trap, she might be satisfied.

The blast of Cooper's grenade raised more screams on the midway, while its shock waves drove the tourists back, sent them in new directions as if riding waves of fear. At Cooper's command, she followed him, running as fast as her trembling legs would carry her, clutching her submachine gun at the ready.

She had failed to estimate the rounds she'd fired so far. A dozen, more or less? She couldn't check the weapon's magazine without unloading it by hand. Say half its thirty rounds were gone, then, hoping for the best. Maia had five more magazines distributed in pockets of her jeans and jacket underneath the poncho, plus her pistol's sixteen rounds and two spare magazines for that. It ought to be enough, but who could say?

Cooper ducked into the open doorway of a booth where rings were tossed at bottles to secure a prize. A small man cowered in one corner—the proprietor, Maia supposed—but didn't challenge them, his wide eyes fastened on their guns and Maia's bloody hands.

"Saya tidak punya uang!" he cried.

"He says he has no money," Maia translated for Bolan, then told the cringing man in his language, "It's not a robbery. Be quiet."

Running footsteps clattered toward the booth, slowing on the approach. Maia expected bullets to come ripping through the walls, but heard a voice instead, speaking Chinese.

"Where did they go?"

Another answered, "This way. But then I lost them."

Her partner was poised and waiting when the two men passed the booth, one barely glancing at its open door. He stepped into the light behind them, and his autorifle stuttered like a jackhammer.

THE BURST OF GUNFIRE startled Huo Zhangke, raising fresh cries of panic on the midway among tourists who were scrambling for an exit or a place to hide. It didn't sound like one of his team's weapons, but at least the firing lasted long enough for him to get a rough fix on its source.

He ran against the tide of fleeing bodies, brandishing his pistol like a scepter as he cleared a path, growling instructions to his soldiers through the wireless headset. They were moving eastward now, back toward the ticket gates and sole official exit from the park. He hadn't seen the targets for some time, but knew from chatter coming through his earpiece that a couple of his men thought they had spotted them.

And that had happened just before the latest burst of automatic fire.

Huo called out to them, using last names only, wishing now that he had designated numbers for his team members. "Chan? Ki? Answer! Where are you?"

Empty air hissed back at him. In place of a response from Chan or Ki, he snapped commands off to his other hunters. "Everyone to me! East on the midway, toward the exit. Hurry!"

Huo's instinct led him to the place where his two silent soldiers lay, shot from behind and lying facedown in a lake of blood. From their position, he surmised they had been ambushed by a shooter hiding in the ring-toss booth, which meant they hadn't cleared the stand before they passed it by. Their own damn fault.

He called directions to his team, then ducked in through the booth's back door himself. A cringing figure hunkered in the shadows there, babbling, "There is no money!"

"Forget the stinking money!" Huo commanded. "Who was in here with you? Tell me! Quickly!"

"Two came in," the frightened man replied. "A man and woman. When the others came, they…left."

Huo thanked him in Chinese, then shot him in the face.

As he emerged, two other members of his team arrived, blinking at Chan and Ki dead on the ground. "We've lost four now," Huo cautioned them. "Remain alert and find the targets. Now!"

The two ran on without him, Huo remaining with the bodies for another moment, while he issued more precise directions to the other members of his hunting party. He had no emotional attachment to the ones who'd fallen—well, except perhaps for Lia Yin—but he would have to answer for the dead when he reported back to Tan Sen Neo.

If he survived, that was. And if he could report success.

But if the targets managed to escape, Huo thought it might be better for him if he simply disappeared. It made no sense to kill the bearer of bad news, but Tan was known for venting his frustration on subordinates. If he believed that Huo Zhangke had failed him…

Better not to fail, Huo thought, and set off running in the footsteps of his men.

How LONG BEFORE the park was flooded with police? Bolan had no idea, but every passing minute brought him closer to a confrontation he could not escape, unless he broke his own long-standing rule against the use of deadly force on law-enforcement officers. And knowing that he *wouldn't* break that rule—that solemn vow—he understood that being caged on any charge was tantamount to death.

The simple answer: don't get caught.

Which wouldn't be so simple, after all.

Four hunters down, and if his first guess was correct, that still left nine or ten in play, at least. They would have found his latest kills by now, extrapolating the direction he and Maia had to be traveling in order to escape from Ancol Dreamland. He'd already seen that they had no qualms about gunning down civilians, and he guessed the same would go for any cops they met along the midway. By the time that butcher's bill was tallied up, Bolan would have a whole new troupe of ghosts to haunt his dreams.

But he was wide-awake right now, in blitzing mode. Maia was keeping pace, her features grim, and Bolan didn't want to think about what might be going on inside her head. As long as she could focus on the task at hand—survival—it was all that he required of her.

More shooting as they neared the Ferris wheel. The giant ride was still revolving, its controllers either unaware of what was happening around them, or already running for their lives, to hell with paying customers stuck on the wheel for the duration. Bolan had no time to help the stranded couples, so he ducked and veered around the ride, Maia pursuing him, as more shots echoed through the park.

He reached another game booth, ducked behind it and came out the other side, his Pindad SS2 leveled and aiming back in the direction that he'd come from. Two Chinese were closing fast, both armed with automatic weapons, firing as they glimpsed him in the glare of neon. Bolan's aim was better, ripping one across the chest with three hot 5.56 mm NATO rounds, swinging across to nail the other as he stopped, turned, tried to dive for cover.

All too late.

Instead of moving on at once, Bolan ducked back around the booth, retraced his steps, and came out on the other side just as a third man reached the killing ground. This one was giving orders through a wireless headset, and it clicked with Bolan that he might be someone in authority.

Still seeking someone who could help him locate Jin Au-Yo, he took a chance, told Maia, "Give me this one," and leaped out of hiding to surprise the runner. Striking with his rifle's butt before the triad gunner could react, he dropped the guy, relieved him of an antique-looking automatic pistol, then reached down to haul him upright once again.

"Speak English?" he demanded.

Fuzzily, the captive nodded. "Yes."

"You tired of living?" Bolan asked him.

Slow blink in response, before the man answered, "No."

"Then send your people off another way. Be quick about it, and you still might see tomorrow."

When the man hesitated, Maia jabbed him with the muzzle of her SMG and snarled, "Do it! No tricks, or you're a dead *koujiao*."

Whatever that meant, it provoked a spark of anger in the triad gunner's eyes before he started jabbering into his headset's little microphone. When he was done, Maia nodded to Bolan, saying, "Yes. It's done."

"All right, then," Bolan told his scowling prisoner. "Let's take a little walk."

THE CHAOS HELPED. Bolan and Maia reached the public exit with their prisoner while hundreds more were trying to get out of Ancol Dreamland and police were rolling up in force, lights flashing, their discordant sirens adding to the general atmosphere of panic. If the park had been surrounded by a chain-link fence, Bolan suspected that it would have been torn down by now. A mob like this could trample you to death and never notice, but it also made fair cover for a getaway.

The good news: people exiting the park weren't required to pass through a revolving gate, which would've jammed in nothing flat and turned into a death trap. There were larger gates, patrolled by private guards on normal days and evenings, abandoned now as every able-bodied member of the staff was scouring the park for terrorists—and finding them, apparently.

Bolan had worried that police might block the exits and screen people individually, but a fresh outbreak of gunfire scotched that plan. It came from somewhere to the northwest of where he stood with Maia and their captive, in the general direction their reluctant guest had sent the other members of his team. On hearing that, the cops abandoned any thought of barricading exits from the park and rushed off toward the sounds of battle with their weapons drawn.

Bolan prodded their captive with his pistol through the fabric of his poncho. Maia had the guy pinned on his right, with the Executioner on the left, prepared to drop him in a cross fire if he tried his luck at running. Beyond the nearest exit, people who had made it through were scattering, putting as much space between themselves and Ancol Dreamland as they could. Cars jockeyed for position in the parking lots, some fenders clashing in the process, drivers jumping out to curse and swing at one another.

"We could be all night getting away from here," Maia said.

"We'll get it done," he answered, hoping that was true.

Still twenty feet before they reached the exit and began their odyssey to reach the SUV. The parking lot had several exits and, unlike the park, it wasn't fenced. If necessary, Bolan thought they could four-wheel it over dirt and grass to reach the nearest access road and clear the scene. First, though, they had to get their triad shooter *to* the car and *in* the car, without attracting any cops.

The exit gate was coming up. Bolan could feel their prisoner bracing himself to make a move, and didn't wait for anything to happen. Clutching the man's left arm with his own left hand, Bolan put his weight behind a kidney jab, the muzzle of his SIG-Sauer biting deep. Their captive squealed in pain and slumped between them, his toes dragging as they steered him toward and through the exit.

"Injured man here," Bolan warned the nervous folk in front of them, while Maia translated.

A moment later, they were out and moving toward the parking lot. Not free and clear, by any means, but getting there. Bolan could only hope it wasn't all for nothing, and the man they'd captured knew something that could advance their cause.

Without that boost, they would be going nowhere fast.

CHAPTER TWENTY

Banten Province, Java, Indonesia

"It's Tan, sir," said Ma Mingxia, sat phone in hand.

"How does he sound?" Jin Au-Yo asked.

"Upset," Ma said, grim-faced.

That meant something had gone wrong. Again. Jin frowned and took the phone from Ma. Said, "Yes."

Tan Sen Neo told him, "Bad news, Jin. They got away."

"Both of them?"

"Yes. I sent the best soldiers available, but they have failed us. Out of fourteen, six are dead and five are now in custody."

Jin did the math and said, "That still leaves three."

"Two managed to escape. They're coming in for a debriefing."

"And the fourteenth?" Jin inquired.

"The team leader," Tan said. "You may not know him. Huo Zhangke?"

"I've heard the name. He dealt with the Moluccans for us," Jin replied.

"That's him," Tan said.

"And where is he?"

Tan hesitated, then said, "No one seems to know. Perhaps he'll call in soon. I've spoken to our man with the police. He's definitely not among the ones arrested."

"So, you're saying that he's disappeared?"

"There was a great deal of confusion at the park," Tan said. "And there still is, I believe. We'll find him."

"What about the other agent from Beijing?" Jin asked.

"He's dead, I think," Tan said.

"You *think?*" Jin challenged him.

"It isn't clear yet. They're still counting bodies at the park."

Which meant civilians dead, as well. Scowling, Jin asked, "Police?"

"One dead, at least," Tan replied. "We don't know yet who shot him."

"It's bad enough with the civilians, Tan. They had to kill a cop?"

"I don't have the details yet," Tan said. "Don't worry. I'll find out what happened."

"With a dead cop, it doesn't matter," Jin replied. "They'll want revenge on top of money."

Tan considered that and said, "We'll come to an accommodation."

"They'll need blood for this," Jin said. "Give them the two who got away, after you've questioned them."

"Alive, or…?"

"I don't want them telling tales outside the family," Jin said.

"I understand, sir. About Beijing…"

"I'll speak with them. They won't be pleased," Jin said.

"Will it require a sacrifice?" Tan asked.

Tan had to have known who would be next in line if Beijing wanted blood.

"Perhaps not," Jin replied. "I'll let you know."

He broke the link without goodbyes, handing the

sat phone back to Ma, and asked, "Do you believe in curses?"

"No, sir."

Of course not. That was mystic foolishness. Still, Jin thought he could trace the moment when his luck had changed, gone sour on him. Was it when his soldiers captured Maia Lee? When she escaped? Or could he trace it further back, to the beginning of his business with the Arabs? By dealing with them, offering to satisfy their craving for a mighty weapon, he'd invited trouble. Now, with several dozen of his soldiers dead and the police involved, as well as agents from the PRC, Jin knew the burden of responsibility fell squarely on his shoulders.

Wu Guchan would sacrifice him, if it came to that, to save the family. Why not? Jin was prepared to do the same with Tan Sen Neo. It was only natural. Whatever happened to a single man or group of men, the Flying Ax Triad survived.

As to *which* man was sacrificed, however, there might be some flexibility. If he could shift the blame to Wu, their allies in the Ministry of State Security might see the wisdom of replacing him.

And who better to fill that role, if he could pull it off, than Jin Au-Yo?

Pluit, North Jakarta

THEY HADN'T DRIVEN all that far from Ancol Dreamland, after all. The storage site where Maia kept a locker paid up for the year was one block off Jalan Pluit Karang Ayu, two klicks west of the theme park that had turned into a battleground. Renters had access to the place around the clock, a sleepy guard on-site to greet them without showing any interest in their business.

Bolan drove between two rows of storage lockers to the far north end and parked outside of number 109. They had the sector to themselves as Maia stepped out of the vehicle, unlocked the unit, then returned to help convey their passenger inside. He didn't fight them, may have known that it was hopeless or perhaps thought that he could bargain for his life.

The unit had internal lighting, and the roll-down door was lockable from either side. Once they were shuttered from the world, Bolan examined the unit, noting the total lack of furniture, some plastic tubs against the back wall and a concrete floor beneath his feet. Someone had thought to put a drain dead center, probably in case the site was flooded. There were no stains on the floor or walls to indicate that that had happened yet.

Bolan addressed their captive, telling him, "We may as well start with your name."

After a moment's hesitation, the triad shooter replied, "I'm Huo Zhangke. You're not police. Why have you brought me here?"

"For answers," Bolan said.

"I don't betray my brothers," Huo informed him.

"Let me guess," Bolan replied. "The thunderbolts and myriads of swords?"

"You mock ancient tradition. No one from the Flying Ax has ever turned informer."

"My only interest in your brotherhood," Bolan said, "is recovering the missile that was sold to terrorists. They want to set the world on fire and don't care if the Flying Ax goes up in smoke along with everybody else. You owe no loyalty to them."

"I couldn't help you if I wanted to," Huo answered. "I know nothing of such things."

"We figured that," Bolan advised him. "Which is why we need some face time with the man in charge."

"He's left Jakarta," Huo said. "I can't tell you where he's gone."

"But someone can," Bolan replied. "Smart money says you know who that would be."

The triad gunner frowned, studied his shoes, retreating into silence.

Maia glanced at Bolan, turned and shot their captive in the left leg, crimson spurting from his thigh an inch or two above the knee. Huo hit the concrete, wailing, making Bolan wonder how far sound would carry from their unit in the night.

"Someone takes charge when Jin is traveling outside Jakarta," Maia said. "Give us the name."

The wounded man glared back at her with teary eyes, then spit out, "Tan Sen Neo."

"What is he to Jin?" Maia demanded.

"Underboss," Huo replied, through clenched teeth.

"So far, so good," Bolan told Huo. "Now, all we need is his address."

Lesser Sunda Islands, Indonesia

A NEW DAY WAS BEGINNING. Would it be the last for Usmar Malik?

He had long since come to terms with death—with the idea of martyrdom in God's name—but in the dark hours, when he was honest with himself, Malik still feared the crossing into unknown territory. It wasn't that he had any cause to doubt his faith, much less accept the counterarguments of Christians serving the

Great Satan. Rather, Malik wondered whether he was worthy of the paradise awaiting those who gave their lives to the jihad.

It's time to sleep, he told himself, deciding on a final check-in with the radar operators to make sure they were awake and paying close attention to their screens. It would be his head left in a basket if the night watch missed the U.S. fleet and let them slip beyond the Brave Wind missile's range.

Where were they? What was keeping them?

Nasir had calculated that it might be days before the ships began to search among the Lesser Sundas. Malik's argument—that they might *never* come unless the lure they had prepared was activated—failed to gain Nasir's approval. Any premature broadcast, the Saudi said, might draw one of the E-3 Sentry AWACS planes—the U.S. Air Force Airborne Warning and Control System aircraft cruising at forty thousand feet and picking out their signal with its various surveillance systems. Once the Sentry had a fix, its Joint Tactical Information Distribution System would direct a Tomahawk cruise missile to the *Thunderbolt* from up to 1,550 miles away, with no risk whatsoever to the fleet.

So, they had to wait. Only when ships were well within the Brave Wind's relatively puny range could they afford to activate the beacon, setting up the largest target for a killing strike.

And after that...

Malik had questioned the escape plan when he heard it for the first time, half expecting that he would be asked to die after the fatal blow was struck, but as Nasir had explained it to him, it made sense. The Sword of Allah was a relatively small group, certainly when you compared it to al Qaeda or Hamas. As such, it couldn't carelessly discard its highest-ranking officers—the brains behind the operation, as it were.

So he and Nasir would escape, or try to, in the speedboats that sat waiting on the far side of their little island. One fleeing in each direction, east and west, to multiply the odds of individual survival. Malik understood that logic, too. And yet, suspicion lingered in a corner of his mind where doubt was prone to fester.

What if Nasir planned on using Malik's boat for bait, the same way they were using the *Thunderbolt* as a staked goat to attract a tiger? Should he cross the island now, before he tried to sleep, and search his speedboat for a hidden radio transmitter that would bring one of the Boeing F/A-18E/F Super Hornet fighters down upon him with its 20 mm Vulcan Gatling gun and its Harpoon antiship missiles?

Was he simply being paranoid?

Perhaps. But it would be an awkward situation, trying to explain his trek across the island if Nasir woke early and discovered he was gone. The next day, while they waited for the fleet, Malik could always dream up some excuse to check the boats. And if he found a hidden homing beacon...then what?

Maybe switch it to the other speedboat, proving by his action that he had the sharper mind and was more suited to survive.

Beijing, China

CHOU HUA TIAN had gone to bed and was already dozing when the phone rang at his bedside. From its tone, he knew it was the green phone, scrambled automatically, its number known to fewer than a dozen people in the world. No matter which of them was calling at that hour, Chou knew that he was about to be confronted with some new emergency.

Because he was a bachelor and lived alone, the late call troubled no one but himself. He cleared his throat, lifted the receiver from its cradle and said, "Yes?"

"It's me," Jin Au-Yo said.

Chou knew why he was calling. It could only be about the trap they'd laid for Maia Lee.

"What news?" Chou asked.

"All bad," Jin answered. "Your decoy is dead. The woman and her American have escaped."

"Again," Chou said, not bothering to cover the re-criminating tone.

"I know," said Jin. "The men responsible are being punished as we speak."

"That is no consolation," Chou replied.

"Agreed. My soldiers are on full alert, as are authorities throughout the district."

"None of which has helped so far," Chou said. He'd come to a decision, most reluctantly, and saw no reason to postpone it further. "I am coming to Jakarta with a group of my own people to resolve the situation."

"As you wish," Jin said. "If you need anything…"

"Certain equipment," Chou acknowledged. "It can be arranged between us on arrival."

"Of course. Call me with details of your flight when it's arranged, and you will be met at the airport. Anything you need will be provided."

"Very well," Chou said. "I'll see you soon."

He cut the link and scrambled out of bed, suddenly anxious to be on his way. It was a move he should have made before this, Chou supposed, but he had hoped that Maia Lee's defection could be covered up without him spending six long hours in the air and sweating in Jakarta's heat to see the job done properly.

Clearly, he had expected too much of the Flying Ax Triad and of Fann Lieu. At least Fann wouldn't be coming home and telling tales around the office. Failure had a price, and Chou didn't intend to be the one who ultimately paid for the fiasco now unfolding to the south.

His team, already placed on standby, would be drawn from the elite troops of the ministry's Ninth Bureau—Anti-Defection and Countersurveillance. Within that unit were one hundred warriors trained as members of the People's Liberation Army Special Operations Forces and detached for service with the Ministry of State Security. They handled any wet work that the ministry required, either on foreign soil or in the PRC itself.

Now, ten of them would be flying to Jakarta under the direct command of Chou Hua Tian, Deputy Assistant Minster for State Security. It was his first time in the field, directing troops, but Chou was confident that he could pull it off.

Especially since failure meant disgrace, displacement and a brutal death.

Pluit, North Jakarta

HUO ZHANGKE HAD BALKED at giving up an address for his boss, but cracked when Maia pressed the muzzle of her PM2 against his still-unwounded right leg and advised him to invest in crutches. They would find the Flying Ax's underboss in Cengkareng, he said, not far from Soekarno–Hatta International Airport. He was cursing himself as a traitor when Maia fired one more shot and the flow of words stopped.

Disposal wasn't all that tricky. Bolan used a pair of

trash bags, pulling one over the triad shooter's shattered skull, down to his waist, the other starting at his feet and coming up to meet the first. They lugged him to the SUV and put him in the cargo bay, considered cleaning up the storage unit, then decided it would be a waste of time.

"I won't be coming back here," Maia told him. "To this place or to Jakarta when we're finished."

"Leave it, then," Bolan said. "If they send someone along behind you, it's their problem."

They were close enough to smell Jakarta Bay and reached it in five minutes flat, spent two more scouting out a stretch of shoreline where the fishermen had packed it in at sundown and gone home. A concrete pier extended thirty yards or so over the water, and they dropped Huo Zhangke from the end of it, not caring much whether he sank or floated. By the time somebody found him, called police and got around to tipping off his friends that he was dead, they ought to have his boss sewn up.

Or they would have a whole new set of troubles to concern them.

Like being dead.

A triad underboss was bound to be protected. Jin Au-Yo would certainly have taken soldiers with him when he fled to Banten Province. Others would be scouring the streets for Maia and Bolan, looking anywhere that they could think of for their enemies. But Tan Sen Neo would retain enough guns to secure himself against attack.

And reaching him meant getting past those guns, or going through them.

Bolan's specialty.

His first job was to find the address Huo had given

them and scout the layout, find the best approach. His goal was to take Tan alive and squeeze him as they had his underling, this time to get a fix on Jin Au-Yo. From there, if they were lucky, Bolan hoped to ID Jin's connection with the Sword of Allah and, perhaps, get Jin's thoughts on the best place to go hunting for the Brave Wind missile still in hostile hands.

He understood that Jin likely had no idea—and wouldn't care—how paying customers intended to use weapons he supplied. As far as learning detailed future plans the buyers might have hatched, he knew they didn't have a hope in hell. But anything would help at this point, with the U.S. fleet in motion and a ship-killer prepared to strike at any moment.

It was the only game in town, and Bolan was all-in.

Beijing, China

COMMODORE FENG JINGWEI sat at his desk at home, inside his den. The only light burning in his apartment was a small lamp on that desk. It sent a pool of light across the desktop blotter, where normally he would lay out correspondence, files, reports—whatever the next day's official business required him to study. This night, however, the blotter was clear, except for a pistol centered precisely within the circle of light.

It was an old Type 64, first issued back in 1980, but a firearm's age was immaterial if it was well maintained. Chambered for 7.65 mm rounds, the equivalent of a 7.65 mm Browning or .32 ACP, it would be more than adequate for what Feng had in mind. A larger caliber would make more mess, and Feng had no wish to unduly aggravate the housekeeper who came on Fridays.

It was only common courtesy, a trait too often lacking from his life as he saw now.

A life which Feng Jingwei intended to cut short.

He had considered every other option, after Chou Hua Tian called to report that he was heading for Jakarta with a team of handpicked men to settle the "unpleasantness" ongoing there. Feng hadn't asked the Deputy Assistant Minister for State Security for any details, left it all in Chou's hands, wished him well and turned his thoughts to personal concerns.

Of course, Chou's scheme was risky. Some might call it ludicrous. Feng didn't know how Chou intended to explain his absence from Beijing, much less the borrowing of soldiers from his ministry for duty in the capital of Indonesia. That sounded like an act of war to Feng, and he imagined that the Minister for State Security would take a dim view of the outing. Not to mention China's president, premier and other ranking leaders of the Central People's Government.

If Chou should fail, or even make his presence in Jakarta known, there would be hell to pay. And Feng had no doubt in his mind that Chou would sell him out immediately, in a hopeless bid for leniency. Which meant that both of them would face a firing squad, but only after fierce, prolonged interrogation and a public trial stage-managed to absolve the Chinese government of any fault.

Feng found that prospect unacceptable.

If he had to die—and who on earth could finally escape it?—he would pick the time, the place, and he would go out in a peaceful haze induced by copious amounts of rice *baijiu,* his favorite liquor. Two large glasses had already dulled his fear, and Feng thought that a third would be enough to send him smiling on his way.

He sipped the liquor slowly, feeling no great hurry now. Holding the tall glass in his left hand, Feng picked up the pistol with his right. It weighed twenty-four ounces with a loaded magazine, but he would only need one of the weapon's seven rounds. His memory told Feng the sixty-five-grain bullet would leave the gun's muzzle at 925 feet per second, delivering 123 foot-pounds of destructive energy on impact. More than enough for his needs when the pistol was inside his mouth, its front blade sight pressed into his soft palate.

No one could possibly miss at that range.

There would be no lingering, no witnessing the shame experienced by family or friends when his corruption was exposed, no pain beyond the first split second. And beyond that? Who could say?

Feng drained his glass, set it aside and cocked the pistol.

He closed his eyes and hoped for the relief of sheer oblivion.

CHAPTER TWENTY-ONE

Cengkareng, West Jakarta

"He should have called by now, if he was still alive," Tan Sen Neo said. "We already know he's not in custody."

"Or not reported, anyway," Gao Chu replied.

"What do you mean?"

"If he was in protective custody…" Gao left the comment dangling, letting Tan draw whatever conclusions came to mind.

"You think that Huo Zhangke is now an informer?" Tan made no effort to conceal his incredulity.

"Not an informer in the common sense," Gao said. "But think of it, sir. If he was charged with murder—more than one, in fact—he faces death. Presented with an opportunity to save himself, he might give names."

"And then *we* kill him *slowly,*" Tan reminded Gao. "What would he gain?"

"We'd have to find him first. If he's concealed by the authorities, it might be difficult."

"Witness protection?" Tan imagined Jin Au-Yo's reaction if that proved to be the case.

Gao Chu shrugged, then replied, "It's possible. I don't say it's a certainty, sir."

"Find out," Tan ordered. "If our people on the force don't know, increase their bonuses to motivate them.

Use the information from our files, if necessary. Someone knows if Huo has turned."

"I'll see to it," Gao said.

"Meanwhile, I want patrols at full strength in the
city. How many Americans can there be wandering
around Jakarta with a Chinese woman? They should
stand out like a boil on Dong Jie's face."

Tan's reference to the Chinese film and television
star made Gao Chu smile, but only for a second. Their
predicament allowed no room for levity. In fact, the task
at hand was deadly serious, and could rebound against
them fatally unless they managed to resolve it soon.

"We still have soldiers checking the hotels," said
Gao. "There are so many that—"

"I can't give Jin excuses," Tan said, interrupting him.
"It doesn't matter if there are a thousand. We must visit
every one of them, then think of something else to try
if that brings no result."

"Of course, sir," Gao said. "It has occurred to me that
since the woman is—or was—an agent of the Ministry
of State Security, she may have access to facilities not
recognized as rented lodgings."

"You mean safe houses," Tan said.

"Why not? We know the ministry maintains a presence in Jakarta. There's no reason to believe they are
restricted to the embassy."

"I have no ready access to that information," Tan acknowledged grudgingly. "But Jin may know of someone who could help."

"Will you contact him?" Gao inquired.

"Not yet," Tan said. "He took the last call badly, as
expected. It's too soon to ask a favor, when we still have
other avenues remaining to explore."

"You're right, of course, sir," Gao said. He didn't sound convinced.

No matter. Tan was still in charge, as long as Jin Au-Yo remained in hiding and didn't relieve him of command. If it came down to that, Tan would have worse problems than making another phone call to his boss. He would be out of work, and likely out of time.

But not yet.

Tan still had a few tricks left, and ample guns at his disposal to eliminate the targets he was tasked to kill. If only he could *find* them now. His best chance had been wasted, but it need not be his last chance.

Not just yet.

Cengkareng

"THAT MUST BE IT," said Maia Lee.

They had followed Jalan Daan Mogot across town, westbound, then wound north on Jalan Bangun Nusa into the Daan Mogot Estate. Mini mansions lined the curving streets, and Bolan eyed the number Maia had picked out approaching on their left.

According to their late informant, they were looking at the lair of Tan Sen Neo.

Which explained the two men idling by the gate that sealed off Tan's driveway from access by unwanted visitors. The wall that stretched away on either side of it, encircling the grounds, was six feet high and made of poured concrete someone had painted beige. No razor wire or other obstacles sat atop the wall, as far as Bolan could discover on a drive-by, but that didn't mean there were no sensors, cameras or other security devices in place.

He drove around the block, came at the place another

way. Tan's property ran downhill toward a spillway that ran like a scar through the landscape, east-west, ready to take in water from the nearby flood-control channel or spill into it if the rain grew too fierce on any given day. Part of Jakarta's overall survival plan, and Bolan thought it might just work against the Flying Ax's underboss this night.

"There's no place here to leave the car unguarded," Bolan said, when they had made a circuit of the ritzy neighborhood. "We'll have to run plan B."

"What's that?" Maia asked, frowning.

"I go in. You drive around as unobtrusively as possible and pick me up when I come out."

"You go in by yourself?" she asked, as if she hadn't understood him properly.

"Won't be the first time," Bolan said. Thinking, *And if I'm lucky, it won't be the last.*

"While I just drive around?"

"We're wasting time," he said.

"All right," she told him, clearly disappointed. "Pull behind that store, and we can switch."

The place was closed at this hour, some kind of Jakarta-style convenience store. Bolan rolled in behind it, left the engine running while he stepped out in the dark and got his weapons squared away, then moved around to take the rider's seat while Maia slid behind the wheel.

He had already changed into his blacksuit, prior to dumping Huo Zhangke back at the waterfront. It fitted him like a second skin, had hidden pockets in convenient places and was sleek beneath the web gear that he wore. As Maia drove him back toward Tan's place, Bolan cracked a can of camo paint, smearing his face and hands with practiced strokes that left them mottled green and black.

"Okay," he said, when Swamp Thing faced him from the mirror on the flip side of his sun visor. "If there's no one behind us, drop me off at the canal. I'll hike back in from there."

"I still think I should go in with you," Maia told him.

"And come back to find the car's been towed, or someone's waiting for us? Sorry. It's a one-man job." Smiling through paint, he altered that. "One-*person* job."

"All right, then. But if you're not back in half an hour—"

"You take off," he finished for her. "Give some thought to getting out."

The SUV slowed, no headlights coming either way. Bolan stepped out and closed the door behind him, moving into darkness that devoured him.

AS IT TURNED OUT, there were no cameras or sensors on the wall. Another break: no dogs patrolling on the grounds. Bolan preferred to deal with human watchdogs when he had the opportunity. They'd made a conscious choice of who to serve, had joined the predators, and when he took them down it carried no sensation of regret.

Over the wall in nothing flat, and Bolan blended with the shadows on the other side. If anyone had spotted him during the two seconds it took to make his move, they sounded no alarm. Bolan counted to ten inside his head, then moved out toward the house with loping strides. A sloping lawn, say forty yards across, and dim lights showing through a couple of the windows on the mini mansion's second floor.

Which didn't mean the underboss or any of his men were tucked up in their beds. Barely two hours since the massacre at Ancol Dreamland, Bolan took for granted that his target would be stewing over what moves he should make to salvage something from the situation, land his prey before the angry weight of higher-ups came down on him.

Expect a concentration toward the middle of the house, then, or up front. As to the numbers, Bolan couldn't say. He'd have to play it all by ear.

Another drawback: the Executioner didn't have a clue what Tan looked like, beyond being Chinese. No help there, in a triad house, but Bolan knew from long experience that Tan—the boss—would be the guy least likely to be fighting on the front lines, *most* likely to be surrounded and protected by his men. Wade through the rest, and there he'd be.

The back door to the house was locked, which was no great surprise. Bolan considered picking it, then changed his mind as voices reached his ears, coming from somewhere to his left. He tracked the noise around the south side of the house, paused at the corner, checking out a spill of light that fell onto a patio through glass sliding doors left open to the night. Some kind of conference in progress, cigarette smoke drifting on the breeze, shadows of pacing figures cast across the paving stones outside.

Wishing that he had a stun grenade, Bolan advanced until he stood within three paces of the open sliding doors. The voices from inside were clear enough now, but he couldn't understand a word. Not that it mattered, since he wasn't there to eavesdrop.

Edging closer, Bolan risked a peek around the door-frame, counting nine men in some kind of recreation

room: flat-screen TV on one wall, chairs and couches,
and a round table designed for playing cards or other
games transformed into a drawing board for strategy.
He tried to size them up, decide which one received the
most respect and deference. Decided that it had to be
the smallish man who sat facing the open portal listening as one and then another of his men suggested plans.

Next step: take the others out, along with any stragglers, while he left the boss man breathing.

Bolan took a deep breath, let it go and stepped into
the doorway.

TAN SEN NEO SAW a shadow drift across the light spill
from the patio, glanced up and blinked once at the vision of a tall man dressed in black, his face smeared
with something that resembled grease, his torso hung
with webbing that supported ammunition pouches. In
his hands, some kind of automatic weapon with two
muzzles pointed toward Tan and his men.

Tan yelped a warning, saw Gao Chu begin to turn,
and then the stranger opened fire. Short bursts and well
controlled, the bullets ripping flesh and fabric, scattering his men as they were hit or tried to save themselves
by leaping this and that way, clawing pistols from their
holsters. Tan, stunned into momentary immobility by
sheer surprise, kicked backward in his chair and hit the
floor with stunning force, his head bouncing off the
concrete under shag carpeting.

He cursed, rolled clear, the sound of gunfire ringing in his ears. Some of his men were fighting back,
but ineffectually, either wounded or so panicked that
their shots went high and wide. Above Tan, crimson
mist exploded from the lurching figures of his soldiers
and advisers. Gao was down and thrashing on the car-

pet, staining it beneath him, like a mangled fish cast up onshore.

Tan rolled and started scrabbling toward the nearest cover. That turned out to be a billiards table on the far side of the room. Halfway across that no-man's-land, he suddenly remembered that he wore a pistol of his own and stopped to claw it from his belt. It might be wasted effort, but at least the man who'd come to kill him wouldn't walk away and say that Tan had taken it without a fight.

Tan owed the brotherhood that much.

He yanked the pistol clear, half turned to fire in the direction of the doorway, but a boot came down upon his wrist with crushing force. Tan gasped, squeezed off one wasted shot before a painted hand relieved him of the weapon, then the boot was off his wrist and hammering his ribs. He grunted, rolled in an attempt to flee the pain and wound up facing toward the ceiling.

Toward the smoking muzzle of a weapon hanging inches from his face.

"I'm guessing you speak English," the intruder said.

Tan thought about denying it, but how would that work, if he didn't understand the question? Grudgingly, stalling for time until his other soldiers reached the recreation room, he said, "I do."

"A second guess—you're Tan Sen Neo."

While his first thought was to lie, Tan realized that a denial of his true identity might end his life and send the gunman off to search elsewhere. He nodded. "I am."

"Okay," the stranger said. He was a white man underneath the paint. No doubt, the American who had eluded Tan's best shooters at the waterfront theme park. "You want to take a little trip with me? Or are you tired of living?"

Stall, Tan thought, and asked, "Where would we go?"

"Someplace to have a private chat."

Pretending to consider it, he bought another fifteen seconds, then replied, "I seem to have no choice."

The soldier took a step back, then said, "Get up."

Tan started to comply, then saw his outer guards rush through the open exit to the patio with weapons leveled at his enemy.

"Perhaps, instead," Tan offered, "you should simply die."

BOLAN SUPPOSED they were the gate guards, though he couldn't swear to it. Wherever they had come from, they were in his face and in his way now. It was time for them to go.

Lying at Bolan's feet, Tan spit an order at his soldiers. Bolan caught the tone and knew they hadn't been told to take him alive.

Split seconds made the difference in combat. One soldier's reaction time against another's swung the balance. Bolan's index finger had been tightening around the 40 mm launcher's trigger as he turned to face the new arrivals, and he followed through the squeeze before they had a chance to fire, his weapon elevated toward the lintel of the doorway where they stood. His high-explosive round went off on impact with the doorframe, like an airburst from artillery, spraying its cone of shrapnel downward while the shock wave rattled through Tan's house. The triad soldiers almost seemed to *flatten* underneath that deadly rain, but Bolan's view was topsy-turvy as concussion tossed him backward, tumbling him to the floor.

Tan was almost quick enough in his recovery to make a break, but Bolan swept his ankles out from underneath him with the Pindad autorifle's stock. Tan hit the deck facedown, cursing a blue streak in his native tongue, and Bolan had him pinned with one knee in the middle of the underboss's back before Tan could recover from the fall.

"Last chance," the Executioner advised the man, while the muzzle of his weapon warmed Tan's nape. "How badly do you want to die?"

"What is it that you want to know?" Tan asked.

"Not here," Bolan replied. "Not now. Get up."

It didn't take cue cards to know that Tan was stalling. In his ritzy neighborhood, it was a lead-pipe cinch that someone would have called for the police already, and response times typically grew shorter as the caller's affluence increased. Even with riot squads tied up at Ancol Dreamland, there'd be cops to spare for a report of gunfire and explosions out of Cengkareng.

Tan struggled to his feet, seeming a little dizzy, but it could have been another act. Bolan clutched Tan's right arm with his left hand and steered his captive toward the patio, beyond the leaking corpses of his soldiers and advisers. They made squelching noises on the carpet and left ruby footprints on the paving stones outside.

Bolan paused there, watching and listening for any sign of further opposition, then asked Tan, "Who else is on the property?"

"No one."

"First shooter we meet, you hit the ground before he does," Bolan replied.

"There's no one!" Tan repeated, angrily. "You've killed them all."

"Not yet," Bolan replied, and steered his prisoner toward the front gate.

A risky move, but it was Bolan's only option. Cov-

ering his captive while they scaled one of the outer
walls—assuming Tan *could* climb the wall—only invited an escape attempt. The last thing Bolan needed at
the moment was a footrace through a residential district
with police expected momentarily. He'd either have to
drop Tan on the spot or let him go, a waste of precious
time, in either case.

Better to haul him out the front, dealing with any obstacles they met along the way, and hope that Maia Lee
would make a pass before the cops showed up.

It was another gamble, and the game was far from
over, but the Executioner couldn't afford to fold.

It was dumb luck that Maia saw them seconds after
they had cleared the gate to Tan Sen Neo's driveway.
She was on her fourth pass through the neighborhood,
reversing her direction on each circuit, after getting
trapped once in a cul-de-sac. Driving with windows
down, she'd heard faint echoes that she took to be gunfire, and then a louder sound, grenade-loud in the still-
ness of the night, that brought her speeding back to
check the property again.

And there they were. She didn't recognize the man
Cooper was supporting and half dragging after him,
but guessed it had to be Tan. She blinked her headlights twice, the signal they'd agreed upon, then braked
as Cooper crossed with his prisoner to her side of the
street. He opened one rear door, checked high and low
for any stray weapons, then shoved Tan forward and
climbed in behind him, settling in the backseat.

"Go," he said. "But don't be obvious."

Maia accelerated to the speed limit, no screeching
rubber, and turned left at the first cross street. Left

again, then right, and they were rolling out of Daan Mogot Estate, then out of Cengkareng.

"Where shall we take him?" she inquired.

"Nowhere," Cooper said. "Just drive around and keep an eye out for police. I don't have many questions."

"Few or many," Tan Sen Neo interjected. "Why should I say anything?"

"Because you'd rather live than die," Bolan said. "And if you choose death, you'd prefer it to be quick and clean."

"How do you know what I prefer?" Tan asked.

"You're human, more or less. I'll play the odds."

"Ask what you wish. I promise nothing," Tan replied.

"Two questions only. Jin Au-Yo has gone to ground somewhere in Banten Province. You know where he is. I need directions to his hardsite."

"And the other question?" Tan inquired.

"How many soldiers should be with him, give or take?"

Tan thought about it, then produced a mocking smile, reflected in the rearview mirror.

"I will answer you," he said at last, "because the truth leads to your death. The place you seek lies twenty-five kilometers southwest of Serang. There is a trading post that marks your turnoff from the Banten highway. Four kilometers from there, you find the camp. As to the force awaiting you, I cannot cite a number, but I trust that it will be sufficient for the task."

"They're better men than you had, then?" Bolan asked.

Tan shrugged and said, "You must answer that your-self. As for me—"

He lunged away from Bolan and had his door open before Maia could brake. The Executioner tried to grab

Tan, but the triad underboss rolled clear and hit the pavement with a squawk. Behind them, traffic swerved, but not in time. Maia saw one car lurch as it ran over him, another driver close behind it slamming on his brakes too late and smearing Tan along the roadway.

Another side street. Maia took it, sped along to reach another and turned there, as well.

"Do you believe him?" she asked when they were clear.

"We'll find out soon enough," Bolan said.

CHAPTER TWENTY-TWO

Banten Province, West Java

Jin Au-Yo switched off the sat phone, gave it back to Ma Mingxia and cursed with bitter feeling.

Ma waited, obviously knowing better than to interrupt and ask the question that was on his mind.

When Jin had calmed himself enough for civil speech, he said, "One of our men with the police. Of course, you know that. It seems that no one else remains to call me with the bad news now."

"Sir?"

"Our enemies have taken Tan from his home and killed his guards. Some miles away, they threw him from a car and others crushed him. Traffic officers identified him from the papers that he carried. They couldn't compare the photo from his driver's license."

Ma said nothing. It occurred to Jin that he had never heard his houseman voice emotions about any subject.

"They may be here, next," Jin said. In fact, he hoped so. Finally, he could confront the vermin who had come so close to ruining his plans.

So close, but not entirely.

They would never find the one remaining missile now, even if they broke through all Jin's defenses and eliminated him. He could die laughing in their faces, with his secret safely tucked away inside his brain.

The plan had hatched from lack of trust, his own doubt that Nasir al-Jarrah would come through with the entire amount owed for the Brave Wind missiles on delivery. In case of any tricks, Jin had attached a GPS transmitter to each weapon with a two-ounce plastic charge and detonator. If the Saudi had absconded with the missiles prior to payment, Jin could press a button and destroy their guidance mechanisms anywhere within a ten-mile range. And far beyond that, he could track the missiles by the homing signals issuing from their transmitters.

Well, *one* of them, anyway.

The first device was vaporized when al-Jarrah had sunk the *Eiland Koningin*. That still left one, however, and its signal echoed strongly enough for Jin to plot its new location on a map. The missile wasn't moving any longer, causing him to think that it had to be on-shore, or else aboard a ship berthed near the nameless island found at the coordinates he'd calculated for the pulsing signal.

Jin had no way of knowing what the Saudi madman had in mind, beyond a vague idea of chaos and destruction, but a thought had come to him while he was idling in his jungle camp, waiting for enemies who hadn't shown their faces yet. If he could sell the Brave Wind missiles once, what would prevent him doing it again?

If al-Jarrah hadn't fired the second missile yet, Jin thought it would be relatively easy to retrieve it, advertise it through his underground communications network and arrange an auction to the highest bidder.

Why not profit twice from one transaction, if he could? And if the Chinese People's Liberation Army Navy bought its own toy back again, Jin thought, he might even become a hero in his nation's eyes. A savior, as it were, who had averted tragedy.

The prospect made him smile, for what felt like the first time in a month.

"Is something funny, sir?" Ma asked.

"It's possible," Jin said. "It just may be."

Tangerang–Merak Toll Road

BACK THEY WENT, westbound along the AH2 Banten highway. Bolan held the Toyota Fortuner at a steady sixty miles per hour, watching out for cops along the way and meeting none. Highway patrol didn't appear to be a top priority on Java, and that was working in their favor now.

He hoped the law would be as scarce when he and Maia found Jin's rural camp.

There was a chance, he realized, that Tan Sen Neo had deceived them, given false directions, but he'd sounded straight to Bolan. Fatalistic, playing out his string and hoping that his brothers of the Flying Ax would rally to avenge him. That was fair enough. You couldn't fault a guy for being pissed when he ran out of time and luck.

They didn't have precise coordinates, but in the end, Tan's pointers brought them to the trading post he had described, a run-down place with signs out front that Bolan couldn't read, a dried and mottled python's skin stretched out across the joint's facade above the door and grimy windows. Bolan didn't know or care what they were selling during business hours. The place was closed now, meaning that no witness saw them make their turn.

He kept an eye on the odometer, slowed and switched

from headlights to the smaller fog lights, then killed those as well when they had covered half the distance to Jin's camp. He found a turnout, made the most of it and nosed the SUV some thirty feet off-road, where drivers passing by from north or south would miss it if they didn't make a special point to stop and peer around.

The night was silent for a little while after they parked, except for engine ticking sounds, then it came slowly back to life. Bolan and Maia stood outside the SUV, its dome light off, and dressed for battle in the dark. When both were squared away, as comfortable as they could be, they faced north toward their target.

Now, the choice. They could save time by striking off along the access road that led directly to the compound, but they might meet vehicles along the way and it was likely to be watched by sentries, maybe even booby-trapped if Jin was really nervous. Option two: hike in the same direction through the forest, risking more noise in the undergrowth, sharing the dark with snakes and who knew what else, while the threat of lurking guards and traps remained.

They settled on plan B, knowing the road would rate more guards. Even if Jin had brought an army with him, they would have to be spread thin along the camp's perimeter, a bunch of city boys jumping at every sound the forest made past nightfall. And the jungle after dark was Bolan's happy hunting ground.

Bolan led the way, using all the tricks he'd learned in Special Forces training and on battlefields around the world to keep the two of them on course. Two klicks came down to a mile and one-third, more or less, a half hour's walk on flat ground for the average person. Bolan reckoned they might double that time, planting one foot in front of the other with ultimate care, and what of it?

The hours from three to five o'clock were perfect for surprises, when the human mind and body went into a slump dictated by biology. More people died in hospitals during those hours than at any other time.

In jungles, too.

The Executioner was hunting. He could almost smell his prey.

MAIA DIDN'T SEE the lookout waiting for them in the shadows. Cooper had picked him out somehow, stopped her with one hand on her arm and leaned in close enough that when he whispered, it was barely breathing.

"Wait here."

Maia nodded, watched him go, her index finger resting lightly on the trigger of her silenced submachine gun. If she couldn't see the enemy, at least she had a fair idea of where he was, and she could always spray the forest with a whole magazine if she needed to. Something was bound to die, in that event.

Perhaps two minutes after Cooper left her alone, she heard a muted thrashing in the undergrowth ahead, perhaps a burbling gasp, then Cooper came back to fetch her.

"Clear," he whispered, and she fell in step behind him once again, trying to place her feet as he did, with a minimum of noise.

The forest wasn't silent as they passed, which boosted Maia's confidence a little. In her mind, she knew she wasn't making that much noise, but she still worried that a rustling bush or snapping twig would loose a storm of automatic fire from hidden watchers, stopping them before they dealt with Jin Au-Yo.

Or his men dealt with them.

They had been bucking lethal odds since she'd

teamed up with Cooper, and each engagement stretched their luck a little further. Somewhere, Maia knew, there had to be a breaking point. If this was it, if she was fated for a jungle death, at least she meant to go down fighting. Take as many of the bastards with her as she could.

The camp was sleeping when they reached it, more or less. A generator grumbled in its shed, but few lights showed around the compound. One was burning in what Maia took to be the camp's communication hut, a satellite dish and several ship antennae mounted on its sloping metal roof. Also a larger prefab building, possibly Jin's private quarters based on size, had dim light showing through a window covered by frosted privacy film.

Cooper chose a spot on the perimeter where everything was visible and crouched with Maia at his side. He spent a moment studying the layout, marking half a dozen sentries at their posts, then leaned close and said, "Stay here. I'll work my way around and start the party when I'm situated."

Maia nodded, was afraid to speak. What would she say? *Be careful? Don't get killed?* The possibilities sounded redundant and ridiculous.

Cooper eased away from her, and in another moment he was gone, swallowed by darkness. Maia couldn't track him aurally and dared not break off observation of the camp to search the shadows for him. She would know when he was ready. It would be no secret.

Seven minutes later by her watch, kneeling beside a giant tree that she couldn't identify, she heard a pop, and then the crump of an explosion in the camp as the communications shed collapsed in smoke and dust.

Sighting on the nearest startled sentry with her SMG, she took a breath and held it. Almost smiling, she cut him down.

THE BLAST WOKE Jin Au-Yo from fitful sleep, from a
dream in which he was pursued by something large
and ravenous, yet seemingly invisible. He rolled out
of his camp bed, found the AK-47 he'd positioned on
the floor within arm's reach and found his balance in
the four long strides it took to reach the front door of
his quarters.

He froze with one hand on the doorknob, listening.
After the shock of the explosion, Jin could hear his
men calling to one another, most groggy from sleep
but struggling back to full awareness in an instant with
the threat of sudden death upon them. None was firing
yet, a sign of discipline, but how long would that last?

All of the men he'd chosen to defend his forest camp
were seasoned fighters, some of them ex-military men,
but Jin had no idea how they would fare against his present enemies until the battle had been joined.

Right now.

He turned the doorknob, eased his way outside,
nearly colliding with a sentry on his way to rouse the
boss. Before his soldier had a chance to speak, a burst
of automatic rifle fire ripped through the camp from
somewhere on Jin's right, to the east. One of his men
fell, crying out in pain, and then a dozen of them started
firing into darkness on the camp's perimeter. They had
no target, Jin could see that much, but they were doing
something, and at least they had the general direction
of their enemy correct.

Or did they?

From his left, another cry of mortal pain, and Jin's
head snapped around in time to see another of his soldiers fall. He'd heard no hostile shots that time, uncertain whether they were covered by the firing by his
men, or if the sniper on that side had used a silenced

weapon. Either way, he saw that they were in a cross
fire, meaning that at least two adversaries were in play.

The woman and her American? If not them, who
else could it be?

Jin ducked off to his right, in the direction of the first
incoming fire. His men needed a leader in the heat of
battle, and the role was his to fill. Anger supplanted his
initial pang of fear as Jin moved toward the dark trees
shadowing his compound, jogging with the sentry on
at his heels. Another moment, and—

Another burst of firing from the woods. He saw the
muzzle-flash this time and knelt to steady his Kalashnikov before returning fire, then rocked off-balance as
the sentry who'd been following him slumped across
Jin's shoulders, bearing him to earth. Warm blood
splashed over Jin, streaking his face and drizzling down
inside the collar of his shirt.

Cursing, he shoved the body backward and away
from him, sleeving a blur of crimson from his left eye,
feeling suddenly exposed. He grappled with his weapon,
looking for the target he had lost, but had not found it
when the world exploded in his face.

MAIA FED her Pindad PM2 a fresh magazine, cocked
the weapon and peered cautiously around the southeast corner of the prefab building she had taken for
the compound's mess hall. Close now, she could still
pick out the cooking smells that lingered there, despite
the cordite reek of gunsmoke and explosives wafting
through the camp.

She had lost count of bodies since the shooting
started, would have claimed seven herself, but couldn't
say for sure that all of them were dead. Say seven hits,
then, understanding that the 9 mm Parabellum rounds

her SMG spit out traveled at 1300 feet per second, striking with 420 foot-pounds of force. Jin's men weren't wearing body armor, so even a flesh wound would ruin one's night. Maybe ruin one's life.

Maia supposed she should feel something other than excitement in the midst of deadly battle, but she'd given up waiting to mourn the men she'd killed since teaming up with Cooper. More than a full day they had been together now, and Maia's only true regret was her betrayal by the ministry she'd loyally served for years.

Or was it the whole ministry?

Fann Lieu had named one man, Chou Hua Tian. Granted, he was a highly placed official, but did that mean that his actions were approved by his superiors? To answer that, Maia knew she would have to speak with someone else inside the ministry, explain what had been happening, and—

Bullets raked across the wall near Maia's face and she ducked backward, rolled out to her right and ran along the mess hall's southern wall, circling to find another field of fire. Ten seconds later she was peering at the compound from a new perspective, and she saw a pair of riflemen advancing toward the spot she'd lately vacated. Watching them duck and dodge, she gave them credit for coordination, but it wouldn't help them now.

She led the forward stalker with her weapon's sights and caught him with a 3-round burst that opened up his ribs beneath his right arm, mangling lungs and heart. Before he dropped, she was already swinging left to catch his partner as the second man recoiled, backpedaling, but any chance he might have had to save himself was gone.

Another burst from Maia's weapon took the second shooter, two rounds ripping through his neck, a third exploding through the lower right-hand quadrant of his face. Bone shards inflicted as much damage as bullet fragments with a solid hit, and he was shocked into unconsciousness—perhaps already dead—before he fell.

Another of Matt Cooper's grenades exploded in the middle of the compound, flinging bodies through the air as if a team of acrobats were putting on a special high-tech show. Except these tumblers didn't spring erect on landing, rather, sprawling where they fell with spastic twitches, crimson mist settling around them from their wounds.

How many triad soldiers left? Scanning the open ground in front of her, Maia saw only five or six still up and moving, at least two of them already slowed by wounds. She took a moment to prepare herself, then rose and left her cover, moving out to meet the enemy.

BOLAN MOVED AMONG the dead and dying, checking faces where they still remained, sparing a mercy round for this or that one if his features varied from the mug shot fixed in Bolan's mind. Across the compound, he saw Maia doing the same. Searching. Relieving misery where it was called for, turning over corpses if they lay facedown.

Bolan found Jin Au-Yo just struggling back to consciousness from a grenade blast, bleeding from a dozen shrapnel wounds. The worst was on the left side of his lower abdomen, where blood had soaked his trousers and a loop of bowel extruded. He was hurting, on his way toward dying, but he wasn't finished yet.

The man's eyes swam into focus, locking onto Bolan's face as Maia Lee stepped up beside him. "You!" he said, twisting his bloodied lips into a kind of smile.

Bolan took a chance, told him, "You're dying. Nothing to be done about it now, this far from any medics."

"So…you think…you win?" Jin challenged him.

"I can't say that," Bolan replied. "But we'll be leaving in a minute. Was it worth it?"

Jin grimaced, then spoke a phrase in Chinese.

"How's that?" Bolan asked.

Maia translated it. "The goddamned Saudis."

"You can even up the score," Bolan said. "Tell us where to find them, while there's still time left."

"Why…should…I?"

"Pay them back for all your triad brothers," Bolan said. "For what you're feeling now."

Jin closed his eyes, considered it so long that Bolan might have taken him for dead, except that blood still burbled from his wounds. His heart was beating, but the pulse was slowing, fading out. Bolan was ready to accept that he'd lost consciousness when Jin's eyes opened and his head turned, squinting toward the smoky west end of the camp.

"My quarters, are they standing?"

Bolan glanced back toward the prefab house. He hadn't blasted it, since it appeared to be unoccupied.

"Still there," he said.

"Inside…the table…GPS receiver."

"Tracking what?" Bolan asked.

"A device…inside the…missile," Jin replied, his voice fading fast.

Bolan looked up at Maia, saw her turn away and jog off toward the dying man's home away from home.

"See…the…chart," Jin gasped, blood trickling from his lips.

"We'll find them," Bolan answered, hoping that the man wasn't feeding him a phony exit line as payback for his suffering. There seemed to be no point in lying, but the Executioner had long since given up on trying to read minds.

"Make them…feel this," Jin said, expelling one last ragged breath before he died.

And Bolan told the corpse, "I'll do my best."

He rose as Maia returned, her submachine gun slung over one shoulder, carrying a GPS receiver and a folded map. "He wanted to keep track of them," she said, handing the map to Bolan. "Why would he do that?"

"No way to tell," Bolan replied. "If he was having second thoughts about the deal, they came too late."

"As we may be," she said.

"Not yet," said Bolan. "If they're still at these coordinates, we've got a shot."

"Why not alert your fleet?" she asked.

"The point of this is keeping them outside harm's way," Bolan replied.

"So, what now?"

"Now, we go back to Jakarta," he said. "And find ourselves a set of wings."

CHAPTER TWENTY-THREE

Soekarno–Hatta International Airport

Island Airways was a one-plane charter operation that combined small freight deliveries with tourist sightseeing excursions. Normally, its office didn't open before nine o'clock, but Bolan's call had caught the owner sitting down to breakfast, and the price that he had offered for a lift from Java eastward to the neighborhood of Flores had been too good to resist.

A thousand miles and change, one-way, with no requirement that the pilot wait around and bring them back again. Toss in the acquisition of a Zodiac inflatable raft or its equivalent and would a payday equal to the best month Island Airways ever had be satisfactory?

Damn straight it would.

The aircraft was a de Havilland Canada DHC-3 Otter floatplane, with seating for one pilot and ten passengers. The plane was old but well maintained, its prop powered by a Pratt & Whitney R-1340 Wasp engine, pioneered in the 1920s and used worldwide since then in smaller private planes, as well as certain military transport craft. Its 945-mile range dictated a refueling stop at Bali's Ngurah Rai International before continuing to their target, another hundred miles due east, near Flores Island.

On arrival at the charter airline's hangar, bypassing

airport security and customs, Bolan gave the smiling pilot/owner cash up front, then checked out the inflatable raft he'd picked up for them on short notice. There was nothing obviously wrong with it, and Bolan let the flyboy—Carmit Dhani—glimpse his holstered pistol as he asked whether Dhani would trust his own life to it on the open sea. A quick, earnest affirmative let Bolan know that Dhani understood his life *was* riding on the little rubber boat's seaworthiness.

They had no other gear to load, aside from duffel bags heavy with ammunition. Dhani recognized those, too, and didn't bother asking why they wanted to be dropped off in the middle of the Lesser Sundas with no way of getting back. Instead, he counted rupiahs and weighed the cash against whatever debts he had outstanding, probably grateful that he would be flying back alone.

Whatever happened to his customers once they had left the plane at sea was their problem, not his.

The tower kept them waiting twenty minutes after they were battened down and ready, Bolan tapping years of self-control to keep from getting antsy in his seat. He had done everything he could to get them back in a timely fashion and arrange the flight. Beyond that, it was in the hands of fate.

He'd also placed a quick call to Brognola, via sat phone from the road, to brief him on their progress. The big Fed, like Maia, had suggested that they pass Jin's GPS coordinates to the Pacific Fleet for any further action, but he'd understood Bolan's objection and wound up agreeing with his soldier on the ground. If Jin was wrong, or if his chart was some kind of elaborate backup hoax, the Navy would be wasting time and fuel. Conversely, if the lone surviving Brave Wind mis-

sile *was* located more or less where Tan believed it was,
approaching it would put the fleet at risk.

Of course, they could lie back and hit it with a Tomahawk—or several—but there would be no confirmation of a kill until they got around to sorting through
the wreckage, likely after some prolonged negotiations
with the Indonesian government. Meanwhile, if their
strike didn't destroy the HF3...

Then they were back to square one, right? Nothing
to show for it.

So it was Bolan's show, at least for now. Until he won
big on the nameless island.

Or he lost it all.

Ngurah Rai International Airport, Tuban, Bali

THE AIRCRAFT'S CRUISING speed of 120 miles per hour translated into a nine-hour flight from Jakarta to touchdown
near Flores. The stop on Bali was required to prevent
them from ditching at sea, but it added more time to the
trip. Despite his own extraordinary patience, Bolan knew
they were cutting it close. Aside from the air time and
stopover, they were crossing the line to another time zone.

He pictured an hourglass, sand running out and no
way to stop it.

The Executioner had convinced Brognola not to tip
off the Navy just yet, but the Third Fleet was searching high and low throughout the region for any trace of
their target. Every minute Bolan spent in transit could
be bringing warships closer to the enemy. They'd have
no difficulty taking out the terrorists after the missile
launch exposed their base of operations, but by that
time it would be too late.

While the Otter took on fuel, Bolan's mind ran
through the various defenses against missiles presently

available on U.S. Navy ships. The RIM-7 Sea Sparrow was a short-range missile powered by a Hercules MK-58 solid-propellant rocket motor, with semiactive radar homing, built primarily for knocking other missiles down in flight. With a top range of thirteen miles, its epic speed—2,645 miles per hour—put it on target in 1.3 seconds, with a proximity fuse eliminating any need for pinpoint accuracy. Still, it might not work.

If the Sea Sparrow failed, there was always the Mark 36 Super Rapid Blooming Offboard Chaff system, a battery of short-range mortars that launched chaff—thin pieces of aluminum, metalized glass fiber or plastic—or infrared decoys to divert incoming antiship missiles. The last line of shipboard defense was the Phalanx close-in weapons system, a 20 x 102 mm Gatling gun whose six barrels had a selectable fire rate of 3,000 to 4,500 rounds per minute, with an effective range of 2.2 miles. The standard Phalanx ammo was an armor-piercing tungsten round with discarding sabots, but high-explosive incendiary tracer rounds were also available.

Overall, the best solution to the Sword of Allah's threat remained stopping the HF3 before it launched. That could be done in several ways, but only one approach kept juicy targets out of range—boots on the ground striking where they were least expected by the enemy.

Unless they came too late, in which case it was all a wasted exercise.

But while a chance remained, Bolan stayed the course.

It was the only way he knew to play the game.

Lesser Sunda Islands

THE ZODIAC INFLATABLE raft worked fine. It took five minutes to inflate and load it, then Maia and Bolan waved off Carmit Dhani as he turned his floatplane around and powered up for takeoff, westbound.

"I think he is glad to see the last of us," Maia said.

"I think he's off to count his money," Bolan said, before he turned on the raft's small outboard motor and nosed the craft eastward.

Another small island lay between them and their unnamed target, neither any larger than an ink spot on the map he carried. Bolan supposed that naming 18,306 islands got tiresome, not to mention being a waste of time, since only five percent of them were inhabited by humans. Anyhow, the mapmakers had given up somewhere around 8,800 and left the rest anonymous. First come, first served.

Maybe they'd call his destination Missile Island, after this. Or Bloody Island.

Maybe Death Island.

Whatever, Bolan knew that they weren't too late. Brognola would have tipped him off by sat phone if the second missile had been fired. Not calling Bolan back, necessarily, but letting him know that the thrust of the mission had changed.

To what?

A blood feud, maybe, ending only when the individuals responsible were dead.

The afternoon was hot. Bright sun reflected from the ocean's surface punished skin and even found its way around their polarized sunglasses. Bolan fought a light chop as he steered the Zodiac around the island they had used for cover, coming up on its companion at an oblique angle, from the southwest.

Now, the tricky part. He couldn't say exactly where within the next small island's acreage, approximately one square mile, his enemies had set up camp. The latest overflight showed nothing, which told Bolan they were camouflaged, prepared for prying eyes overhead. The GPS receiver would direct them to the missile once they got ashore, but first they had to get past any guards that might be placed around the island, staring out to sea.

Amphibious landings were always dicey, whether it was two invaders in a rubber boat or hundreds alighting from armored personnel carriers. The approaches to islands were always exposed, which made any unwelcome visitors prime sniping targets. Beyond hostile fire, beaches could be defended in a wide variety of ways, from underwater razor wire to mines, tank traps and trenches packed with rude surprises such as explosive charges, punji stakes, whatever. Or the occupants of any given island might sit back and watch a landing party come ashore, then cut them up with automatic fire the second that they dropped their guard, believing they were home and dry.

Too many ways to die.

Bolan and Maia had to risk them all this afternoon, on their approach to No-Name Island.

So it was that even when they'd beached the Zodiac, dragged it above the waterline and camouflaged it with a mass of stranded kelp, they didn't feel secure. They'd traded one threat for another, that was all. Reaching the treeline as they followed the silent flashes from the GPS receiver toward a point inland was a bonus.

And they were watching every step they took along the way.

HARIS BACHDIM slapped a mosquito that was feasting on his neck, studied the blood smear on his palm, then wiped it on his trousers. He was happy not to be a Hindu, forced to treat all forms of life as sacred, even when they fed on him and made *his* life a misery. Also, Bachdim didn't think he could survive on vegetables alone.

Patrolling in this heat was tiresome. Bachdim stopped frequently to rest and felt no guilt about it, since he knew the island to be uninhabited. As far as enemies from the outside, even if they suspected that the Chinese missile was somewhere in Indonesia, how would they select one island in particular among the many thousands in the archipelago? Although himself an Indonesian, Bachdim could name only a dozen of the major islands, maybe less.

Of course, he had dropped out of school when the studies proved too arduous. What did he need with further education once he chose a life of dedication to jihad?

The shoulder strap on his Kalashnikov was chafing at Bachdim's shoulder through the fabric of his shirt. Another mosquito had already found him, its infernal buzzing in his ear grating on his last nerve. He watched the shrubbery around him for a hint of movement that would mark the presence of a krait or viper. As for noise, he knew the island's giant predatory lizards made a plodding, thrashing sound as they moved through the forest, though he hadn't actually seen one for himself. It was enough to make his skin crawl, and he cursed Usmar Malik for sending him to search the woods, then instantly felt guilt for disrespecting his superior.

"God forgive me," he muttered.

As if anyone was listening.

More blasphemy, and Bachdim was disappointed in himself, a warrior on a holy mission so distracted by an insect and a forest filled with silent shadows that he let his standards suffer. How could he be fit for mar-

tyrdom and its celestial rewards if he was vexed by a
mosquito to the point where he abandoned basic mental discipline?

Bachdim slipped his rifle off its sling and tucked
the weapon underneath his arm, its weight a physical
reminder that his job was serious. He had been chosen to protect the Brave Wind missile and its operators
from whatever infidels might seek to spoil the Sword of
Allah's plans. Determined not to fail, Bachdim scanned
the forest with new eyes, half hoping that an enemy
would show himself, give him the chance to spill some
blood before the main event.

But all in vain. The island was deserted, except for
al-Jarrah and their assembled company, the missile crew
and its small force of guards. There would be no excitement until launch time, then a mad dash for the speedboats and to freedom, if the Great Satan's warplanes
hadn't found them yet.

Buoyed by newfound confidence, Bachdim barely
noticed the mere whisper of a scraping sound behind
him, might have blamed it on a forest rodent if the sound
had registered. Too late, he felt the presence of another
body close behind him, as a hand was clasped across
his lower face, twisting his head sharply to the left and
backward, exposing his throat.

The blade was razor-sharp. It penetrated deeply,
severing his jugular and the carotid artery en route to
find his brain stem, where it probed, stirred briskly and
withdrew. Bachdim didn't feel its exit from his flesh,
already dead before the unseen hand released him and
he toppled face-forward to the forest floor.

CHAPTER TWENTY-FOUR

Bolan bent down to wipe his knife blade on the dead man's pants, then sheathed it. In the treetops overhead, birds called and monkeys chattered as if nothing of great interest to them had occurred. Another life lost, more or less, meant nothing here.

"Northeast from here," he told Maia, after a consultation with the GPS device. "It can't be very far ahead. There's not much island."

Even so, a square mile was 640 acres, close to thirty-one hundred square yards. Walking at a steady pace, with no great obstacles before them, Bolan reckoned they could cross the wooded island in an hour, maybe less—but searching it, even if they split up, could take the best part of a day.

More wasted time. A greater risk that targets would appear on the horizon and the Brave Wind missile would lift off, roaring toward impact with a U.S. warship.

The GPS would have to lead them home.

"Okay, we're clear," Bolan told Maia, speaking softly. She responded with a nod and fell in step behind him as he moved out from the kill site, rising ground beneath his feet that would eventually take them to the island's high point if they kept on climbing.

But the GPS wasn't directing them to seek the topmost heights. Instead, it set a course for Bolan that would take them to the left, nearly due north, into the forest that cloaked most of No-Name Island. Bolan tried to picture how and where a missile would be launched from there, then gave it up, deciding anything could be accomplished with sufficient preparation and advance time.

Who could say how long the Brave Wind plot had incubated prior to execution? Given months, weeks— even days, if you were dealing with determined workers and the right equipment—you could slash a clearing in the midst of any jungle, mount your launcher where you wanted it, and…what? Lure targets into range with some kind of enticing bait, perhaps. A radio broadcast could do it, if you let the tape run long enough for trackers to triangulate, lock onto it and move in for the kill.

For all he knew, the lure had been deployed by now. Brognola couldn't tell him if the Third Fleet had a target and was closing. Stony Man would have to snatch that message from the air, decode it, pass it on to Washington…by which time, it would likely be too late to help a warrior on the ground. If Bolan couldn't find the launch site and disable the Brave Wind before it flew, then his whole Asian exercise had been a waste of time.

As far as taking out the Brave Wind, any significant damage should keep it from landing on target—or, better yet, keep it from launching at all. Its warhead was supposed to be an explosively formed penetrator: basically a shaped explosive charge inside a metal plate, whose detonation turned the plate into a hurtling armor-piercing projectile. In this case, the warhead weighed five hundred pounds and would normally be triggered by a smart fuse.

Unless the Executioner got to it first.

In which case, all concerned were in for a surprise.

MAIA HOPED the GPS device was accurate, not leading them astray. She knew some people swore by them, but she'd had problems with them in the past, trying to navigate her way around downtown Beijing. Cooper seemed to trust it, and she trusted him, but still…

Aside from her immediate concerns, another problem weighed on Maia's mind. She had used Cooper's sat phone to call the ministry from Bali's airport and a comrade there, while seeming cagey, had delivered more disturbing news. The Deputy Assistant Minister for State Security, no less than Chou Hua Tian himself, was en route to Jakarta, and the word was that he didn't fly alone. While nothing was confirmed—or spoken of, above a whisper—rumor had it that he was accompanied by members of the People's Liberation Army Special Operations Forces.

Coming, Maia presumed, to rub her out.

Which raised a question in her mind and prompted her to make a second call, this one to a specific officer she trusted with her life. So far, at least. She'd reached him, given him the broad strokes of events since she was captured by, then rescued from, the Malay pirates. News of Chou's departure for Jakarta spread an icy silence over the long-distance link, before her contact said that he'd look into it.

Meanwhile, Maia followed Cooper across a tilting landscape, through the clutches of a mini forest that presumably had never seen a white man or a Chinese woman treading on its soil before. As for the rest—Saudis or Indonesians, soldiers from the Sword of Allah—well, she knew *someone* was here, since Cooper had killed one of their lookouts moments earlier.

Ahead of her, Cooper slowed his pace, and Maia followed suit. It could be anything. Another sentry, possibly a snake, or some fluke in the landscape that required negotiation. Only when he beckoned Maia forward did she close the gap between them, step by cautious step, until she stood beside him, touching-close, and peered around his shoulder.

At first, she didn't fully understand what she was seeing. In the middle distance, call it thirty yards in front of them, a clearing had been cut out of the forest, then concealed with high-strung tarps in a camouflage pattern. Beneath that false canopy, men dressed variously in fatigues and denim, mostly bearded, moved with purpose in the open space they'd carved out for themselves.

And at the center of that space, a launching platform held the second missing Hsiung Feng III missile, aimed skyward, though it would be forced to pierce the camouflage tarp before it could escape and do its work. It seemed to her almost innocuous, just sitting there, but Maia knew the awesome power it contained and all it represented if the launch succeeded.

But they were still in time. It hadn't happened yet.

Cooper edged back from the clearing, bent to put his lips beside her left ear and began to whisper rapid-fire instructions. Maia listened, nodding that she understood and would comply.

They had one chance to do it properly, and only one. Whether they lived to see another day, what she would do about Chou's little army in Jakarta—nothing took priority over their mission of the moment.

Stop the Brave Wind where it sat, and no mistake.

NASIR AL-JARRAH LIT a brown cigarette and inhaled its smoke deeply, ignoring the glares from some of the workers around him. It wasn't his fault that Indonesia's

Muhammadiyah group had banned Muslims from smoking in 2010. Brethren in Singapore had rejected that *fatwa* by an overwhelming majority of votes, and the rest of the Islamic world was divided on the subject of tobacco. His own Saudi homeland, despite its small population, was the world's twenty-third leading consumer of cigarettes, and al-Jarrah had caught the habit early.

Besides, with wine and liquor forbidden, what else did he have?

Only war.

Usmar Malik had prodded him once more to change the deadline for broadcasting their lure to the fleet, and al-Jarrah was considering it. For all his talk of patience to the others, it was true he found their time spent on the nameless island tedious, uncomfortable—a misery, in short.

If they could only glean something of the Third Fleet's movements from their radios, at least he'd have a fair idea of where the warships were. But so far, nothing.

He could always try the beacon, see what happened, first ensuring that he was prepared to flee as soon as—

"Guru! Guru! Musah!"

Someone was shouting from the forest, and he turned to see one of their Indonesian sentries burst into the camp, wild-eyed, his shirt torn from running through dense undergrowth.

Al-Jarrah had quickly learned that *guru* was the word for *master,* but he had to wait for Malik on the rest of it. His local second-in-command debriefed the lookout quickly and returned to al-Jarrah, frowning.

"He says that enemies have found us, sir. One of our men is dead. Stabbed on patrol."

The obvious inquiry would be stabbed by whom? But if the sentry knew that, clearly, he would have ex-

plained to Malik in the first place. As for enemies, al-
Jarrah found it difficult to think that anyone had found
their island hideaway. If that had been the case, where
were the swooping jets? The Tomahawk cruise missiles?
Stabbing spoke to him of primitive assailants, possibly
some throwback tribesman from a nearby island who—

He heard the pop and nearly recognized it, even
with the babble of excited voices rising all around him.
Given four or five more seconds, he could probably have
named its source, but he was out of time.

The blast that followed, although relatively modest in
the scheme of warfare, sounded thunderous beneath the
camouflage tarpaulins covering the launch site. Spinning toward the Brave Wind missile on its launcher, al-
Jarrah saw that one of its tailfins had been sheared off at
the base, leaving a wound that gaped and smoked. The
missile shivered, as if seeking to escape that wound,
its blue-gray shaft and white nose cone still angled toward the sky.

Al-Jarrah felt his heart stop for a moment, then resume its beating with a stutter-step that left him short
of breath. A secondary blast, and he was bellowing with
rage, his voice lost in the greater noise of solid propel-
lant exploding, hurling fragments of the missile's fuse-
lage across the clearing. Staggered by the shock wave,
al-Jarrah dropped to his hands and knees, cursing the
day when he was born.

MAIA COULDN'T BELIEVE IT. After all that she had risked
and suffered, all she'd done to reach this moment, Cooper had brought the Brave Wind down in seconds flat.
One shot from his grenade launcher had maimed the
missile, rendered it inoperable, then the fuel had caught
and detonated with a roar that deafened her. Concussion

from the blast had knocked down most of the assembled guards and workers, several of them transformed into flaming twists of blackened flesh, but most were struggling to their feet again, shaking their heads, groping for weapons they had dropped.

Now was the time to take them.

Even deaf and shaken from the blast, Maia was able to control her trembling hands and aim her weapon. From the cover of the treeline, she dropped one man, then another, before anyone caught on to what was happening. Dazed as they were, however, some of those before her had to have been trained soldiers, for they bounced back from their shock and started laying down a spray of automatic fire that raked the forest. Marking her position, she supposed, from the direction that her first two victims fell.

And it was close. The fire from half a dozen AK-47s ripped through shrubbery, slashed bark from ancient trees and filled the air with humming death. Maia lay prone behind one of the forest giants, waiting out the storm, knowing that if she stayed in place too long they had a chance to flank her, and she wouldn't know they'd done it until searing bullets cut her down.

She rolled out, staying low, wincing as stones beneath the forest's leafy carpet dug into her knees, ribs, elbows. Dimly, as if they were miles away instead of yards, she heard the men who meant to kill her shouting back and forth among themselves. They would be cautious moving in, but driven by the rage and disappointment of their grand scheme's demolition. Eager for a bloodletting to compensate for loss.

Maia reached a point where large roots heaved out of the earth and formed a natural depression, heaved herself across one of the brawny tentacles and rolled into the swale between them. Seconds later, she heard running footsteps closing from her left and right together, one hunter a little slower than the other. Angrily, they spoke back and forth, rushing to meet each other at the spot where she had dropped from sight.

It was an all-or-nothing moment. Maia drew her pistol, switched it to her left hand, while she clutched the submachine gun with her right. Bracing her heels, she lurched up from the ground with arms outstretched, firing in both directions, barely seeing targets as they froze stock-still, surprised.

Both of her guns were silencer-equipped, their coughing sounds inconsequential by comparison to the screams, the roar of flames and automatic weapons firing from the camp behind her. Still, the silent bullets found their marks, two shooters twitching from the impact, crying out in pain and impotent frustration as they died and crumpled to the forest floor.

Stop wasting time, Maia thought, as she scrambled from her makeshift foxhole and prepared to join the fight once more.

THE BRAVE WIND MISSILE's warhead detonated with a bang that rocked the forest clearing and sent shrapnel skyward, ripping through the tarps that masked the clearing like a charge of buckshot tearing sheets on a clothesline. It also dropped a couple more of the camp's dazed defenders, shot through with chunks of red-hot metal as they were recovering from their initial shock.

Disposing of the missile had been Bolan's first priority. Whatever happened after that, whether they won or lost, the mission would be rated a success. He might not get a chance to update Brognola, but one way or another, when the Hsiung Feng III wasn't used against a

U.S. ship at sea, the point would get across. The Sword of Allah would be claiming no jihadic victories from this attempt to wound the West.

But taking down the missile wasn't all of it. Somewhere in the confusion of the forest compound, Bolan reasoned that he'd find the individuals who had conceived and carried out the hijacking, with the destruction of the *Shenyang,* the *Eiland Koningin* and their respective crews. As long as he had strength and ammunition left, eliminating them was job two on his list to make the mission a clean sweep.

And it was time to hunt.

The chaos helped him. Coming out of cover, through the smoke and haze, finding his adversaries shaken and disoriented, Bolan let his autorifle do the talking, spitting 5.56 mm NATO rounds in short precision bursts. He wasn't taking prisoners, had no more need of anyone to grill for information. It came down to scorched earth now, ensuring that the men behind this waking nightmare never had a chance to try again.

Of course, they weren't *all* down and out. In fact, most were recovering their senses as he broke out of the treeline, spotting individuals and dropping them as they woke up to yet another danger in their midst. Most of the camp's inhabitants were armed, if not exactly ready to defend themselves. The first one who got off a shot missed Bolan by at least a yard, then died trying to get it right the second time around.

By then, others were scrambling for whatever cover they could find, taking advantage of the dark smoke from the missile's immolation, some retreating toward the trees, while others tried to put the flaming wreckage of the Brave Wind and its launching platform in between themselves and Bolan.

All good efforts. None sufficient to outwit the Executioner.

Bolan wasn't keeping score—notching a gun had never been his thing—and there'd been no time for a head count of the camp's inhabitants when he'd arrived with Maia. Still, he had a feeling for the numbers, running low, making sure to double-check the bodies as he passed them, to prevent a rude surprise. If he went down this day, it wouldn't be because he let a dead man shoot him in the back.

And there would be dead men aplenty by the time his work was done.

USMAR MALIK KNEW a losing proposition when he saw one. Prepared as he had been for martyrdom in God's name, he saw no value in the simple act of dying, once the mission was aborted and had no hope of success. No missile meant no death blow to the Great Satan's Pacific Fleet. The cause—at least for now—was lost.

Malik was getting out.

The speedboats waited for him, one equipped with a homing device that would draw fighter planes, but he had switched the small black box from his boat to Nasir al-Jarrah's. Both were cigarette high-performance boats, built for offshore power racing, identical in all respects except that one was painted blue, the other green. Al-Jarrah had stashed his small homing device inside the blue boat, but Malik had switched it to the green.

Why not, when al-Jarrah meant to betray him? Where was the brotherhood in that?

And al-Jarrah had fled the killing field already. Malik saw him go, flitting through smoke and flames to reach the treeline while his men died all around him, none presumably aware that they had been abandoned by their fearless leader. Malik could have stayed to lead them, sacrificed himself to help Nasir escape, but why should he?

An officer led by example, and Malik was following his master's lead.

Armed only with a Skorpion machine pistol and two spare magazines of .32 ACP ammunition, Malik scuttled after Nasir al-Jarrah, hoping no one would see him go. Their soldiers—anyway, the few who still survived—were busy fighting for their lives, but Malik thought about the enemy, wondered how many of them lurked around the forest camp, and whether one of them was tracking him right now.

If so, would they pursue him? He wore nothing to identify himself as second-in-command of the missile launch team, no special uniform or insignia. He had been knocked around by the explosions, just like everybody else, clothes torn and dirtied, his face smeared with a residue of soot and grime. Malik supposed he looked like any other frightened peasant in the circumstances, a disguise—though unintentional—that might help him escape.

He needed time and luck. If only—

When the bullet struck him like a hammer blow beneath one shoulder blade, Malik gasped a cry of pain and sprawled facedown on stinking leaf mold. Spastic fingers lost their purchase on the Skorpion, and he had no idea where it had gone.

Behind him, footsteps cautiously approached. His slayer, coming to confirm the kill. Malik wondered if he had strength to fight and got his answer as a strong hand rolled him over on his back, great bolts of agony turning his limbs to rubber while he sobbed.

"Speak English?" asked the rifleman who towered over him.

"Ye—yes."

"Leaving the party early," the gunman said. "Who is—or *was*—in charge?"

Malik considered lying, even claiming credit for himself to help al-Jarrah, but what would be the point? What did he owe the Saudi, after all?

"That way." He pointed toward the cove, across the island. "Boats. Escaping."

The shooter eyed him for another moment, then said, "Thanks," and turned away. Left Malik where he lay, a living feast for insects or the island's giant lizards, if they found him soon enough.

Maybe the fighter planes would come.

Maybe they'd strafe and bomb the stranger who had killed him.

Maybe Malik's heart would stop before the lizards came.

He closed his eyes and offered up a hopeless prayer.

CHAPTER TWENTY-FIVE

Bolan believed the dying man, in part because he'd seemed sincere, and equally because Bolan had seen another runner leave the camp seconds ahead of his last target, headed in the same direction. South, across the island's girth, to reach the farthest shore.

Call it three-quarters of a mile from where they'd started, over moderately rough terrain. The clinging undergrowth would slow passage—might even trip and maim a careless runner—but the man Bolan was tracking would have checked it out beforehand, blazed or memorized a trail between the Brave Wind launch site and the bay or cove where the escape craft would be stashed.

Bolan supposed that he and Maia had to have missed them by a whisker, coming in from the southwest. A few yards farther east, they might have seen the waiting boats, detoured and disabled them as a precautionary measure. It was too late now, of course. Another of those little ironies and glitches that could turn a battle's outcome one way or another in a flash.

Bolan still didn't know his final target's name, nor did he care. His mission was successful on its face, whether he caught the guy or not, but the soldier didn't like loose ends. Unfinished business had a way of coming back to bite him when his mind was elsewhere.

Why put off till tomorrow killing someone he could deal with here and now?

The runner had a fair head start, and Bolan couldn't say what kind of shape the other man was in, but once he found the game trail—recently improved with a machete, it appeared—Bolan began to pick up speed. Still wary of a trap, knowing the guy might know he was pursued and try to spring an ambush, the soldier jogged ahead, his long legs eating up the yards.

And thought of Maia, still back at the camp, maybe alone by now with only corpses left for company. There'd been no time to look for her, communicate where he was going, what he had in mind. Experience had told him that the fleeing men were likely to be leaders of the pack, escaping while their lackeys stood and died to cover them, and Bolan hadn't planned to let them flee and plot again some other day.

If he had anything to say about the outcome of this fight, it ended here, for good.

And someone else would plan the next hit for the Sword of Allah, sure. That was the way it worked in real life, where ideas could only be frustrated and diverted for the moment, never killed. Each time the U.S. made a move or issued a pronouncement on the Middle East, it spawned more enemies.

War everlasting, to the death of one and all.

But this one plotter, somewhere up ahead of him and running for his life, wouldn't be sitting at the table when the next mass-murder plan was sketched out and debated. Not if Bolan found him first.

Another half mile, no great distance, and the runner should be visible. Unless he'd reached the boats already and secured one, speeding on his way. Then what?

Go after him, what else?

Leave Maia where she was and come back for her, if and when he could. And if he couldn't, for whatever reason, she still had the Zodiac.

A chance, at least.

Bolan wished her all the luck that he could spare, and ran on through the forest, following the man he meant to kill.

Jakarta

"He's dead? You're certain?" Chou Hua Tian asked the young man who stood nervously before him.

"Yes, sir," the triad soldier said. "There is no doubt. We have word from inside the Indonesian National Police."

Chou swore bitterly. "Who is in charge, then?"

"That should be Jin Au-Yo, sir."

"Should be?"

With a helpless shrug, the gangster answered, "He is also dead."

Chou felt his anger simmering, preparing to boil over. "So, is *anyone* alive?"

"No one with clear authority, sir. Perhaps you should contact our master of the mountain."

"Wu Guchan is in Beijing," Chou said, stating the obvious. "How can he help me in Jakarta?"

Yet another shrug, this time without a verbal answer.

"Very well, get out!" Chou commanded, turning from the young thug as he left.

Five hours on the ground now, in Jakarta, and he had accomplished nothing. Jin Au-Yo had run off to another province and been killed, his second-in-command was lying in Jakarta's morgue, and it appeared that there was no one left to help Chou except himself.

He blamed all this on Maia Lee, first for surviving when she had been captured by the Malay pirates who were meant to kill her, then for teaming with the American—still unidentified—who'd helped her carve a swath of carnage from Johor to Jakarta and beyond. For all he knew, they might even succeed in tracking down the final Brave Wind missile and destroying it, but that wouldn't help Chou. By this time, his rogue agent knew that he had planned to kill her, to prevent her from recovering the missile, and that knowledge was a time bomb ticking down to doomsday. If she reached the ministry and told her story...

Feng Jingwei had already taken the coward's way out. A call from Beijing had alerted Chou to the commodore's suicide, which slammed the door on his plan B: framing the naval officer for everything from start to finish. No one in the triad or the Sword of Allah would have contradicted him, but now, without his scapegoat, it was a pathetic plan at best.

And useless, anyway, while Maia Lee survived.

Chou's soldiers were standing by in their hotel suites, with the weapons furnished by the Flying Ax Triad, but Chou had no targets for them to stalk and kill. He'd kept his visit secret from the Chinese embassy on Jalan Mega Kuningan, anxious as he was to operate without official notice. Now, it seemed, his trip had been a costly, risky waste of time that might expose him after all. He'd made excuses in Beijing—a family emergency, the soldiers needed for a special training exercise to keep them fit—but it could all unravel in a heartbeat and undo him if he failed to silence Maia Lee.

Where was she? After all the havoc she had wreaked across two countries, how could she just disappear without a trace?

That mystery could be the death of Chou Hua Tian, unless he solved it soon.

No-Name Island, Lesser Sundas

NASIR AL-JARRAH WAS winded, cursing the addiction to tobacco that had left him short of breath. Was this his punishment for smoking? Would almighty God be so petty, in the face of all that al-Jarrah had done for Him?

Gasping, he pushed on through the forest undergrowth that snagged his flesh and clothing, tearing both. The trail seemed narrower this afternoon than when he'd walked it the previous day. He supposed his fright produced that feeling, yet another thing that galled him. He was running for his life like some thief in a village marketplace, an act of cowardice that shamed him.

A root reached out to trip him. Al-Jarrah pitched forward, flayed his palms breaking the fall and spit an angry curse. Against all odds, it made him laugh at his ridiculous position, but the terrorist swallowed the rasping cackle, recognizing that it sounded like hysteria.

How much farther to the cove and waiting speedboat? Al-Jarrah thought he had run for half a mile, at least. Perhaps four hundred yards to go, and that was nothing. Up and down a football pitch four times, and all downhill from where he was. He would let gravity assist him, pull him toward the shoreline and his vehicle to freedom.

Without U.S. planes and warships to prevent it, Nasir al-Jarrah believed he could escape. Traveling at top speed, the cigarette boat could carry him two hundred miles before it ran out of fuel. Depending on his direction of travel, he could reach Flores, Sumba or Sumbawa. All three had airports where al-Jarrah could catch a flight to East Timor, Papua New Guinea or perhaps even Australia. If need be, he could fly back to Jakarta, using his reserve ID, and leave Indonesia from there.

But first, the boat.

A hissing lizard six or seven feet in length lunged from the bushes on his left and snapped at him. Al-Jarrah screamed and leaped over its head, as if he were an athlete running hurdles on track. He landed on his feet and picked up speed, driven by desperation to escape. A thrashing on the trail behind him told al-Jarrah that the reptile was in pursuit. He thought of stopping on the trail to kill it with his pistol, but he was uncertain whether he could manage it and feared drawing attention from his human adversaries with the noise of shots.

Better to run and offer up a hasty prayer for assistance in his hour of need.

The lizard snorted somewhere close behind him, driving al-Jarrah toward the cove.

MAIA SAW Matt Cooper leave the camp and knew she had a choice to make: remain and finish off the compound's last few wounded men, or follow him. She glanced around, saw no one fit to rise and walk, much less put up a fight, and left them to the task of dying on their own.

What did it matter if a couple of them crawled away to lick their wounds and wait for nightfall to conceal them or bring scavengers to feast upon their flesh? The missile was destroyed, catastrophe averted. All that mattered now was keeping track of Cooper and getting off the island in one piece.

He wasn't leaving her behind; Maia knew that much as she followed him along a narrow trail that led her southward from the forest camp. The only explanation for his flight was that he'd seen someone escaping from the compound and had given chase, which meant the man or men he was pursuing had to be worth the added risk and effort. If he caught them, *when* he caught them, Maia would be there to help him finish it.

Whatever happened next, she recognized that they were headed in the right direction for their own evacuation from the island, moving more or less toward where the Zodiac inflatable raft was beached and hidden. Once they caught whoever Cooper was chasing, there would be no need to backtrack. They could simply leave and make their way to Sumbawa. It would be dark before they landed, granting cover while they stashed their boat and larger weapons, keeping only pistols for the inland hike to reach the island's airport and arrange a charter flight.

Simple. Assuming that they got that far.

But first, there was more bloody work to do.

She kept expecting to catch sight of Cooper, but he eluded her. The forest, pressing close on either side, whispered and whistled at her passing with the cries of birds and monkeys, the incessant droning sound of insects. Maia strained her ears for any human sounds, but heard none that would guide her. She began to wonder if she'd missed a turnoff from the trail, but dared not stop to search for one, much less retreat. Barring an obvious diversion, she would press on toward the island's southern coastline and the Indian Ocean beyond.

Something was keeping pace with Maia, to her left, concealed by undergrowth and forest shadows. Maia hesitated, whispering Cooper's name, but there was no reply. The *something* shifted closer to her, and she fired a nearly silent 3-round burst into the bushes there, rewarded with a kind of honking growl from an inhuman throat.

She cursed and ran on southward, gaining speed as fear propelled her. Whether she found Cooper and his elusive prey or not, she wanted out of the jungle, into open space with blue sky overhead. It didn't matter if her back was to the ocean then.

At least she'd have a chance to stand and fight an enemy that she could see.

AL-JARRAH CLEARED the treeline and paused for a moment, slumped forward with hands on his knees, while he fought to control his breathing. His throat felt as if he had gargled acid, and his lungs ached with each panting, wheezing breath. Dark spots spun in his field of vision like a swarm of jungle gnats.

A cool breeze off the water saved him, nearly chilled him as it played over his sweat-soaked face and clothing. For a moment, he stood shivering, then shook it off and started down the clear slope toward the cove and the speedboats waiting at the simple wooden dock. He angled toward the green boat, limping slightly, his ankle throbbing from his fall along the trail, but it was strong enough to bear his weight.

And he was getting out of there regardless, even if he had to crawl the last few yards.

A crashing in the shrubbery behind him startled al-Jarrah. He turned in time to see the seven-foot Komodo dragon that he'd thought he had eluded in the forest charging down the hillside with its jaws agape. The Sword of Allah's field commander raised his pistol, fired too hastily and shot a chunk out of the monster reptile's whipping tail. Before he could adjust his aim, its jaws clamped on his injured ankle with a crushing force.

The lizard shook its head and hurled al-Jarrah to the ground. He nearly lost the pistol in his panic, shrieking curses at his scaly nemesis, before he reasserted self-control and sat bolt upright, sobbing from pain as he steadied the gun with both hands. Three shots ripped apart the dragon's skull in rapid fire, the third round drilling through its snout and soft palate, ending its flight in al-Jarrah's already mangled leg.

Even dead, the beast wouldn't release its grip, however. Al-Jarrah was forced to pry its jaws apart by hand, slashing his fingers on its razor teeth. More pain to make him weep as he lay bleeding on the hillside, still some thirty yards from the green boat and freedom.

Could he make it? Was there any other choice?

If he was captured, it meant jail for a start. Most probably in one of Indonesia's filthy prisons. And when they'd wrung him dry of information, if the torture didn't kill him, al-Jarrah would die before a firing squad.

No. He wouldn't submit.

On hands and knees, dragging his wounded leg behind him, Nasir al-Jarrah crawled toward the dock and waiting cigarette boat, trailing blood behind him all the way.

BOLAN CLEARED THE TREES just as a green speedboat roared off westward from a small dock where a second cigarette was moored. Raising his rifle, Bolan tracked the disappearing vessel, trying to lead it, and fired two quick shots before a promontory masked the craft from view.

Both wasted rounds, as far as he could tell.

He sprinted down the slope, veered left to miss the carcass of a man-sized lizard with the best part of its head blown off, a blood trail leading on from there downhill, across the wooden planking of the dock, to disappear where the green speedboat had been tied moments earlier. His boots were on the pier when Maia called out, behind him.

"Matt! Wait!"

He turned and shouted back at her, "Come on! No time! He's running!"

As to who *he* was, the Executioner still didn't have a clue. Someone in a position of command behind the missile hijacking, the sinking of the hapless *Eiland Koningin,* and the intended massacre of everyone aboard a massive U.S. warship.

Someone who was overdue to meet the Executioner.

He hopped into the blue speedboat, fired up its twin high-performance engines, and was checking the fuel gauge when Maia arrived on the dock.

"Cast off and get in, if you're coming," he told her.

Maia untied the bowline and dropped in beside him, pushed back in her low seat as Bolan gunned it from the dock, cranking the throttle up until the massive engines roared behind him, raising plumes of water from their screws.

"Who is it?" Maia asked him, shouting to be heard over the growling engines.

"Has to be the guy in charge," Bolan replied, "whoever that is. If he gets away, our job's not done."

And they were gaining on the other speedboat, though it seemed to take forever with the green vessel's head start. In fact, the first boat should have held its lead, no problem, but it seemed to Bolan that the pilot must be having trouble. From the blood trail on the beach and dock, he reconstructed the scenario and wondered whether blood loss from the giant lizard's bite would kill their adversary, or if it had merely slowed him.

Whichever, they were gaining now, closing the gap as Bolan held the speedboat's throttle open, fairly flying over blue-green water at a hundred miles per hour, still accelerating. If they struck a rock at that speed, or if any other obstacle ripped through the hull, they were as good as dead.

Ahead of them, the green boat had begun to yaw and swerve, its pilot seemingly incapable of holding to a steady course. Bolan leaned close to Maia, asked her, "Can you drive this thing?"

She nodded, scooting over to his seat and taking the controls as Bolan shifted forward, took his autorifle with him to a spot where he could aim across the speedboat's low windscreen and long, sleek forward deck. Two hundred yards and closing as he found his mark, then saw the boat veer off to the left, then track across his line of fire once more and keep on going to the right.

With no way to anticipate the boat's erratic movements, Bolan picked a spot and zeroed in on it, holding steady as his target veered from right to left and back again. The trick was to anticipate the next move, firing off a measured burst before the cigarette was in his sights, and to put the slugs where it would be when they arrived. The Pindad rifle's 5.56 mm NATO rounds traveled at 3,100 feet per second, so call it one-fifteenth of a second to cover the distance from muzzle to target at 150 yards out. If he could make that shot...

Bolan saw the speedboat begin to drift leftward, squeezed off one 3-round burst and then another as it came. Downrange, the fleeing speedboat's pilot seemed to twitch, and crimson spray painted the inside of his windscreen, just before his body slumped across the wheel and throttle.

With a foaming roar, the green boat veered off-course again, then steadied on a straight line to the northwest. Maia had begun to turn in that direction when their target struck some underwater object—coral, a jutting boulder, they would never know for sure—and its hull disintegrated on impact. A split second later, the fuel tanks went up with a roar, spreading a lake of blazing gasoline across the ocean's surface.

Maia throttled back until their craft was idling on the swells, their view obscured by drifting smoke. A moment later, she asked Bolan, "So, what now?"

"Head for the nearest island with an airport," he replied. "We still have people in Jakarta that we need to see." Then added, "If you're up for it."

"Try me," she said, and aimed the speedboat westward.

EPILOGUE

Intercontinental Jakarta Midplaza Hotel

Chou Hua Tian woke well before the morning alarm, which he'd set for six-thirty. If the truth were told, he'd barely slept all night, thinking about what might be waiting for him when he got back to Beijing.

Nothing, perhaps. Or possibly a firing squad.

On one hand, he had felt relief on hearing news of the Brave Wind missile's destruction. Later reports claimed that all of the terrorists involved were dead. Which, if true, should bring the international investigation to a close. And with Feng's suicide—a simple bullet to the brain, no whining note, as Chou had verified by telephone—any suspicion of an inside job fell naturally on the commodore.

Still, there was Maia Lee.

Had she survived the final raid that brought the missile down? Chou had no proof that she had even been involved, though simple logic told him that she had to have been. Chou would have known if Chinese troops were on the move, or if a special strike force from his ministry had learned where the missile was hidden.

Maybe she was dead. If not, the evidence that she had worked with an American, unsanctioned by the ministry, should be enough to put her well out of the way. An accident could always be arranged for her in custody, if she was fool enough to show her traitor's face again. Meanwhile, as no one had been credited so far with breaking up the plot, Chou wondered whether he could turn it to his own advantage.

Could *he* be the hero of the hour in Beijing? It would require collaboration from his special forces unit, strict adherence to a script already being written in his mind, but with the right incentives—heroes' medals all around, with guaranteed promotions, extra benefits, a bonus payment to each man determined by his rank—Chou thought the soldiers would be happy to oblige him. Later, if Chou thought they might be having second thoughts, they could be shipped off to some danger zone where anything might happen.

Chou showered, dressed and called room service with a breakfast order. He had yet to book a flight back to Beijing, but that could wait. First, he would have to speak with the commander of his handpicked team and see if they could come to some accommodation.

Failing that, the Flying Ax Triad still owed him several favors. It could be arranged for Chou alone to come back from his covert mission. As a rule, the last man standing wrote the history of what had gone before.

There came a rapping on his door, a female voice announcing room service. Chou marveled at their speed, opened the door and blinked in shock to find himself confronted by a tall American—and Maia Lee. Both held pistols leveled at his chest, their muzzles fat with sound suppressors. The agent Chou had tried in vain to kill spoke one more word—*traitor*—before the unexpected callers fired as one.

Chou was surprised to feel no pain as he sprawled backward, gaping at the ceiling, where a vast dark hole was opening, preparing to consume him. Waiting for a glimpse of the light the old stories had promised him, he died.

Soekarno–Hatta International Airport, Jakarta

"YOU THINK IT'S SETTLED, THEN, at home?" Bolan asked, his voice low-pitched despite the racket of a heedless mob that bustled past them, up and down the concourse of Terminal 2.

"I'm fairly confident," Maia replied. "Of course, I can't be certain until I am at the ministry."

"And by then, it's too late to change your mind," Bolan reminded her.

"I have assurances from Chou's successor, the new Deputy Assistant Minister for State Security," she said.

"Who could be lying through his teeth."

"I must trust someone, sometime," she replied.

"If you say so." Bolan could only hope she wasn't making a disastrous mistake. "You know, you could—"

"No, thank you," Maia said emphatically but with a smile. "Defection is not me, I think is how you say it."

"Close enough."

Her flight was scheduled to start boarding in nine minutes. Bolan's was a later flight, leaving at noon, but he preferred killing time in a crowded airport to roaming the foreign streets on his own.

Maia began to speak again. "I wish to thank you for—"

"Enough said," he cut her off. "I'm not much for goodbyes and fare-thee-wells."

"A man of action," Maia said, "not words."

"Whenever possible," he said.

"An action, then," she answered back. Stepped close,

rising on tiptoe, for a quick kiss planted at one corner of his mouth. "In payment for my life."

Without another word, she turned and joined the flow of passengers en route to their departure gates. Maia didn't turn back to wave or look at Bolan as she left.

Smiling, the Executioner moved off to find a place where he could sit and rest, before the long flight home. Back to his neverending war.

* * * * *

TAKE 'EM FREE
2 action-packed novels plus a mystery bonus

NO RISK
NO OBLIGATION TO BUY

Reader Service.com

Manage your account online!

- Review your order history
- Manage your payments
- Update your address

> ### We've designed the Harlequin® Reader Service website just for you.

Enjoy all the features!

- Reader excerpts from any series
- Respond to mailings and special monthly offers
- Discover new series available to you
- Browse the Bonus Bucks catalog
- Share your feedback

Visit us at:

ReaderService.com

RS13